Dear Reader,

This collection of stories has been a special project that we—Lyn Cote, Lenora Worth and Penny Richards—started several years ago. Just as in "Wed by a Prayer," when Aunt Becky prays for her niece, Jo, and Jo's friends, Hannah and Elizabeth, prayer has been a powerful force in our lives.

Our stories show that even when we're disillusioned and hurting, sometimes a prayer from a friend or loved one can help get us through. In "The Dream Man," Elizabeth felt abandoned because her father left her, but Jake taught her that our Father is always with us. His example gave Elizabeth the ability to find her faith again. And to find a happy ending!

In "Small-Town Wedding," Hannah refuses to grant the forgiveness to Griff that God had granted to her. Through prayer, friendship and a lot of growing in her faith, she was able to forgive, put the past into its proper perspective and find a real, mature love.

I hope you enjoy this series of stories as much as we enjoyed writing them. God bless!

Lyn Cote
Lenora Worth
Penny Richards

Since childhood, **Lyn Cote** always wanted to be a writer. She began work on her first book in 1983 when her daughter (now in college) was thirteen months old. After writing five manuscripts and being rejected by editors everywhere, Lyn discovered that a whole new market for inspirational fiction had opened in the 1990s. This brought together her desire to tell stories and the desire to reach out to others with the encouragement that the good news brings. That is the wonder of writing for God. Lyn writes light romances, romantic suspense and her favorite, historical sagas. Visit her at www.booksbylyncote.com or drop her a note at P.O. Box 864, Woodruff, WI 54568 or at 1.cote@juno.com.

Lenora Worth knew she wanted to be a writer after her fourth-grade teacher assigned a creative writing project. While the other children moaned and groaned, Lenora gleefully wrote her first story, then promptly sold it (for a quarter) on the playground. She's written fifteen books for Love Inspired and Steeple Hill, including the 2004 release of *After the Storm* as a single title. Married for thirty years, Lenora has two children. Before writing full-time, she worked in marketing and public relations. She has served in her local RWA chapter and as president of Faith, Hope, and Love, the inspirational chapter of RWA. She also writes a monthly column for a local magazine.

Penny Richards has been an active member of her church for more than thirty-five years. She's sung for weddings and funerals, led ladies' class discussions and home Bible studies. Through the efforts of a good friend, Penny was involved with the parish jail ministry for almost two years. It was during this time that she began to understand why Jesus fraternized with sinners: it's impossible to reach others with a holier-than-thou attitude. Penny likes writing about all kinds of relationships and hopes her writing shows readers that no matter what the situation, God is in control and that His grace truly is sufficient. The author and her husband have been married almost forty-one years. They have two sons, a daughter and eight grandchildren—six boys and two girls.

Blessed Bouquets

Lyn Cote
Lenora Worth
Penny Richards

Steeple
Hill®

Published by Steeple Hill Books™

STEEPLE HILL BOOKS

**Steeple
Hill®**

ISBN 0-373-81218-3

BLESSED BOUQUETS

Copyright © 2005 by Steeple Hill Books

The publisher acknowledges the copyright holders
of the individual works as follows:

WED BY A PRAYER
Copyright © 2005 by Lyn Cote

THE DREAM MAN
Copyright © 2005 by Lenora H. Nazworth

SMALL-TOWN WEDDING
Copyright © 2005 by Penny Richards

www.SteepleHill.com

Printed in U.S.A.

CONTENTS

WED BY A PRAYER

Lyn Cote

In memory of Betty Gray, the best boss
I ever had—who gave so much joy to others
and who possessed an unmatched zest for life.
Thanks for everything, Betty!

To have faith is to be sure
of the things we hope for, to be certain
of the things we cannot see.
—*Hebrews* 11:1

Prologue

Jo Woodward couldn't bear another mournful glance or pat condolence. And, from their strained expressions, neither could her friends, Elizabeth and Hannah.

"Let's get out of here," Hannah whispered and led the way. Jo and Elizabeth followed her, fleeing the church basement where the ladies were cleaning up after the funeral luncheon.

The three burst outside into the May afternoon. The bright spring sunlight of the Arkansas day dazzled their eyes after the dim church basement. Gentle breezes played with their Sunday-best skirts. Jo looked at her two stricken friends—Elizabeth with golden-brown curls and Hannah with beautiful dark hair. How could the world look so happy on this awful, hateful day?

"Do you want to walk home now?" Jo asked, touching Hannah's soft brown hair, brushing it back from her beautiful face.

"I don't want to do anything ever again," Hannah

said. Pulling away, she walked over to the ancient oak tree on the church's front lawn and leaned against it, her back to them. As children, they'd often played around the tree's twisted and gnarled roots after Sunday school.

Jo and Elizabeth exchanged glances and moved up close to Hannah. How did one comfort a friend who'd lost her one true love? Three days ago, Johnny Harrison had been killed in a car accident the night of Elizabeth and Hannah's senior prom. Jo, only a sophomore, hadn't heard the shattering news until the morning. Griff, Johnny's brother, had been driving which only added to the horror everyone felt.

"Losing Johnny," Hannah said, her lower lip trembling, "it's a sign."

"A sign?" Elizabeth repeated.

Hannah turned to face them, leaning her back against the coarse-barked tree. "We all knew that falling in love and putting all our trust in a man was risky at best. Look at our mothers."

Jo considered Hannah's words. Each of their fathers had abandoned their mothers in one way or another. Too choked with her own sorrow, she couldn't think of anything to say to counter or comfort Hannah. And obviously neither could Elizabeth.

"We thought God could make the difference for us," Hannah said fiercely, "You two prayed with me that we'd find men who'd be true, who wouldn't leave us...."

Like our fathers did, Jo added silently.

"Then Johnny fell in love with me and we thought

it was starting. God was going to bring us everlasting love. But Johnny's death says it isn't going to work out for us." Tears dripped down Hannah's face. "Don't you see?"

Unfortunately, Jo did see. The three of them had prayed that Hannah and Johnny would make it, that their love wouldn't fail. Now Johnny was gone. "We didn't have much hope in the first place," Jo conceded.

"Right. And I'm not wasting my time praying anymore," Elizabeth agreed, an edge to her voice. "Some families just don't get happily-ever-afters. And that's us. God just doesn't care about us I guess."

Jo didn't like what Elizabeth said, but she couldn't argue. This wasn't the time to discuss God's faithfulness. Whatever her friend thought, Jo knew God had carried her through the loss of her father and then her mother. Diplomatically, she groped for some words of solace. "But we've got each other," she offered at last, breaking the terrible aching silence. "We've always had our friendship."

"That will help us through this," Elizabeth said, nodding. "We won't bother trying to do the impossible. We'll just stick together."

Hannah grabbed one hand of each of her friends. "A pact then." Her pretty face shone with tears. "We won't put ourselves through something like this again. No men, but friends forever?"

"No men, but friends forever," Elizabeth promised.

"No men, but friends forever," Jo agreed solemnly.

* * *

From the church's open doorway, Jo's Aunt Becky had overheard everything. She felt her heart breaking for her niece and Jo's two lifelong friends. Becky knew from her own experience that love could be lost. She'd lost hers to Viet Nam. But she'd never given up hope that she might find a new love.

Now her sweet Jo, Elizabeth and Hannah's hopes had been shattered by one of those terrible end-of-senior-year tragedies that seemed to happen every May. Becky tried to take a deep breath and couldn't. Sorrow for her niece and her best friends pressed down on Becky's heart.

Oh, Lord, she prayed silently. *Heal these three crushed hearts and bring them the loves they deserve.* Her attitude then turned gritty. *I'm going to pray this prayer until you grant it. These three girls have suffered enough from selfish hearts. Bring them three men with honest and loving spirits. Amen. And I mean it.*

Chapter One

❧

Ten years later

On Valentine's Day in the late afternoon, Jo Woodward, reluctant maid of honor, tried to concentrate on the wedding couple to her right. Fettered in yards of peach satin, she fought the urge to fidget. But thoughts about what was scheduled at her shop after the wedding ceremony kept prickling her mind.

To distract herself, she looked past the bride and groom and caught a glimpse of the best man. What was with him anyway? Tall, dark and handsome, Bramwell Dixon, standing opposite her in a black tux, looked as if he'd sucked lemons for breakfast—vigorously and daily for at least the past ten years. If he didn't want to be the best man, why had he said yes? But then who could figure out men? *Not me. Not now. Not ever.*

Jo accepted her cousin's bridal bouquet as the

solemn groom took the bride's hand in his and began to recite his vows in a deep, quavering voice. Still not wanting to call attention to herself, Jo bent her head over the two dewy bouquets. She stifled a yawn. This week had been an endurance test as she'd prepared floral orders to go out on Valentine's Day plus crafting all Leta's wedding flowers in her shop yesterday.

White roses dominated the bride's bouquet—white roses that symbolized eternal love. For contrast, she'd included pink carnations which denoted "I'll never forget you" and had intertwined abundant delicate baby's breath, bringing the hope of everlasting happiness. All of these sentiments and more she wished for her cousin. Well, a maid of honor could hope, couldn't she?

Motion to her right caught her eye. She glanced sideways and watched Bram hand his friend the gold wedding band. Again, Bram snared and held her attention against her will. How could any woman ignore him? He was well over six feet tall, broad-shouldered and slim-hipped. He looked just like what he was, a former high-school and college football player and now the local high-school football coach. Make that the highly successful and popular new football coach.

The rest of the ceremony proceeded without a hitch and soon Jo prepared to follow the happy couple down the steps and up the aisle of the small church. Jo preferred jeans to bridesmaid gowns and the one she was wearing was a doozy. Why had her cousin chosen such a full skirt—and hooped at that? With care, Jo moved her feet, making a graceful turn in her billowing dress and its antebellum hoop.

Bram stared at her, his arm crooked, waiting for her hand. "What's taking you so long?" he murmured.

Jo beamed an artificial smile up at him. "This is a wedding, not a race." She took his arm and he tried to start off, pulling her along with him. She countered this with a tug on his sleeve. "Whoa, I've got to go slowly to control the swing on this crazy skirt."

He halted. "Sorry, I didn't realize. Sorry."

"And be careful not to step on my hem," she cautioned him. "If you do, the hoop will lift up my skirt."

Obviously appalled at this possibility, Bram looked at her hem as though it might spring to life. "Okay." He again offered her the use of his strong arm, now for support as she negotiated each step.

"Thanks, Bram," she whispered at the bottom.

He gave her a little smile and she forgave him. Of course, a man wouldn't know that a hoop skirt could be tricky. Finally, they were on their way down the aisle. Leta and her groom Don were stopping to greet people on their way out of the church, letting each pew empty after they'd greeted the happy couple.

"What's taking them so long?" Bram grumbled.

"Lighten up. This is the new way of avoiding a formal receiving line," Jo said, switching her bouquet into another hand and running quick fingers through her short red hair. She liked it to look just a bit spiky rather than curly.

"What's wrong with a receiving line?" He tugged

at his collar which seemed too tight for his formidable neck.

Poor man. He probably didn't like formal dress. "They're boring," Jo explained patiently, "and we'd be standing shaking hands for over an hour. This way, the bride and groom alone perform the civilities, so when we arrive at the reception hall, the party begins on time."

"Who invented big weddings anyway?" Bram asked in an obvious rhetorical aside.

As a florist who did many weddings a year, she was ready for Bram's question. She gave him a playful grin. "Obviously men."

"Men?" He stared at her, both dark eyebrows lifted.

"Yes, centuries ago, men realized weddings were big business. They purchased all the fabric, designed all the clothing, hired the seamstresses to sew milady's gowns and tailors to sew m'lord's raiment, sold the flowers, crafted the rings and then they pocketed all those hefty profits." She knew she was being provocative and she was enjoying it. Just try to blame all the wedding stuff on women.

Bram shook his head at her and then smiled at last. She could sympathize with him. Bram wasn't that unusual. Few men enjoyed weddings. He just put into words what most men thought. And he didn't seem to mind that their eyes were almost at a level. Some men didn't appreciate her being almost six feet tall. But Bram didn't look one bit intimidated.

So, letting the happy occasion restore her mood, she grinned at the wedding guests. Finally, they stood on the steps of the church in unusual February sunshine. People were blowing bubbles from little plastic bottles in the direction of the bride and groom. Leta was laughing. Don was smiling as they got into the streamer-decorated limousine which would drive around Prescott, honking.

Jo and Bram sat in the limo facing the newlyweds. Jo waved out the window and laughed at the people who stopped in their tracks to watch the wedding party drive by. But her mind lurched back to fretting over the recent threat to her business. Would what she'd planned for today work? Would it be enough to make a difference?

At last, they drove up to Jo's floral shop on its quiet side street. Don helped Leta out of the car and Bram did the same for Jo, looking puzzled. She didn't have time to explain. The photographer she'd hired was waiting for them, looking antsy. The weather, at least, had cooperated with the festiveness of the day.

"Where do you want us?" Jo called to the photographer.

"Let's do a shot of the bride and groom beside your front door first," replied the harried-looking man with an assortment of cameras hanging around his neck.

Leta and Don obligingly posed by the door. Behind them was the window with the name Jo's Bower emblazoned in shades of pink and red. While the photographer snapped still after still, Bram leaned toward her and asked, "Why are we here?"

"I wanted to use Leta's flowers in a round of new media commercials for my shop."

"Yes," Leta chimed in, "isn't it a great idea? Don and I will be on TV and in the paper."

Bram muttered something Jo couldn't hear, for which she should probably be thankful. She didn't have time right now to deal with any distraction. This had to go quickly and smoothly so the newlyweds could get on to their reception within fifteen minutes or so.

The photographer motioned Jo and Bram to join the newlyweds in front of the shop window. Bram obeyed, but stiffly. The photographer took several more shots, his camera clicking away. "Now I want only the bride and maid of honor together holding their bouquets. That's right. Face each other. Have the bouquets touching. Look happy. Look pleased." More furious clicking.

The wedding party of four went through various poses inside and outside the store. All the while, Jo's van came and went, loading up to deliver sweetheart gifts. Why Leta had asked her to be a bridesmaid on the busiest day of the year for florists escaped Jo. But her part-time helper and driver were doing a great job. Jo concentrated on the photo shoot. At last, the photographer said, "That's all I need. Great. Really great stuff, Jo. This should give you the edge you want right when everyone is gearing up for summer weddings."

"Thanks," Jo said. "I'll be looking forward to seeing the proofs."

"I'll give you a call as soon as I've got them," the photographer replied, starting to collapse his tripod.

Don helped Leta back into the limo. Bram nudged

Jo in after the bride. Just as Jo bent to enter, the best man stepped on the back of her hem. The metal hoop reared up and smacked Jo's nose. "Ouch."

"Sorry. Sorry," Bram apologized. "Are you all right?"

Over her shoulder, she gave him a disgruntled look as she edged into the limo. Surely he hadn't done that on purpose, had he? Then both of the men climbed inside with the ladies and the driver pulled away from the curb, heading toward the country club for the reception. Bram said nothing. His expression was stormy and held a trace of chagrin.

The man was unhappy about something and she guessed that the chagrin was from his stepping on her hem. She gave him another smile, saying "No hard feelings." Then she turned to the bride. "Thanks again," Jo said, ignoring the masculine thundercloud beside her. "You're such a great-looking couple I couldn't see passing up a chance for such a good shoot."

"Well, I hope it does the trick," Leta declared. "I can't believe that Henderson's is trying to grab your business. Don't they have enough customers over in Hope to keep them busy? Why do they think we needed another florist in Prescott?"

Jo shrugged, her stomach burning. Henderson's had opened another shop just down the street from her place over a month ago. "Competition is just part of being in business."

The limo pulled up in front of the country club. The

wedding party got out and paraded up to the door. Inside, Jo was swept up into the festive occasion. After dinner, the groom led bride to the table where they cut the cake and fed each other a tidbit. Then the staff began distributing the tempting dessert. At the head table, Jo forked up one of the pink roses and savored the sweetness.

"I can't see how you can eat that," Bram said with a look of distaste.

Trying not to react negatively, she looked over at him and smiled. "I get the feeling weddings aren't your thing."

He grunted.

She chuckled. "If you didn't want to do all this, then why did you agree to be best man?"

"I like Don. He's a good friend."

"He seems like a good guy." She forked up more gooey frosting, just to tease him. "You were friends when you lived here before, right?"

"What? Do you want my life history?" he asked.

Jo didn't disguise her displeasure, stabbing her cake with her fork. "I'm just trying to make polite conversation. I see it's lost on you."

"At least, *I* don't use my relatives on their wedding day for cheap publicity for my business."

His scathing tone sliced through Jo and the explanation of his obvious displeasure was now revealed. For once, she couldn't speak. Too many words jammed in her throat. She picked up her cake before she tipped it into his lap and swished away to her best friends, Hannah West and Elizabeth Sinclair, sitting at a table in the rear.

"What's eating you?" Hannah, a striking brunette and owner of the local Mimosa Manor Bed and Breakfast, asked as Jo sank into the chair beside her.

To her horror, Jo felt tears start in her eyes. Bram's cutting words echoed in her mind. She pursed her lips. "Do you think I was awful to ask Leta to pose for publicity photos today?" she asked Hannah and Elizabeth.

"It was up to Leta. I think she loved the idea," Hannah replied immediately.

"It was a great idea," Elizabeth, a successful local Realtor and a very pretty one with golden-brown curls, joined in. "Leta's lovely and the bouquets! Jo, you outdid yourself."

"Absolutely," Hannah agreed. "If the bride and groom liked the idea, that's that."

"What made you think anything was wrong with the shoot?" Elizabeth asked.

"Bramwell Dixon." Jo felt her face drawing down into a grim expression. "He's the rudest man I've ever met. I was just trying to make polite conversation—"

"He hates women," Hannah interrupted. "Didn't you know that? He even glared at the cheerleaders during all the football games." Hannah grinned.

"I'm not into sports." Jo grimaced. "I know he's done a great job with his first year as coach because that's all anyone talked about all fall and winter. Big deal."

"He's notorious," Elizabeth added. "He gave all the

single mothers of his team short shrift. Turned down every invitation to a 'home-cooked meal.'"

Jo grinned suddenly. "I'll just bet he did."

The call for all the single women to come forward for the tossing of the bouquet trumpeted through the hall. Jo, Hannah and Elizabeth didn't even flinch. Their eyes met in a unanimous "not in a million years" look.

Aunt Becky fluttered over. "You girls get up there."

"We're not girls any more, Aunty," Jo objected.

"And we aren't interested in catching Leta's bouquet," Hannah said airily.

"I pass, too." Elizabeth held up one hand and waved away the idea.

"No, you don't." Aunt Becky literally pulled them up and herded them to the small cluster of giggling single women. Jo rolled her eyes. Elizabeth shook her head. And Hannah folded her arms.

"Ready or not," Leta called out and let loose her bouquet.

Startled, Jo looked up just as the bouquet landed in her hands.

Chapter Two

"Tassie, get down here!" On Monday morning, Bram shouted once more up the stairwell of the two-story house he'd bought last fall. "We have to leave in ten minutes and I want to see you eat breakfast!" He'd tried and failed to keep the exasperation out of his tone.

"I don't want any breakfast!" his nearly fourteen-year-old (as she kept reminding him) sister yelled back at him.

"Then I won't drive you to school. You'll be stuck with the bus. Take it or leave it." He walked back to the blue-and-white kitchen and picked up the weekly *Nevada County Picayune* again. He turned the page and there he was smiling back at himself in front of Jo's Bower. His aggravation boiled up again. *I should never have signed that permission form,* he thought.

But what could he do when Don asked him right in front of Leta and that bridesmaid of hers? Why hadn't Don realized he was letting that bridesmaid use a private, very personal moment for cheap publicity? Why hadn't the groom put his foot down? Was Bram the only one who got it?

Even though more than a week had passed since the wedding-slash-photo shoot, he still couldn't free himself from his irritation or from thinking about Jo Woodward. Her image—red hair cut short and a little spiky and skin like rich cream—flashed into his mind. He brushed aside the memory of how she'd walked gracefully down the altar steps in spite of having to deal with a hooped skirt.

"All right." Tassie appeared in the kitchen and said with true teen-age disgust, "what do I have to eat?"

Bram looked over his newspaper and ran his eyes over the wrinkled black T-shirt and blue jeans she was wearing. Fortunately for her, she hadn't tried his patience again by exposing her navel bright and early this morning. "Try a bowl of cereal."

Tassie huffed her displeasure, jerked the corn flakes box from atop the fridge, jammed it down onto the table and flung open the fridge door to get the milk.

Bram refused to rise to the bait. Tassie didn't carry an extra ounce of weight that he could see, so her concern over eating too much and gaining weight baffled him. But he'd weathered Tassie's first full teen year. Only six more to go. The words of an old hymn came to mind. *Lord, with this kid—I do need thee every hour.*

Tassie dumped herself into the chair opposite him and began to spoon up cereal noisily. With one hand, she pushed her long hair, the same dark brown as his, behind her shoulders. "What's the deal with eating breakfast? Tasha never made me eat any."

Bram ignored the reference to the sister who had taken care of Tassie for a few months after his parents' disappearance until Bram had bought this house and moved into it. If he knew Natasha, she had probably never given a thought to what Tassie was eating. And they might not have eaten at all if he hadn't sent her regular checks. "We've had this discussion too many times before. You will eat breakfast before you leave for school in the morning...period."

Bram felt waves of Tassie's smoldering dissatisfaction lapping against him, but he clung to his patience and his newspaper. He turned the page. Again, his face looked back at him. The article was about how he was spending time with his se-niors prepping them for their college entrance exams. Why was that big news? *The season's long over. Why don't they give us a rest?*

The timer on the stove buzzed. Tassie leaped up and poured what was left of her cereal into the sink and hurriedly ran the water, probably so he wouldn't see how little she'd eaten. Bram said nothing. She'd at least gotten a few spoonfuls down her. He'd have to be satisfied with that.

He folded the paper and glanced down once more at the ad of Leta, Don, him and that Jo. He recalled the feel of the florist's small hand on his arm. She'd been so willowy, so effortlessly feminine. *Stop right there.*

He'd already found out that she was a woman who had her own agenda and who took advantage of her friends and relatives. Bram shook his head as though sweeping his memory of Jo's infectious giggle out of his mind. He headed grimly out the back door.

As they arrived in the circle drive in front of the middle school Tassie was half out the door of his red pickup truck when he caught her hand. "I'll pick you up here right after school."

She tugged free. "I can just walk home."

"No, I'll pick you up," Bram repeated the same sentence he did every day which for some reason his little sister couldn't seem to remember.

"You act like this is a dangerous place. Isn't it safe to walk home from school in this dinky little town?"

There's safe and then there's safe. I'm not taking any chances with you, Tassie. Every one of your older sisters was pregnant before she graduated high school and I'm not giving in to that statistic. Someone special is going to love you and treasure you the way you deserve. Of course, how could he say that to her? For some reason he couldn't identify, he and his sister never discussed their family; it was a painful subject for both of them.

"See you later." He shut the door and drove away. Then for no reason at all, that bridesmaid's dimpled smile popped into his mind. A thought came to him. He brushed it aside. Crazy idea. Nuts.

On Monday morning, over a week after Leta's wedding, Jo sat like a lump at her work table in the rear of her cozy shop. Pots of azaleas and cyclamens in all possible shades of pink and lavender bloomed around her. By this time of the morning, she should have been juggling the phone, making up an order and handling walk-ins. Instead she sat alone and idle.

In front of her was a copy of today's *Picayune* with the wedding party ad featuring Leta, Don, Bram and herself. To her mind, good-looking Bram Dixon stood out and made the ad eye-catching. So the man had his uses. Unwillingly, her mind took her back to the time they'd shared, his strong hand helping her in and out of the limousine. She cut the string on that line of thought.

She made herself study the ad. It certainly should bring in new business. This fact should have cheered her. But after listening in vain all morning for the phone to ring or the bell on the door to announce a customer, she couldn't generate any glimmer of hope. A daunting silence reigned absolute.

"Stop fretting," she muttered to herself. "It's a weekday in late February. The Valentine rush is over for the month." Still, she couldn't quell her uneasiness.

She slipped off her stool and went to the computer in the back of her small but bright showroom. Clicking on her mouse, she brought up the file for last February's income and then this month's. Last year's numbers far exceeded this year's. Jo tapped the mouse, shutting the file. "Why am I torturing myself?"

Her alter ego replied, "Because you can't stop worrying that Henderson's will put you out of business."

Jo turned cold with fear. "I have to do something."

She moved to the front of the store, sat down on the high stool behind her counter and opened her book of contacts. In it, she always noted the name and phone number of every person who called or stopped in inquiring about a possible order.

She paged back to the beginning of the year and dialed the first number. "Hello, Sarah? This is Jo at the flower shop. I was wondering if you'd decided on using my wedding flower service."

"Oh…oh," the young bride-to-be stammered. "We…my mother and I decided to use that new shop for my wedding."

"Fine. I was just checking to see if I could help." Jo hung up and her heart beat fast. "That was just a fluke, an unhappy coincidence."

Unable to stop herself, she moved her finger down to the next name, the younger sister of a family that Jo had already done two weddings for in the past five years. The sisters had raved about her flowers. Confident that this call would go better, Jo dialed the number.

"Hello, this is Jo calling from the flower shop. May I speak to Corinne?"

A heavy silence came in response.

"Hello?" Jo prompted. "Corinne, how are you today?"

"Hi," came the tentative voice of Corinne, "I was supposed to get back to you about the flowers for my wedding, wasn't I?"

"Only if you wanted me to do them," Jo kept her voice cheerful.

"Well, I guess I decided on using Henderson's. I mean I couldn't beat their new customer discount."

"New customer discount?" Jo's heart now pounded like a tom-tom, a war tom-tom.

"Yeah, with my tight budget, I couldn't pass up twenty-five percent off."

"I see your point." Jo kept all hurt and frustration from seeping into her voice. "I hope you have a lovely wedding, Corinne." She hung up, feeling winded.

Jo dialed the phone again.

"Sinclair Realty," her friend greeted her over the line.

"Elizabeth," Jo wailed into the phone, "I'm in trouble. I don't know what to do."

"Jo, can I call you back?" Elizabeth said in her professional voice. "I'm with clients now."

"Sure. That's fine. I'm at the shop." Jo hung up. She reached to dial again and stopped herself. "I shouldn't spread my good cheer around. Hannah's busy, too. And if I want to, I can have a great pity party all by myself."

Refusing to give into her anxiety, Jo closed her eyes and bowed her head. *God, I don't want to let this helpless feeling win. But I've poured everything into this business and I love it so. I'm plum out of ideas. You're going to have to do something to help me out. Thank you, Father. I know you love me and would never forsake me.*

Confident that her prayer would be answered, Jo leaped up, tangled one foot around the base of her stool and fell to the concrete floor—hard. "Oowww," she moaned. She pushed up to stand and sagged against the counter. She tested her right ankle; it was swelling before her eyes, and she found that it couldn't support her weight. Tears welled up in her eyes. *God, she complained, looking heavenward, this wasn't what I had in mind.*

She reached for the phone and dialed a familiar number. "Aunt Becky, can you come to the shop and drive me to the clinic? I did something to my ankle."

Jo reclined on the cream-colored sofa in her small apartment above her shop. A pair of aluminum crutches was propped beside the sofa. Her right ankle, which was wrapped in an elastic bandage, rested high on a cushion to keep it from swelling more. A couple of blue ice packs also adorned the painfully throbbing ankle. Jo sighed.

"Now stop that sighing," Aunt Becky said. "The doctor said you can go back downstairs tomorrow."

Jo nearly gave in and poured out her problems to her dear aunt. Becky, her mother's sister, had raised her since she'd been orphaned when she was twelve by her mother's death from cancer. Her sweet aunt worried about her enough as it was. She didn't need to hear Jo's litany of anxieties. Besides, Elizabeth had already called and she and Hannah had promised to bring over supper and sympathy after five.

"I'm going to need someone to help out at the shop," Jo began, focusing on practical matters.

"I'll be happy to come—"

"No," Jo said firmly. "I'd let you if you'd take pay for it, but I know you won't. Besides, I can do my floral work and handle customers and the phone sitting down. What I really need is someone to come and neaten everything up and sweep at the end of each day. Even a teenager after school would do. I'll call the school counselor and see if she can recommend someone."

The next afternoon, Jo sat behind her counter with crutches propped nearby. The bell above the door jingled and a shy slender young girl with long dark hair entered.

Jo had seen the girl around town though they'd never spoken. "Hi, are you the student who'd like to work an hour or two after school every night?"

"Yeah." The girl looked up and then down again.

Jo held out her hand. "Call me Jo."

The girl who still wouldn't meet Jo's eyes took her hand and held it loosely. "I'm Tassie Dixon."

The fact that this girl was related to Bramwell Dixon niggled at Jo's better sense. She noted that the girl's hair was the same color as Bram's. She recalled too vividly sitting beside him during their limousine ride and how she'd wanted to finger his dark cocoa-colored hair.

Why am I having these thoughts about a man who thinks I'm a selfish manipulative woman? So this girl is his sister. That doesn't mean I'll have to have anything to do with her brother, right?

Chapter Three

"Tassie, breakfast!" On Friday morning, the last day of February, Bram followed his usual frustrating school-day ritual. The promise of sleeping in late tomorrow and reading the Texarkana and Little Rock papers while lounging around in his sweats lifted his end-of-winter weariness.

"Okay! I'm almost dressed," Tassie's reply floated down to him.

Bram raised one eyebrow. Tassie had sounded almost polite. *I must be imagining things now*. Wish fulfillment. He walked back to the kitchen table. He'd just sat down when he heard his sister bounding down the stairs. Without a fuss, she walked into the room, snagged the box of corn flakes and made herself breakfast.

Bram eyed this from over the top of the Texarkana newspaper. Something looked different about his little sister. Should he say anything or ignore it?

Tassie met his gaze. "Do you like them?"

He couldn't read the expression in his sister's eyes. But she wasn't glaring at him for a change. "Them?"

Tassie shook her head, her nose wrinkling in amusement. "You didn't notice, right?"

He studied her, analyzing her. Bingo. "Your hair's different."

"I've got bangs now." Tassie looked pleased.

"That's right. You do." The bangs flattered his sister's face, made her look…prettier.

Tassie chuckled.

This brought Bram up short. He hadn't heard his sister chuckle in a long time and *never* at the breakfast table. He figured she must laugh sometimes, just never around him, the big bad brother. "I should have thought of that." He'd remembered school physical and dentist appointments, but there was so much "girl stuff" he didn't think of that he wanted to do for his sister. He didn't want her to go without anything she needed. He voiced a sudden and startling idea, "Did… do you want to go to a…beauty shop?"

"No." She watched him, obviously enjoying his being at sea.

"Then how did you get bangs? Did you cut them yourself?"

Tassie gave him another impish grin. "Miss Jo cut them for me yesterday. She told me to wait and see if you noticed. She said you wouldn't."

Bram gritted his teeth. Miss Jo, the I'll-use-my-cousin-for-profit florist and now obviously the expert on men. Irritation jabbed him like a hot needle. "I only let you take that job at her place because it's not going to last more than a week to ten days." His voice had come out sounding more disgruntled than he'd intended. And this wiped the teasing smile off his sister's face.

He backpedaled fast. "Sorry." Did Jo have something to do with the pleasant change in his sister? "Do…do you like Jo?"

She gave him a resentful look. "Yeah."

Bram searched his mind for a way to defuse the tension. Jo had been a…pleasant companion at the wedding. For a second, he pictured her laughing up at him about something he couldn't remember. But he couldn't seem to forget her smile. Maybe Tassie needed more smiles in her day. "She seems like a nice person," he said at last.

"She's not like most adults," Tassie asserted with a lift of her chin. "She's *nice.*"

I'm sure I didn't make the cut on your nice list. Was it good that Tassie was being influenced by Jo? Well, she was the cousin of Leta, his friend's wife. But he was still uneasy. "I'm glad," he said pouring more oil on the troubled waters. "I wouldn't want you working for someone who wasn't nice." The tension eased slightly. Bram took refuge behind his paper, not wanting to stir the cloudy waters again.

Later that morning when he had his planning period in his coaching office, he looked up the phone number for Tassie's school counselor and dialed the number.

"Counseling office," came the answer.

"Hi, is this Miss Adams?" he asked.

"Yes, how may I help you?"

"This is Bram Dixon. I wanted to talk to you about this job you arranged for my sister."

"What do you want to know?" Miss Adams's voice became strained. "Isn't Tassie happy at Jo's?"

"She's happy. I just wanted to know why you *specifically* chose to ask Tassie if she wanted to take the job."

"Ah." The counselor's voice relaxed. "I've known Jo all my life. We went all through school together. I thought Tassie would enjoy getting to know her—especially since your sister doesn't have a female role model in her life right now."

"Oh. But the job's only going to last until Jo's sprained ankle heals, right?"

"That's right, but even for such a short time, I thought Jo's cheery personality would be good for Tassie. Is there a problem?" the counselor asked, sounding cautious again.

"No, I just wondered. Thanks." He hung up slowly.

Female role model. He realized that he'd been actively trying to keep Tassie from following her three older sisters' poor examples, especially that of Natasha, who had three children by three different men, none of whom she'd married. He'd never thought about trying to provide his little sister with a better example. But was Jo a good female role model for Tassie?

* * *

"Yes, that's right, Tassie," Jo said from her stool in the rear work area of her shop late on Friday afternoon. "Now add some greenery."

A last-minute order for a dozen long-stemmed roses from a local businessman (who'd just remembered it was his anniversary) had been called in only minutes before closing. He wanted roses delivered to him to carry home to his "bride." And this had provided Jo with a chance to let Tassie learn how to put together a vase of fresh flowers.

Jo enjoyed having Tassie come every afternoon; the fact that she lived with Bram Dixon curried her sympathy. Out of a vague feeling of sisterhood with Tassie, Jo had tried to do a little extra for the sweet child. Jo was sure that having Bram for an older brother would be a sore trial for any female. His acid comment still stung. *Why am I still letting him get to me?*

"Now I always include a little baby's breath to soften and give contrast to the red roses," Jo explained. "Red roses make such a bold statement."

Tassie nodded, turned to the cooler and took out a few sprigs of baby's breath. She tucked it in and around the thirteen red roses and the greenery already standing in the crystal vase.

"Now some sheer white ribbon," Jo said, enjoying Tassie's intense concentration.

The young girl reached for the spool of white ribbon. She chewed her lower lip as she measured it along the yard stick glued to the edge of the work table and then snipped it.

"Now ease it around the vase and tie it in a pretty bow and clip each end into a V." Jo watched Tassie follow her instructions. "Well done." She patted the girl's shoulder and then, needing a change of position, stood up.

That was when, through the large archway between the front and rear, she noticed Bram Dixon standing at the front window looking in at them. The coach's handsome face at her window jolted her. A scintilla of the resentment she'd felt when she last saw him flashed through her afresh. Bram usually waited out at the front curb in his red pickup for his sister. "What's he doing at the window?" Jo asked with suspicion coloring her tone.

Tassie looked up, but didn't answer her question. "You were right, Miss Jo." The girl grinned in an obvious us-against-them way. "He didn't notice my bangs."

Pressing her lips into a tight smile, Jo shook her head. "Men. Just remember, Tassie, they're all alike."

Bram left his place beside the window and set the bell over the door jingling. He joined them in the work area.

Jo braced herself for his opening salvo. He probably didn't like the bangs. Probably thought Jo should have asked for written permission.

"Hi, Jo, nice to see you again," he said, sounding ill at ease.

Yeah, right. I'm just as happy to see you here as you are to see me. But Jo couldn't stop an unexplained excitement that shivered through her when he had looked at her. She merely gave him a polite smile. "You're here early today."

"It's Friday night. No football in February. And I thought I'd wait inside until Tassie is done."

"Oh, okay," Jo faltered, realizing suddenly that Bram had managed to breach her defenses. Her pulse raced as her mind screeched, "Danger! Danger! Step away from the man!"

Bram felt very much the intruder in Jo's shop. It reminded him of the aggravating photo shoot. He wondered if Jo held a grudge against him for what he'd said to her later that day during the reception. Well, if she had a grudge against him, she hadn't taken it out on his sister. He drew hope from that.

"Bram, look," Tassie pointed out, "Miss Jo let me put together this bouquet of roses. Isn't it pretty?"

"I thought Tassie would only be doing clean-up for you," he said in an accusing tone.

Jo bristled visibly. "Your sister finished up early and I thought she'd enjoy arranging her first bouquet—"

"And I did," Tassie flared up at him and turned to Jo. "My brother doesn't like it when I have fun."

Bram felt like hitting himself in the head. *Why do I always say the wrong thing, Lord?*

Jo placed a hand on Tassie's arm. "I think your brother is just afraid that I'm taking advantage of you. I'm paying you minimum wage for cleaning. Maybe he—"

"No," he spoke up trying to think of a way to redeem this awkward situation and besides he wanted to ask Jo a favor. Instead, with both females, he was sinking deeper and deeper. "I thought Tassie should know how gracious it is for you to take time to show her how to do something creative."

Tassie looked as if she were trying to decide if he were telling the truth or not. Jo merely gave him a completely unconvinced smile.

"Well, if you don't mind," Jo said as if daring him to put his foot in it again, "I'm going to send Tassie down the street to deliver these along with the gift card to the customer."

"Fine. That's fine," Bram said, backing away. Tassie put on her jacket and left the shop. His sister was unable to hide her smile of satisfaction as she walked out proudly, holding the festive arrangement high. An awkward silence followed the jingling bell as Tassie departed.

"Been busy lately?" Bram asked, trying to make conversation, trying to think of how to broach the topic on his mind.

Jo flushed up and glared at him.

"What did I say?" he asked, taking another step backward.

She looked away from him. "Sorry. You couldn't know," she said, sounding ruffled. "I'm just a little touchy lately on that subject of being busy."

"Oh. I remember. You're getting hit with some stiff competition."

"More than that." With her hands, Jo began sweeping up the debris from cutting the roses. "I think Henderson's, the florist from the next town, is trying to put me and the other florists out of business with a storefront here."

"Really? How?"

"They're offering a twenty-five-percent discount to new customers." Keeping her eyes lowered, she swept all the debris into one hand and then tossed it into the receptacle beneath the work bench.

"Do you think they're committing unfair business prac-tices?" He lounged against the work counter.

Jo frowned at him. "What do you mean?"

"If a competitor is really intending to put his competition out of business by undercutting prices, that might be against the law."

"Maybe, but that might be hard to prove," she said.

At last, he'd said something right around her. One point for his team. He better go for it now while she wasn't angry with him. "I was wondering—"

The jingling of the bell on the door interrupted him.

"He loved them!" Tassie enthused. "And he gave me a dollar tip for delivering them." Tassie showed the crisp dollar bill in her hand. "That was okay, wasn't it?"

"Great." Jo smiled that engaging smile of hers. "A dollar tip is very appropriate."

Bram recalled being a recipient of a few of Jo's beaming smiles at Don's wedding. They were hard to resist. It seemed as if Jo really liked Tassie. And just because he didn't approve of her asking her cousin to pose for advertisements didn't make Jo a bad person. Maybe he could get Jo to agree to his proposal. But he couldn't make that request now. Not here with Tassie looking on.

"Well, you're done for the day, Tassie." Jo handed his sister a check. "Here's what I owe you for the week. Would you go lock the rear door and turn off the light?"

"Sure." Tassie ran toward the rear of the shop.

Jo held out her hand. "Thanks for your suggestion about my situation, Bram. I will find out if I have a leg to stand on about unfair competition."

He took her soft little hand and shook it. Then he stood holding it, gazing into her blue eyes. They were not the usual blue, but the color of robins' eggs.

Bram experienced a stab of insight. Some sort of connection was forming between them. He abruptly dropped Jo's hand. No woman had gotten to him in a long time. *Maybe I should rethink this. I don't need any more complications in my life right now,* he thought. And a "cute as a button" redhead with blue eyes could cause all kinds of chaos in his well-ordered life.

Tassie came back. "Anything else I can do, Miss Jo?"

"No, you've been a great help today. Come in Monday and I'll let you know what the doctor says about how many more days I'm going to need your help. But I know I'm going to miss you when this ankle is back to normal." Jo patted Tassie's arm. His sister glowed with unmistakable pleasure.

Bram took a deep breath. He'd be back later—when he'd shored up his defenses.

Chapter Four

Later that night, after dropping off Tassie at her best friend's house, Bram stood outside at the back of Jo's shop. He steadied his nerves and then knocked on Jo's door. It was almost nine o'clock and the darkness held a chill. He pulled up the collar on his jacket even though he shivered from nerves and not from cold. He didn't like asking for favors, especially not from a pretty woman.

"Who is it?" Jo called out.

"It's me," he replied in kind, "Bram. Bram Dixon."

Within a few seconds, Jo pulled back the window curtain and squinted out at him. The light cast by the window gleamed in the night. He heard the lock being turned and the door opened.

With crutches under her arms and dressed in light-blue sweats, Jo stood in the doorway, her expression anything but welcoming. He recalled a story he'd been forced to read in college about a guy who'd woken up in bed one morning and found himself changed into a cockroach. Bram figured that Jo eyed him as if he'd had a similar transformation.

"Can I…may I come in?" Bram managed to say. His throat was as dry as Death Valley. Even on her crutches, the slender redhead made for an appealing sight. He wanted to help her walk, but kept his hands at his sides. *Keep your distance. Remember that.*

Jo maneuvered away from the door and allowed him in as far as her postage-stamp-sized kitchen. Then she halted, facing him. "Is something wrong? Is this about Tassie?"

"Well, yes, to both." He swallowed to moisten his parched mouth. "I need to talk something over with you." He forced himself to keep his eyes on hers.

With a piercing gaze, she weighed and measured him. Finally, she motioned for him to sit down at one of the two chairs at the small round kitchen table.

Relieved that he'd passed her test, he took off his brown leather jacket and hung it on the back of the chair. After he sat down, he rubbed his moist palms on his blue-jeaned thighs.

"Would you like something to drink?" she asked.

"Water," he croaked, dry-mouthed. "I'll get it."

"No, the exercise is good for me." Jo moved slowly over to the counter, her crutches thumping on the dark wood floor. She poured him a glass of water from a pitcher in the refrigerator and handed it to him.

"Now tell me what you want." She stunned him with a teasing grin.

He stood again and helped her take her place at the

table. Standing behind her, he was caught by her nape, the pale skin and auburn wisps of hair. Turning away, he propped her crutches against the counter. He sat down across from her, frowning. How to begin?

"It's Tassie," he took the plunge. "She's my youngest sister. I'm the oldest in the family and then I have four younger sisters. Tassie's the youngest." He was babbling. It hit him then that he was going to have to trust this woman with some personal information about him, about his family. His stomach congealed at the thought.

"Am I doing something, saying something to Tassie that you don't want me to?"

"No, no, quite the opposite." He held up both palms toward her. "Tassie is almost human since she began working for you."

Jo glared at him. "Tassie is a very nice young girl," she retorted. "I've found her to be quite human."

He'd blown it again. He might as well admit it. "I never seem to be able to express myself well when I talk *about* Tassie or *to* her." He pressed his lips together.

Jo watched, evidently waiting for him to go on.

It brought him the familiar empty-stomach jittering he'd always experienced at the line of scrimmage— waiting for the snap. Could he persuade her to help him? He groped for words. "I want Tassie to have a bright future."

"From what I've seen, she has one." Jo watched him.

He'd never opened up to anyone about his family. But Tassie needed him to be honest with this woman.

Bram stared at the table top and then committed himself. "My parents weren't...very steady people. They were carnies."

"What?"

"They worked the carnival circuit, handling games on the midway."

"I didn't know that," Jo said.

He analyzed her tone and found it sympathetic, not at all shocked or condescending. Though he was older than she and they hadn't been close in school, she must have heard rumors about his family. He appreciated her sensitivity. He gulped another deep breath and continued. "We kids were only with them every summer. Otherwise, we stayed with my grandmother here in town and went to school—until she died and then we stayed with our widowed aunt."

She nodded encouragingly, still making no comment.

His heart pounded as if he'd just completed ten yards pursued by an opposing team that was down by twenty points. "Our aunt was good to us, too. But at her age, it was hard for her to keep track of me and my three sisters and then Tassie came to her when she was still only a toddler." He looked into Jo's eyes.

She seemed to understand how much it was costing him to reveal all these personal details to her. She nodded as if asking him to continue.

"When my sisters were in their teens," he said, trying to make his voice sound normal in spite of his breathlessness, "they started traveling with my parents. They got into trouble." Bram hunched up a shoulder.

"Do you mean in trouble with the law or—"

"I mean pregnant and unmarried in their teens." Bram's grim expression set like concrete.

"I see."

His pulse throbbed. Yard by yard, word by word, he was ripping himself open, revealing himself to this near stranger. "The long and short of it is that they all got into trouble in one way or another. When my aunt died while I was finishing college, Tassie spent a couple of years traveling with my parents until they disappeared after dropping Tassie off with my oldest sister."

"Your parents disappeared?" Surprise laced her voice.

He shrugged, trying to appear unconcerned. "They took off for California and we haven't heard from them since. I think they're dead, but we don't know."

"My father disappeared when I was ten." Jo covered the top of her mug with her hands as though warming them.

"What happened to him?" Bram asked. Maybe this woman could understand Tassie's feelings of loss.

She shrugged. "He left for work one day and never came home. Mom tried to find him, but we never did. She died two years later from cancer."

His own sympathy bubbled up. He had to clench his hands to keep from reaching out to her. "What happened to you?"

"My mother's sister, Aunt Becky, took me in and raised me." Their eyes met with understanding. Bram took heart. "How did Tassie end up here with you?" she asked with evident sympathy.

Almost home free, he sprinted toward the goal, now so near. "When Tassie was still so little, I thought she needed to be with a woman. But none of our sisters could really keep her full-time, so she went to live with each in turn. Then she ended up with Natasha, her next oldest sister…." He halted there, not wanting to go into detail about Natasha's shortcomings. "Anyway when I got this job, I decided I'd better take Tassie under my wing." He saw Jo soften completely. He tasted victory.

Jo thought the man across from her looked exhausted. From revealing so much personal history? She ached for Tassie…and Bram. Still, she tightened her resistance. Everyone had suffered. Everyone had a story. She folded her hands to keep herself from touching him. *Why do I always end up reaching for him? I thought I had more sense than that.* "It sounds like you've taken on a big job."

"I don't want Tassie to get into trouble." His words rushed out, tumbling over each other. "I want her to do well in high school and go on to college. I want her to have a good life."

He looked as though he were appealing to her for something. *What?* "From what I've seen of your sister I don't think that will be a problem."

"She needs a woman in her life."

This struck Jo as ominous. *What do you want from me, Bram?*

"You see," he continued, looking down, "because I had someone who cared about me, believed in me, I didn't fall into the traps my sisters did."

"Your grandmother?" She tried not to let any emotion color her expression or her tone.

"Yes, when I was little. But in high school my coach was the one who pushed me and made me do right. He made me think I could be somebody. I could do more than live from day to day. I could have a life, a good life."

Jo nodded, feeling solemn as she recalled all her Aunt Becky had done to encourage her. "What do you want from me?"

"I want you to help Tassie. She needs a good female role model."

Jo opened her mouth, shocked. "You hardly know me."

"I've heard a lot of good things about you. And what's more important is that Tassie respects you. Will you help me with…all the girl stuff I don't know about? I mean, you cut her bangs. She looks cute in them, but it never dawned on me that I should take her to a beauty shop or something." He ran his hands over his dark hair.

"It's a long way from cutting bangs to be a young girl's role model." Jo didn't want to say no, but how much did this man really want from her?

"I don't expect a lot from you. I'm not asking you to adopt her or anything. I just want to be able to ask you about feminine stuff. And if you could, after she stops working for you, let Tassie visit you. You don't know how much her attitude has changed already in a week."

Jo chewed her lower lip. She felt woefully inadequate about being someone's role model. *I'm only twenty-eight. Am I even old enough?* "I don't know if I'm really the person that Tassie needs."

"She needs someone," Bram insisted, "and you've already started the job." His tone turned fierce. "Didn't you ever need help?"

His impassioned question jolted Jo. *Yes, I needed Aunt Becky.* And then she realized her decision had already been made. Refusing Bram and Tassie would be impossible.

"Okay, I'll give it a try," she said with a profound hesitance still dragging inside her. "But I'll just go on doing what I'm doing. And after my ankle's better, I'll ask Tassie to stop in occasionally. Would that do it?"

"Yes." Bram gave one big inaudible sigh. "Thank you." As though sealing the bargain, he took both her hands.

His palms folded over hers, making her feel the difference between them—his roughened large hands around hers. Jo realized that she wanted Bram's touch. She tilted her head up as though seeking a kiss.

Stop right where you are, Jo. With bone-deep fear she was careful not to show, she slipped her hands from his. Her heart beat in a rapid two-step rhythm, dan-ger, dan-ger.

A week later, Jo sat in the doctor's office, looking at the X-ray he'd clipped over a lighted panel. "My ankle's broken then?" Jo despaired.

"Yes, just a hairline crack really." He ran his finger along a barely visible white line. "The first X-ray missed it."

"So that's why I'm still unable to put weight on it." Jo felt cold waves of helplessness rush over her.

"Correct. A sprain would have healed within seven to ten days. As soon as you called me, I knew we'd missed something the first time. Sorry."

Jo shrugged. "It's just one of those things." What else could she say? She couldn't throw herself on the floor and have a hissy fit.

"The good news is twofold. Everything we did for the sprain was good for a break, too. So you just need to keep the ankle in the soft splint I put on it today and keep using the crutches until you don't need them."

"How long will I need the crutches?"

"With a hairline crack like this, a month to six weeks." The doctor looked cheerful at this news.

But Jo groaned inwardly. She'd been looking forward to getting back to normal and only seeing Tassie and Bram once or twice a week. Now Tassie would have to continue to come every day. Jo would have to see Bram daily and show no evidence whatsoever of the havoc his nearness caused her.

In addition, the ads had finally brought her some business and she had several spring weddings to do. She didn't know if Henderson's had given up the new customer discount or what. And she didn't have time to find out. She could still work, but crutches would slow her down. Now she'd need Tassie more than ever. *I can do this. I can keep my emotions under control.* Then Bram's face came to mind and she felt her resistance to his effortless charm crumble like a sand castle under the tide.

The third Friday afternoon in March, Jo sat at the counter, taking a phone order. "Now, how many centerpieces did you need for the luncheon?"

"Twelve," the chair of the local women's club replied. "We've been so happy with what you've done for us in previous years. You have our theme for this year. Just stay within my budget and I'm sure I'll be happy."

"I wish all my customers were as easy to please," Jo said in all sincerity.

"I wish everyone I contacted were as reliable as you. Thanks, Jo."

"Thank you!" Jo couldn't help herself. She was beaming as she hung up the phone.

"Another order?" Tassie asked from the doorway into the work room.

"Yes!" Jo felt like jumping up and dancing, but instead picked up her crutches and waved them high as if they were legs in a chorus line. "We need to celebrate. Lock the back door. We're going to walk down the street and get malts at the ice cream parlor."

"Cool!" Tassie ran to the rear and then returned, pulling on her red lightweight jacket. The first enticing breath of spring had arrived with the morning.

The two of them reached the ice cream place, ready

to indulge. "Two chocolate malts, my good woman," Jo ordered airily, "and whipped cream on top of both." The waitress smiled at them and quickly whipped up their treats.

"So how is school going?" Jo asked, remembering she was supposed to be helping the girl, not just filling her with tasty sugar.

Tassie shrugged one shoulder and looked down.

"It's hard making many friends when you're the new kid," Jo said, trying to draw out the girl.

"Yeah," Tassie grunted.

Well, the direct approach wasn't working. Another thought came to Jo's mind. She studied Tassie's complexion. It had the teen look. A stray blemish here and there.

"Why are you looking at me like that?" Tassie looked puzzled.

"What skin care products do you use?"

Tassie's eyebrows lifted. "I wash it with soap."

Jo made a sound of despair. "Good grief, I'm glad I asked. We've got to get you busy taking care of that lovely skin of yours."

Tassie grunted again. "My skin isn't lovely." She pointed at one of the blemishes.

"Proper skin care can help with that. The most important thing is to get you started taking care of your skin. It's never too young to start a skin-care regimen."

Tassie looked intrigued in spite of herself.

"We'll go to Holly's someday soon after work. You'll need cleansing cream. Every evening and morning, apply it in circles over your face and neck. Then rinse with warm water and pat your skin dry."

Tassie listened intently while drawing on her straw.

"Never, never rub your skin with a towel," Jo lectured. "After you cleanse, then apply moisturizer. We'll get you one made especially for skin like yours—not too dry, not too oily and one moisturizer with a hint of menthol to dry up any blemishes. But you will have much fewer if you start taking care of your skin."

Tassie looked worried. "I don't know if I have enough money saved."

"No problem. You can pay me out of your next check. I really appreciate all your help. It seems like since I can't get around easily, everything I touch I drop."

"Hey." Bram walked in the door. "I was coming to the shop and saw you two."

His entrance shook Jo. She almost dropped her malt.

"Oh, Bram, Miss Jo's teaching me about how to take care of my skin. Can you lend me some money for moisturizer and stuff and I'll pay you back when I get my check?"

Bram seemed uncertain, and Jo gave him a look, reminding him that she was only doing what he'd asked her to.

"Sure, sis," Bram agreed promptly. "Jo must know what she's talking about. Her skin looks great."

Jo felt herself go pink at his compliment. *He doesn't mean it. He's just going along.* "You're early," Jo pointed out, not voicing the final word she was thinking which was *again*. It seemed that the more she tried to distance herself from Bram, the more she found him underfoot.

"Tassie mentioned that your work-counter sink was leaking underneath." He pulled a jar out of his jacket pocket. "I brought some plumber's compound. That might take care of it without your calling a plumber."

"Really, you don't need to—"

"My pleasure, ma'am." He smiled at her.

Her insides melted under the onslaught of his approval. She'd have to get him alone and tell him he didn't have to do this stuff just because she was helping his sister. She preferred him to wait outside in his truck as he had at first. Getting him to do this again would be simple self-defense.

Chapter Five

Back at her shop, Jo fidgeted on her workbench. She tried to concentrate on a fresh-flower arrangement, a last-minute order she needed to get out before six. But her eyes kept drifting away from the project at hand to Bram's long legs encased in khaki chinos, stretched out on the floor beside her stool. His head and upper torso hidden under her work sink, Bram had overborne all her objections and was fixing the leaky pipe. *Thank heaven, today is Friday and this week is almost over. Tassie won't be coming Saturday.* And tomorrow, Jo had something to look forward to, breakfast at the Mimosa Bed and Breakfast with her two best friends—Hannah and Elizabeth. She took strength from this thought

"How's business?" Bram's muffled voice drifted up from below.

"Better." She put the final touch on the arrangement of lavender hyacinths and daisies.

"The ads helped, then?"

Jo had asked herself the same question. "I guess. I just know that my customers started coming back to me."

"Why not?" Bram demanded. "You're really good at this stuff."

His words weren't poetry but she couldn't help herself. She sparkled, zinging with his praise.

Tassie walked in. "I swept the front area." She paused by her brother's legs. "How's it going, big brother?"

"Almost done," Bram grunted as though working hard at something.

"Bram," Tassie continued, "Miss Jo invited me to church this Sunday. Can I go?"

Silence.

Jo said a quick prayer for Bram to agree. For a bright future, Tassie needed more than lessons on being a lady. Jo hoped she could give her a taste for the faith that did not fail.

"Which church is it?" he asked in a cautious voice.

"The big church around the corner," Tassie replied.

"Okay. What time's the service?"

Tassie turned to her.

Jo cleared her throat. "Nine o'clock for Sunday school. I'd be glad to pick Tassie up. Or I should say my Aunt Becky is going to pick me up and we can stop for Tassie."

Bram slid out from under the sink. "No, I'll bring her. I've thought several times this year about getting into a church, but I haven't followed through. Thanks for the nudge."

Jo looked down on Bram, stretched out in all his masculine glory just inches from her feet. He gazed up at her with those dark, serious eyes of his. Suddenly she felt as though she'd run around the block ten times. Despite her galloping emotions, she wanted Tassie and Bram at church. After all, Aunt Becky had taken her to church as a child and God had brought Jo through all her hard times. He could do the same for Tassie.

People needed God—to know his love and redemption. And Jo was happy that Bram hadn't fought her on this. *But I didn't think he'd come, too*. She pressed her lips together tightly, though she hadn't spoken a word aloud. *Don't be petty, Jo. It isn't attractive.*

"Great!" Tassie did a brief cheerleader-type jump. "I'll deliver that for you." She pointed to the arrangement in front of Jo.

"Okay. It's just two blocks away. And then you'll be done for the day."

"I can drive you." Rising in one fluid motion from the floor, Bram reached into his pocket for keys.

Jo had trouble breathing.

"No! I know where the person lives," Tassie objected. "I'll be there and back before you know I'm gone." With that, Tassie picked up the arrangement and left via the front door.

Only inches apart, Bram and Jo looked at each other. The space between them vibrated with tension.

Jo felt frozen in place. She rarely let herself be alone like this with men. That must be why an overwhelming awareness of Bram lapped over her in waves. Everything about him shouted masculinity! His strength and the force of his personality rolled through her like thunder. It wasn't just that he was a good-looking man. He was a man who loved his sister very much and was willing to put that love into action by caring for her.

Jo realized she was clutching a roll of floral tape like a life line. With trembling fingers, she forced herself to lay it down on the counter. She racked her brain for something to talk about, any topic. She closed her eyes. But her brain only taunted her as she imagined Bram pulling her close, leaning down and…kissing her. She opened her eyes. And found Bram's lips only a breath from hers. "Bram," she whispered.

"Why can't I get you out of my mind?" he murmured in reply.

"I…I…"

He kissed her—softly. Just a touch of his lips over hers, the brush of a dragonfly's wing.

Jo's world stood on end. *Don't kiss me. Kiss me again.* But all she managed was a sigh.

The kiss ended and Bram gazed into her eyes. "I shouldn't have done that." But he didn't sound sorry, just…surprised. Did he feel the way she did—astounded?

"Jo!" Aunty Becky's voice interrupted the moment.

Bram took a step backward and Jo swiveled her stool to face Aunty Becky as she walked in from the rear.

The woman stopped in her tracks and grinned. Jo's flushed face and Bram's guilty expression must have told her all she needed to know.

The next morning, Jo sat at Hannah's table in her breakfast nook. Usually Jo felt at her best when spending time with her two lifelong friends. Now, however, she felt like a traitor to them. She couldn't let on about her secret kiss. Consequently, she couldn't relax. She felt as if she'd swallowed a beehive.

Her stomach buzzed and she wondered if she could keep down more than a cup of coffee. But only inches away, Hannah's delectable pecan rolls beckoned with an indescribable fragrance. Jo gave in to temptation and reached for one.

"What's up with you, Jo?" Elizabeth asked.

Jo stopped with the roll halfway to her mouth. Busted. Had Bram's kiss left an indelible mark on her—only visible to her two dearest friends?

Stalling, Jo took a bite of the roll and savored its buttery caramel sweetness and rich pecan flavor while thinking of a good alibi. "I'm bummed about this ankle," she excused herself. "I'll be going into my busy season soon—Easter lilies, spring weddings, graduations, proms, bridal showers, Mother's Day."

"Hey! Spring is my busiest season, too," Elizabeth, the most successful and sassiest Realtor in town, interrupted her. "But you look...I don't know...different somehow." Elizabeth looked to Hannah. "Is it just my imagination?"

"No," Hannah said as she scrutinized Jo, "something's got her upset. What is it?"

Acknowledging defeat, Jo dropped the roll onto her plate. "Well, if you must know—it's Bram Dixon."

"Uh oh," Hannah intoned. "He isn't getting to you, is he?"

"That's what I want to know," Elizabeth joined in. "What's this I hear about him camping at your shop every afternoon?"

Leaning her elbows on the embroidered tablecloth, Jo put her head into her hands. Her thoughts whirled in her mind. "He haunts the place. I can't get rid of him."

"Doesn't he trust you with his sister?" Hannah asked. "Everyone says he's overprotective. He positively hovers over the poor child."

"That's not fair," Jo snapped, putting down her hands. "He loves Tassie very much."

"Are you weakening on us, Jo?" Hannah demanded.

"No," Jo placed her hands on her hips and stared her friends down. "I have no intention of giving in to this sudden frailty. But I'm still human, aren't I? And Bramwell Dixon is temptation spelled out in big bright-red capitals."

"We all pledged to keep away from men," Hannah said. "Year after year, I host weddings in the house and my gardens. And year after year, I watch those marriages break apart." Hannah frowned, but she seemed to be inside herself, deep in remembrances.

Jo waited.

Hannah looked up. "You have a good life, Jo. Do

you want to ruin it by getting involved with a man just because he's good-looking? And you know he almost went pro. He must have an ego the size of Alaska."

"He does not," Jo defended him in spite of herself. "Bram was irritating at my cousin's reception, but since then I've found him to be kind and caring." The truth was the truth.

"Honey, don't get sucked in by his finer qualities." Elizabeth gripped Jo's arm. "Just remember no matter how pleasant it feels in the beginning, it will only bring you tears and regret in the end."

Jo's intransigence crumbled. Her hands slid from her hips and she took Hannah's hand and one of Elizabeth's and gave her friends a tremulous smile. "That's what I needed to hear."

"You're not giving in to this, right?" Hannah met Jo's eyes.

"No, not an inch." Jo said staunchly, feeling hollow all the same. Bram had devastated her with just one kiss.

Hannah squeezed Jo's hand and so did Elizabeth.

"Just remember what happened to our mothers," Elizabeth reminded her. "Our daddies all betrayed them."

"Yes, it's unpleasant, but true," Hannah pronounced, "in the end, men bring only trouble. We learned that from our own families and from Johnny…." Hannah's voice faltered and she looked away.

"So are we standing by our pledge—no men, friends forever," Elizabeth asked.

"Right," Jo assented. *But that kiss possessed an unforeseen power over me and that makes it all the*

*harder. This is going to be tough, Lord. But help me to
keep my emotional distance from Bram, especially at
church tomorrow. It wouldn't work out between him
and me. I'm sure Bram will make some woman a great
husband someday. I can't be untrusting and have a
marriage turn out right. That alone would doom us to
failure for sure. And I just don't have the faith it takes
to trust a man with my heart.*

"Amen," the congregation said together at the end
of the pastor's prayer. And they all sat down, rustling
and whispering to children and spouses. Jo sat in her
usual pew halfway up the aisle on the west side. She
liked to have a good view of the stained-glass window
depicting John the Baptist baptizing Jesus in the Jor-
dan River. Jo had always loved Christ's sweet expression as he looked heavenward. Today, she drew as
much peace as she could from it.

On one side of her sat Aunt Becky, as usual. On the
other sat Tassie and Bram. Did they have to sit with
her? Didn't Bram realize that this would start the gossip grapevine churning out all kinds of foolish spec-
ulation about them being a couple?

At that moment, she glanced toward him and their
eyes met. She felt her face flood with a warm blush. *All
she could think of was how his lips had felt on hers. I
shouldn't be thinking about that in church of all places.*

Bram found he was having a hard time keeping his
attention forward. Jo's short, spiky red hair acted like
a beacon in the church. His eyes kept turning to her.

Why did I kiss her? What was I thinking? I shouldn't mislead her into thinking I want to start a relationship with her. I don't have what it takes to keep a woman. I learned that years ago.

Bram shut down his mind and focused on the pastor. *That's what I'm here for anyway—to listen to the sermon.* It felt good to be in the house of the Lord again. Throughout his childhood, his grandmother and aunt had herded his sisters and him to church every week. This would be good for Tassie, too.

"Our scripture today," the pastor said, "is found in Hebrews 11:1, 'To have faith is to be sure of the things we hope for, to be certain of the things we cannot see.'" The man at the pulpit looked out over them. "Our trust in God is crucial to our joy and outlook in this life and our relationships with those around us. Christ promises us a peace that passes all understanding, but only if we keep our hearts turned to him, only if we have faith in his ability to work for our good—no matter what the circumstances. What men tear down because of their imperfection, God can rebuild. Do you believe that?

"What problems are you trying to solve without God's help? What sorrows have you found yourself unable to heal from? What areas of your life haven't you surrendered to God?"

Bram felt each of the pastor's gentle words burn him like a fiery dart. The problem he was trying to solve was how to help Tassie grow up and have a good future. As the last few weeks had passed, he'd tried to keep his focus on that. But his unruly mind drifted back to his ex-fiancée Marsha, to his last year in college when they'd been engaged to marry. The same year he'd been forced by an injury to give up any thought of a pro football career. That old ache hadn't released its hold on him. And it still gripped him painfully. He nearly rubbed the area around his heart.

What a fool I was to think that I was lovable and that Marsha loved me. She saw right through me. I wasn't anybody special even if I could run with a football. He glanced once more at Jo. Could he trust her? Why am I asking myself that? I'm not looking for love. I just want to do a good job with my team and in raising Tassie. That's enough.

Finally, the pastor signaled them to rise for the closing hymn, "Under His Wings." Bram shared a hymnal with Tassie and sang, "Under His wings I am safely abiding, though the night deepens and tempests are wild. Still I can trust Him. I know He will keep me; He has redeemed me and I am His child." Bram let bittersweet memories of singing this hymn with his grandmother, aunt and all his sisters around him come. His family had splintered and now he only had Tassie, but for such a short time. Then he'd be alone again.

The song ended with the chorus, "Under His wings who from His love can sever?" *Not alone. I was forgetting you, God.* Bram's heart swelled with a sudden feeling of God's pleasure. *Sorry I've been away so long, Lord. But I'm back.* "Under His wings—" Bram filled his lungs with air, letting the joy of finding God again come up through him with the song's melody "—my soul shall abide, safely abide forever."

The organ swelled with the postlude and then chatter broke out all around him. "Hey! Coach!" Adam Norton, one of his freshman players, bounded up the aisle and grabbed his hand. "Great to see you in church today, sir." But Adam's gaze merely grazed Bram and settled onto Tassie.

"This is my sister, Tassie," Bram said.

"Hi," Adam said, his gaze not wavering from Tassie's face.

"Hi," Tassie returned, blushing bright pink.

Bram tried to figure out if Adam had said something to embarrass his sister. What was upsetting about "Hi?"

"You should come to our youth group, Tassie," Adam said, his voice coming out in a rush. "It's on Wednesday evenings at six-thirty. I never miss it."

"I'll th-think about it," Tassie stuttered and blushed more.

Bram finally got it, and was amused. Puppy love at first sight. And in church. What could be safer?

He looked over Tassie's head and made eye contact with Jo for the first time that day. He read his assessment of Tassie and Adam reflected in her eyes.

This gave him a swift kick. He'd asked Jo to help him with Tassie, but he hadn't realized how nice it would feel to have someone to share his sister with. It was almost like having a real family.

Chapter Six

Late the next Saturday afternoon, Jo reclined on her sofa while Bram ran the vacuum back and forth over her living-room carpet. Bram was free to come over because Tassie was at the brand-new library with a friend doing homework. Jo clutched her mug of tea with both hands which itched to yank the vacuum's cord out of the wall socket. Why wouldn't the man take no for an answer?

The wail of the sweeper cut off suddenly. "Thank you, Bram," she said, steel in her tone. "You've done enough. You don't have to do anything more. This is your day off."

Her words evidently fell on deaf ears because with a snap, the man wound up the cord and put away the vacuum in the broom closet. Then, with intense concentration, he began swinging the sagging door to her bedroom back and forth, watching it as it scraped the carpet.

She in turn couldn't stop herself as she also concentrated on the way the muscles of his back moved under his shirt. She clutched the mug so tightly her fingertips felt numb.

"This door needs planing," he said, completely unconcerned about his effect on her, "I'll go out and get my planer from the truck. And I need to tighten the hinges."

"Bram!" Jo called to his back already in the kitchen, "you don't need to do this."

He halted and turned around. He braced his hands on both sides of the door frame, leaning toward her. His broad shoulders filled the doorway. "Jo, just relax and drink your tea. Why fuss? You're helping me. I'm helping you. What's the big deal?" He left her, running down the wooden steps outside, making them rattle.

"The big deal, Bramwell Dixon, is that you are a constant temptation to me," she muttered to herself. "This is wearing me out." And worst of all, she felt herself weakening under wave after wave of Bram's tender care over the past week. One by one, he was repairing all the little things around the shop and apartment that had long needed the attention of a handyman. Now, none of her sinks or faucets dripped. She had new electrical switches. Today he'd mopped her floors and vacuumed her carpeting. And now he was doing something to her sagging door. It was more temptation than she could bear!

Whistling, Bram came back inside, letting the door slam behind him. "It's a lovely day outside. April is almost here. It's too bad you can't get out for a walk. How's that ankle doing? Any better?"

His jaunty whistling did things to the hair on the back of her neck. She ignored his question. Did he have to be concerned about her health and happiness into the bargain? Was he trying to drive her stark raving mad?

She again stared helplessly at him as he began removing screws from her bedroom door hinges with a whirring electric drill. When he finished and put down the drill, he turned to her. "Did Tassie say anything to you about youth group?"

She tried to block out the high wattage of his smile and how it sent shivers through her. "You mean did she say anything to me about Adam Norton?" she asked archly.

"Well, did she?" Bram picked up his drill.

"She enjoyed it very much, and yes—" Jo watched how his deep-brown eyes didn't leave hers as he listened to her "—she had a few nice…very carefully chosen words to say about your freshman quarterback."

"Which were?"

She hesitated, feeling herself warm under his gaze.

He grinned suddenly. "Come on. Don't make me beg, just tell me, okay?"

"She said that he introduced her to everyone, that everyone was very nice to her and that Adam was a gentleman. Evidently, he opened a few doors for her." Jo smirked in spite of herself.

"You women are so easy." Bram chuckled and turned away. "We open a few doors for you and you fall at a man's feet."

Jo tried to analyze his tone. It was in part teasing and in part something else. What? Bitter?

Bram lifted the freed door off its hinges and then stood it up against the wall. "I'll take this outside into the alley. I don't want to get wood shavings on this rug." But, making no move to leave, he leaned his shoulder against the vacant doorjamb. "This is okay, right? I mean Adam and Tassie getting to know one another. He's a good kid. But…" He shrugged. "Help me out here."

His sincere love for his sister whirled, swirled through her, taking no prisoners. "Why aren't you married?" Jo blurted out and then felt like clamping her hands over her mouth. Where had that come from?

Bram eyed Jo. Why had she asked him that? It didn't sound like her. And not all women had marriage on their mind. Some just liked to add another name to their list of conquests. He'd learned that sobering fact long ago. But he wouldn't talk about that to an innocent like Jo. "I'm not much for romance."

"Me neither."

Bram nodded, feeling solemn. The little she'd revealed to him about her father abandoning her family gave him a pretty good idea why she agreed with him on this subject. When she didn't look away, he dredged up some words to satisfy her. "I guess I got…I think *jaded* is the word. You know, when you're a football player, women act strange around you."

"You mean they throw themselves at you?" Jo's mouth quirked into a wry smile. "What does it feel like to be a rock star?"

He grinned back at her, but felt the familiar dull sadness inside. "Mick Jagger—I'm not. But I did feel often that they didn't care anything about the man inside the jersey. They didn't care about Bram, just the quarterback. It's a humiliating experience."

"I hadn't thought of that." Jo looked abashed. "I guess I thought men don't care about a how a woman feels about them—"

"As long as we're getting what we want?" His light tone had converted into harsh sarcasm.

She blushed and lowered her eyes. "Sorry. I should know by now that you're not a taker. You're a giver."

Her words blessed him. "Thank you, Jo." His voice thickened with feeling. "That's the nicest compliment I've ever received."

She shook her head as though shaking off his thanks. "Tassie needs new clothes."

"What?" Jo's swift switch of topics caught him unprepared. "What do you mean?"

"She has a number of dress occasions looming ahead." Jo's tone became brisk, businesslike. "Most notably the eighth-grade spring fling and her graduation party."

"Dress occasions. You mean she needs some new dresses?"

Jo's face crinkled into one of her irresistible smiles. "Yes, quick on the uptake as always—you got it. She needs new dresses, shoes, stockings, jewelry and I think a manicure. And a gift. You need to get her an eighth-grade graduation gift, some keepsake of the occasion."

Feeling out of his depth, he asked, "What would be good for that?"

"I was thinking of a gold locket."

"You mean like a necklace?" He pictured his sister with a nice gold necklace.

"Yes, that's it." Jo wrinkled her nose at him as though mocking. "But a locket opens and she can place a picture of her and a friend or you inside."

He doubted Tassie would want his photo around her neck. "Would you help me pick it out?"

Her face fell and she looked away again.

"I'm sorry." He hurried and sat down in the armchair near her. "I didn't mean to upset you. You're doing more for Tassie than I'd even dreamt of. I know I'm asking a lot—"

She looked up at him. "It's not that."

"Then what is it?"

"Don't you see what you're doing to me?" she whispered, not meeting his eyes. "You're making me care about you."

The words shimmered like fireflies in his mind. He couldn't think of anything to say.

"You and I both know that we aren't meant for each other," Jo continued, sounding and looking as if he'd driven her up against the ropes. "This isn't a movie or a romance novel. We're just trying to help your sister grow up a little, gain confidence. But when you come here and you do so much for me, don't you realize you're tempting me to care about you?"

No, I didn't know. But he felt the tug of his own

conscience. He'd been all too aware of the attraction she'd become to him, drawing him nearer—step by step. "Jo, when I see you with my sister—" the words came out slowly, haltingly "—I feel something for you, too."

"Gratitude?"

"No." He reached for her mug and lifted it from her fingers, setting it on the coffee table. "More." He knelt down and framed her pretty face within his hands. "Much more."

His hands trembled. To mask this, he ran his fingers through her short red hair, the color of burnished copper. It warmed his hands. His mouth hovered over hers. "May I?" he whispered. "Please?"

Her delicate hands found his, covering them. When she nodded, he felt her silky hair sliding within his palms.

He took a shuddering breath and let his lips touch hers. Fireworks exploded inside him. He craved her like sweet honey to a starving man.

And she was kissing him back. A miracle.

Had he ever kissed anyone before? No, he hadn't. He'd never kissed anyone like Jo, never kissed anyone the way he was kissing her. It was more than a kiss; it was an invitation, a plea—*Care about me, Jo. I want to care about you.*

"Y'all home?" a woman called from the doorway. "Jo?"

Bram shot to his feet.

But too late. He recognized the woman as one of Jo's

friends. And she'd seen them kissing. Now the fat was in the fire. He'd worked so hard to discourage Prescott's groupie-wannabes. Would gossip now begin?

"Hi."

Jo swiveled her office chair at her computer desk in her shop to look at the man who'd just entered.

Bram, looking disconcerted, stood with the counter between them.

"Hi." Jo felt herself turning warm crimson under his gaze. She'd come into the closed shop on Sunday afternoon to do some bookkeeping. But the computer mouse had sat idle under her palm. This man's face, the memory of his Saturday-afternoon kiss had distracted her all day yesterday and today. Concealing a shiver of recognition, she clicked Close and shut the file.

"I wanted to talk to you about that shopping trip." He wouldn't meet her eyes.

"Oh."

"When did you want to take her?" He stared at the counter between them.

"I thought we'd go during her Easter break from school. The doctor says he'll be taking off my cast by then. Aunt Becky will man the shop for me. I thought we'd go to Little Rock." How could such bland words hide such longing?

"That sounds good," he said, his tone stilted.

"Right," she said.

"How much should I give her to spend?" he asked. He looked as nonplussed as she felt.

"Well, how much will your budget allow?"

"Money's not a problem."

"Okay. I'll use my best judgment then."

"Right. And about this graduation locket. Did you want to go ahead with that?"

She wanted to refuse but couldn't. "Fine. I've just been looking at some on the Internet. Or we can go to Mitchell's."

"Great." He stared at her and she stared back at him. He braced his hands against her counter. "I'm… afraid I…embarrassed you yesterday," he said, looking pained.

"You mean…" She was not going to say, "when you were kissing me?"

"Your friend looked shocked."

"I guess she was." An understatement. Jo had begged Elizabeth not to tell Hannah.

"I didn't mean to embarrass you." He stared at his hands.

"No." Of course, he hadn't. *Why did you kiss me, Bram? Just to prove you could? To see that I had no defenses?*

"Well, I guess that's all I came to say." He pushed away from the counter.

"Okay." She gave him a bright artificial smile. She hadn't felt like this in a long time, not for years. Pain squeezed around her heart, nearly wrenching a groan from her.

"Okay. See you." He lifted a hand in farewell and then turned away.

Her hand reached for him, but of course, he didn't see that. Just as well. "See you," she mumbled.

The bell jingled and the door shut behind him. *Lord, I don't think I can survive many more conversations like that one. Couldn't you just blot out my feelings for this man? Hannah and Elizabeth are counting on me to remain strong. I'm not going to give in to temptation. The fleeting joy would not equal the loss when we parted. I can't foresee a happy ending for Bram and me.*

Chapter Seven

April had come with fragrant Easter lilies and early-blossoming crepe myrtle bushes cascading with crinkly pale-pink and deep-rose blooms. Despite the spring rains, the sunshine glistened all over Arkansas—sparkling and fresh. And Jo's hairline fracture had healed and the rented crutches had been returned.

Feeling the balm of springtime, Jo and Tassie, both in jeans and denim jackets, strolled through one of nearby Little Rock's glittering department stores, their mission—Tassie's new clothes. Jo entered the juniors' department and looked around. "Where are the dresses?"

The salesgirl, who appeared to be the same age as Tassie, looked at Jo as if she were an alien life form. "Dresses? Over there."

Jo shook her head and followed hanging signs to the right place. Immediately, Tassie gravitated to the flashy "cool" dresses—very short. Jo hung back, trying to come up with a strategy to point Tassie in the right direction.

"Isn't this cool?" Tassie held up a hot-pink dress made of cotton knit that looked like a T-shirt with a hem.

"Yes, it is, but it will only be cool for about ten minutes and then it will be out of style. You don't want your daughter giggling when she looks at photos of you, do you?"

Tassie looked puzzled. "What does that mean?"

"Haven't you ever seen photos of girls from the fifties wearing bright pink felt poodle skirts?"

"Ooh, you mean those big skirts that stuck out?" Tassie pantomimed a flaring skirt with her hands.

"Yes, let's find something that will not look ridiculous twenty years from now."

Tassie hung up the T-shirt dress and followed Jo to another rack of dresses. After much discussing, trying on, and haggling, Tassie said she would be content with a simple ivory linen-blend dress with a matching jacket.

"Good choice." Jo patted the girl on the back. "You can wear it to church and it will stay in style a lot longer than that first dress. Come on. We can go back to juniors' now. I did see a few things I thought you might like there."

Finally after buying shoes, dresses and a couple of pairs of pierced earrings, Jo and Tassie walked out of the department each loaded down with stylish bags. The bright sunlight glinted off metal on the tall buildings around them as they walked to the parking lot.

For a moment and for the first time in weeks, Jo felt

like looking skyward and twirling around on her toes—giggling. Guiding Tassie's purchases today made Jo feel old in one way, but in another privileged to have been given a role in Tassie's transition from child to young woman. "Tassie, I've enjoyed this so much. It was so good to get outside again and be able to walk without crutches."

"Miss Jo, can I ask you something?" Tassie asked, sounding subdued.

The two of them reached the parking lot and began looking for Jo's car. "What?" Jo hoped Tassie wouldn't be asking about the birds and the bees. Jo didn't feel up to *that* talk right now.

"How do you know if a boy likes you?"

Bram's face flickered in Jo's mind—the way he'd looked at her that day weeks ago when he'd knelt beside her sofa and kissed her. "A perennial question," Jo stalled.

"I mean, it's hard for me 'cause I'm Bram's sister."

Jo could think of several different ways being Bram's sister might make this aspect of life difficult. While she led Tassie to her car, she waited to see exactly which Tassie was addressing. "Go on," she coaxed.

"I mean he's the coach and everybody looks up to him." After stowing her bags in the back seat, Tassie got in the car. "Like, he's really special."

"Ah." So Tassie had figured out how Bram's position could help her. Jo put the key in the ignition.

"I'm nobody special."

"Yes, you are," Jo insisted, interrupting. She backed out of the parking place.

Tassie shook her head and kept talking, "Guys talk to me. And I don't know if it's 'cause they like me or just want to—" the girl's voice faltered "—I don't know."

"You mean guys might want to get to know you in order to make a favorable impression on your brother?" Jo drove onto the busy street. "That's a tough one. I don't think there is any hard and fast rule that I can give you. Each case will be judged as an individual."

"How?" Tassie asked, sounding woeful.

Jo took time to consider what to say. Tassie had a very valid concern. *I'm not really the person she should be asking. I've never even taken the chance of falling in love.*

"Tassie," Jo finally said, "I think you'll have to pay attention to your own instincts. If something doesn't feel right about a guy, then you should keep him at arm's length until you have time to get to know him."

"What do you mean at arm's length?" Tassie asked.

"I mean just be friends and take time to get to know him as a friend first." She headed down the highway that would take them back to Prescott, back to Bram. Suddenly, she realized that the advice she was giving Tassie was the advice she needed herself. What was wrong with taking a wait-and-see approach to her feelings for Bram?

"You mean not date him officially?" Tassie asked, pushing her long hair back from her face.

"Right." Jo's spirit lifted inside her, a sudden fluttering, an elation. *I don't have to make a decision about Bram right now. Why can't we just take time to get to know each other? Time will tell, they always say.*

"That makes sense."

It does. "And also you can analyze what the young man has to gain by getting to know you." Jo again thought of how Bram had revealed being used by women who were only interested in his jersey, not him. That had wounded him. What woman in her right mind could mistake how deeply Bram cared about people he loved? It was the main thing that attracted her to him.

"I mean," Jo went on, "if he's already on the team or not interested in football, that might lead you to the conclusion that he has no reason to try to impress Bram."

"Yeah." Tassie grinned. "Yeah."

Jo grinned at the relief in Tassie's voice, but more so from her own sensation of being suddenly set free. *That's the secret, Bram. We'll become friends, and if he wants more he can wait a few years. Why not?* "Let's get home and show your big brother how much of his money we were able to spend." Jo looked heavenward. *Thank you, Lord, for showing me the way.*

"Let's." Tassie laughed out loud and rolled down her window, letting spring in.

Driving down the familiar highway, Jo hummed, letting herself drink in the moment—Tassie's innocent pleasure at spending a day shopping for happy occasions and at having a boy interested in her. And her own joy at making a wise decision about Bram.

Outside Bram's house, an older two-story bungalow on a quiet street of tall maples and pines, Jo let Tassie entice her to come in to show off her new purchases to her big brother. Inside, Jo looked around with interest. This was a bachelor's house, clean but no frills. No pictures hung on the walls, no knick-knacks on the mantel. Utilitarian shades on the windows. White paint on all the walls. Bramwell Dixon was in serious need of an interior decorator.

Bram sauntered down the stairs, masculine to the max and devastating as usual. Jo tried to keep her mouth closed.

"So, did you two break the bank in Little Rock?" he teased.

His deep voice made little darts speed through her veins. "Well, we burned up the bills you gave us. Sorry, no change." Jo waved the bags she still held in each hand.

"Bram," Tassie said, "look at my graduation dress." The girl lifted the bottom of the large gold-and-white plastic bag which covered the simple ivory dress.

"I like that." Bram looked sincerely pleased. "It's…elegant. But I knew Jo would get just what you needed."

Jo couldn't help herself. She glowed with his praise.

After showing him the shoes and a few other purchases, Tassie threw her arms around him. "Thanks for everything! I never had so much money to spend and Miss Jo was great. We got shoes and everything, even underwear!"

Bram looked sincerely relieved that he hadn't been included on the shopping trip. "Good. Good."

"Well, I guess I'll be going then." Jo put down her bags.

"Oh, Jo—" Bram stopped her "—I was hoping you'd go out with me and Tassie and Adam tomorrow night."

Out with me, Jo echoed silently. A date?

"Adam?" Tassie exclaimed.

"Yeah, he dropped by looking for you. He wanted to know if I allowed you to go out on dates yet." Bram knew Tassie would not like that Adam had applied to him first.

Suddenly glaring, his sister started to fire up.

"I told him," Bram cut in, "that you won't be allowed to date one on one until you're sixteen. But…" He held up one hand. "I told him that I didn't mind him coming along on a double date—you and Adam and Jo and me—to celebrate your graduation maybe next Saturday. I thought we'd go to that new supper club in Little Rock." He turned to Jo. "What do you say?"

Chapter Eight

A week later, on Saturday night in the chic new supper club in Little Rock, Jo sat across from Bram at a crisp-linened table for two. The romantically darkened dining room was elegant in shades of burgundy and pale rose. Flute-shaped sconces of frosted glass with bands of bronze augmented the flickering candlelight on each small table. The aroma of delicious food floated over all and filled Jo with a keen anticipation of her dinner. And the murmur of intimate conversations and the chink of ice in glasses lulled her tense nerves.

Bram had been insistent that she demonstrate to Tassie how to dress and behave on a formal date. So Jo had overseen Tassie's choice of dress and Jo had worn her favorite ivory silk sheath with a mandarin collar. But she couldn't decide if she'd agreed for that reason or if in all honesty, she'd accepted the invitation primarily because she wanted to have dinner out with Bram.

In any event, he hadn't hog-tied her and dragged her

here. She'd made her decision and must face up to it. She tried to summon up her defenses against the hunk decked out in a gleaming starched white shirt and black suit and tie sitting across from her. But it was hard work.

Nearby, Adam and Tassie sat stiffly across from one another at another table for two. Jo leaned forward, "Why didn't you reserve a table for four?"

Bram glanced at his sister who appeared to be strangling the linen napkin in her lap. "Because I thought it would be nice to give them privacy. They might not want to hang out with old folks."

Jo recalled the back seat conversation she'd overheard on the drive here. Musical groups, movies and actors she'd never heard of. "I see your point."

He grinned.

And she couldn't argue with the fact that the man looked *fine* tonight. Mighty fine. Bram Dixon did clean up well. If possible, he was more dangerously handsome tonight than he'd been at her cousin's Valentine's Day wedding. She gripped the end of her swizzle stick strung with crimson maraschino cherries and stirred her rosy Shirley Temple.

"I'm glad I was able to persuade you to come with me," Bram said, "I thought it would do Tassie good to see how a lady behaves on a formal date."

"So you said—repeatedly." She bit off the first cherry and chewed, its tangy sweetness flowing over her tongue.

He chuckled. "Well, you did take some stiff persuasion."

She nodded, but did not reply. She couldn't. Gazing at Bram's sculpted features in the flickering candlelight had suddenly blocked her throat. She wanted to trace his sun-highlighted eyebrows with her fingertips and tease the dark hair that dipped low over his forehead.

Jo pushed away the thought. They were in a public place. Bram was unlikely to lean over and kiss her here and now. And on the way home, the teens in the back seat would be adequate chaperones. Why not just relax and enjoy the evening?

A tall, silver-haired man appeared at their table and cleared his throat. "Miss Jo?"

Snatched from her comfortable mood, she stared up into the face of Mr. Henderson of Henderson's Florals. She recognized him from his TV ads. She gaped, keeping her mouth closed by biting her lower lip.

"May I sit down for just a moment?" He pulled out the chair. "I have been meaning to drive over to Prescott and apologize in person, but things keep coming up."

Jo opened her mouth, closed it and tried again. "Apologize?"

Mr. Henderson sat down. "Yes, I don't know if you were aware of it, but I started semi-retirement at the end of last year. My wife and I spent most of the winter in Florida."

"Oh?" She tried to come up with his motive for telling her this.

"And so my son is buying me out and taking over

the business. I'm afraid in trying to impress me with his ability to turn a hefty profit that he caused you to lose some business this winter by opening that store in Prescott."

Oh. That. Jo looked down into her Shirley Temple, not trusting herself to reply.

"And his twenty-five-percent-off new-customer rate?" Mr. Henderson prompted.

"Well, I did think that was…rather…" Jo couldn't come up with a word she wanted that was polite.

"Thoughtless," Henderson supplied. "I'm afraid my son didn't realize that giving such a deep discount on top of investing in another store cut way into our profits."

"I see." This had all occurred to her and she'd put it down to vindictiveness by Henderson for some unknown reason.

"Plus, since the discount was only for new customers," Henderson continued, sounding put out, "your customers would most likely only use us once. You are well-established. So what was the purpose in the first place? We only realized a tiny profit and really no new lasting customers."

Jo took strength from his words. "I wondered when—"

"When your customers started coming back to you, you wondered what we had gained by cutting into your trade the first part of the year? Is that it?"

"Yes." She smiled as she sipped her drink.

"We gained exactly zero—except the hostility of

some of the customers who didn't like our grabbing your customers, and the same from Prescott florists. I hope you won't hold any hard feelings. The shop is going to close as soon as we complete the final few obligations." Henderson offered her his hand.

"Of course." Jo shook his hand.

"And if your date will permit me, I'd like to pick up the tab for your dinner tonight?" Henderson looked inquiringly to Bram.

Jo looked to her date. *My date. That's right. For the first time in years, I'm on a date.*

"No thanks," Bram declined.

Henderson rose. "As you wish. Again, my apologies." He bowed his head and walked away.

"Well—" Jo looked at Bram with wide eyes "—what do you think about that?"

"I think it's about time," Bram added, hitting each word hard, "and that he owes you more than a dinner."

Jo laid her hand over Bram's. "I'm just glad to have the mystery solved and my customers back."

Bram claimed her hand and drew it to his lips.

Her nerve endings screamed, Warning! She glanced over at the teen couple. Had Bram forgotten that they were supposed to set them an example tonight? But she couldn't draw back her hand. His touch flowed up her arm, warming her, making her even more aware of him, if that were possible.

"Do you have any idea of how you've turned my life upside down?" he whispered.

Jo couldn't reply. She could barely breathe. So

much for the protection of a public place and teenaged chaperones.

"I never thought I'd find a woman like you—honest, caring, giving. You think of others, not just yourself. Jo, I've fallen in love with you."

She clutched his hand and choked back sudden tears. Half-heartedly, she tried to pull her hand from his. But another glance told her that Tassie and her date had no eyes for anyone but each other.

"I know you don't trust in a man's love," Bram went on. "But won't you give me a chance?"

Her world as she knew it, as she'd constructed it began crumbling. Jo found her voice. "I need time."

"That's fair." Bram's thumb traced slow circles on the flesh of her palm. "We don't have to rush into anything."

"Let's take time to get to know each other better." With each sensible word, she felt the noose around her heart and lungs loosening.

Bram drew her hand to his insistent lips again. "Time is relative."

His touch was doing things to her pulse. She checked the teens. They were still oblivious. She closed her eyes, letting her whole being concentrate on where his skin met hers. "What does that mean?" she breathed.

"It means that no one can predict how long it takes to get to know another person." He kissed the sensitive inside of her wrist.

"Bram," she whispered silently.

"Some people you never know. They keep themselves hidden. Other people, like you for instance, are easy to know. You're all out in the open, sincere. I know you, Jo." His grip became more commanding. "I know I care for you."

His deep voice stirred her pulse. "I need time," she murmured again. He rubbed her hand against his cheek. She reveled in the sensation of the hint of his beard and the firm line of his jaw. But thinking of Tassie, she drew her hand back.

"Okay, Jo. I want to give you whatever you want. Even time. But just remember my feelings won't change because I know you won't turn out to be someone I couldn't love. My heart is sure that this time is different. Because *you* are different. I've never known any woman like you before. Let me love you, Jo. That's all I want."

She wanted to ask him what he meant about this time is different. Who had he loved before and why had it ended? But she couldn't pry like that, not now. "You'll give me time?" She opened her eyes to read his.

Bram nodded, though everything inside him shouted for him to disagree. In her lustrous cream-colored dress and her auburn hair, Jo glimmered like a burst of fireworks frozen in the darkened room. He wanted Jo in his arms now. He wanted to put a ring on her finger. He wanted to kiss her sweet lips good night tonight and every night.

Her hesitance only made him firmer in his decision. Jo wasn't chasing the hot new high-school football coach or erstwhile quarterback who'd almost gone pro. She cared about him even if she denied it. He saw it in the way she closed her eyes when he kissed her hand. In the way she'd reached out to Tassie. Even in her plea for time. *But, Lord, I don't want to wait. If I can't persuade her, would you do it for me?*

Later, in the spring moonlight, Bram walked Jo up the steps to her door.

"I know why you asked me to drop you off at home first," he said with a grin. "You're not fooling me and you're not getting off without a good-night kiss."

"The kids are watching us." She nodded toward the motion-activated lamp that had flickered on at their approach.

"Then I better show Adam a good example."

"Right—"

Bram gripped her shoulders tenderly and pulled her to him. "I better show him how to do it up right." He cradled her chin in one hand and kissed her.

Jo felt her knees soften to jelly. She kissed him back slowly, forgetting her resolve, forgetting everything but him.

He finally lifted his lips from hers. "Good night… my sweet Jo."

"Good night." She felt winded and wondered if she could walk without his support.

He unlocked her door and she managed to slip inside. Bram's kisses packed way too much power. They might be illegal. Grinning, she slumped into the kitchen chair. *How am I ever going to be able to take time to get to know him when he keeps kissing me like that? How can I think when he turns my knees, my brain to mush?*

Her phone rang. She stood and answered it.

"Jo," Aunt Becky said, "I'm glad you're home. I've been calling you every half hour this evening."

"I was out with—"

"I know. I know. Come over right now. Please."

"What? What's wrong?"

"Just come." Aunt Becky hung up.

Chapter Nine

In the balmy night, Jo didn't even get a chance to knock on Aunt Becky's back door. Looking perfectly distracted, her aunt threw wide the door. Aunt Becky was wringing her hands. "Jo, I didn't read my mail when it came today. Too busy."

At her aunt's troubled tone, Jo's worry quotient zoomed. "What's wrong?"

Aunt Becky lowered her eyes and then pulled away. From the coffee table in the living room, she handed Jo an opened letter. "He must have given my name as next of kin to be notified upon his death."

Her aunt's words made no sense to Jo, so she opened the tri-fold letter and began reading. At first, it appeared to be just an official letter from an Illinois hospital to her aunt. Then she read her father's name. Shock like an invisible needle pierced Jo's lungs. Still clutching the letter, she bolted out to her car.

Aunt Becky didn't call after her. But when Jo looked in her rearview mirror, her aunt stood in the door, the light behind her outlining her silhouette. Her aunt held out one hand as though beckoning her to return, as though throwing out a lifeline.

Jo put her hand over her heart. The pain was excruciating. Was this what a heart attack felt like? She knew logically that the shock of what she'd read hadn't actually ruptured her heart. *But that's what it feels like. Why the truth, the horrible truth now, Lord, after all these years?*

Still in her pale-blue pajamas, Jo huddled, battered and crushed, under her afghan on her sofa. She'd hidden away all day Palm Sunday. Now on Monday morning, she couldn't bring herself to get dressed and go down to work. The phone rang. With effort, she lifted the receiver. "Jo's Bower," she muttered.

"Hi, Miss Jo, it's me, Tassie."

"Hi." Jo tried to infuse her voice with warmth and failed.

"I'm calling from school. My counselor said you didn't need me today."

"That's right." Jo rubbed the back of her neck; it was so tight a dime would have bounced on it. "I'm not opening today. I'm sick."

"Oh." Pause. "Could I come over anyway?"

Jo shut her eyes, fatigue and despair rolling over

her again. "I'm sick, honey. I'll be back to normal tomorrow."

"Oh, okay. Bye."

There was something in Tassie's voice. What? "Tassie—" But Jo was too late. Tassie had hung up. Jo put down the phone and buried her face in the sofa pillows. She didn't have the strength to deal with her own problems, much less Tassie's. Bram would have to handle his sister.

Some time later, the phone jangled again. Jo lay still. Let the machine pick up. The machine did, and Jo heard: "Hi, Jo, it's me." Bram's rich voice came into the shadowy room.

Just as it had Saturday night, that needle of pain pierced her. She squeezed her lips shut, trying to hold back an agonizing moan. *Bram, don't call me.*

"I just wanted to tell you how much I enjoyed Saturday night."

In her present state, she only vaguely remembered that they had shared an evening. But the memory of it caused no response in her. She was flat, filled with sawdust and ashes.

"I'll drop over early this afternoon to pick up Tassie."

No. Jo grabbed the phone. "Bram, I'm not open today. I called the school. Tassie knows."

"Jo, you're there? What's wrong?" His palpable concern didn't soothe her. She didn't want him to show concern for her.

"Some twenty-four-hour bug probably." She tried to sound casual as her pulse pounded through her. "I'll be fine tomorrow. I've got to hang up and lie down again."

"Okay. Call me if you need anything—"

"I will." She hung up. Lying back on the sofa, she pulled her afghan around her and shivered as if it were January again. *I can't face this, Lord. I can't.*

That evening, Elizabeth and Hannah flanked Aunt Becky as Jo opened her door. They filed in silently and went to the living room. Still in her pajamas, Jo sat down facing them and lowered her eyes again. Feelings, sensations, emotions she'd long forgotten gushed over and through her—cold, so cold. She felt abandoned, emptied, unprotected again—as if she'd been stripped naked for all the world to see. That was how it had felt all those years ago, to have her father walk away then. Now it all came back too vividly, too wrenchingly.

"I won't beat around the bush." Aunt Becky clasped her hands together. "Jo, you read the letter. Your father left you and your mother because he was suffering mental problems. He was severely depressed and was suicidal."

"But why was he depressed?" Jo blurted out. "What was so wrong with his life?"

"Your aunt says that the letter called his depression a clinical one," Hannah said gently. "I looked that up on the Internet today and it means that it was triggered by a chemical imbalance in his brain, not by his life."

"I don't understand." Jo looked away.

"Depression is an illness, Jo." Elizabeth sighed.

"So he left us because he was sick?" Jo snapped. "Was that better for Mom and me?"

"He didn't want the stigma of his mental illness to rub off on you or your mother." Aunt Becky reached for Jo's hands. "Attitudes are changing. Years ago admitting that he had mental problems would have affected you, tainted you. In a small town like this, people would have wondered if you'd turn out like your dad. Some people would even have shunned your family."

"Stop!" Jo jumped up. "Was that—the stigma— worse than leaving us without a word? Mama faced terrible gossip. Everyone whispering, 'What has she done to make her husband desert her?'"

Aunty Becky stood. "Your father's mind wasn't working the way it should have." Aunt Becky approached Jo with her hands held out, beseeching Jo. Elizabeth and Hannah had let Aunt Becky take center stage. But Jo felt their concern like a warm blanket around her. "He had to make a terrible decision."

"But why didn't he ever write us? No one would have had to know."

"He didn't suffer only from depression. The letter said he'd been diagnosed as manic-depressive or bipolar. The doctors spent years trying to get the right mix of medications so he could live a normal life. But he died before that could happen. Maybe he couldn't bear you knowing."

Jo sat back down, her head in her hands. "I needed him. Mama…"

"Do you realize, Jo," Aunt Becky asked, "That before he left town, he made sure all your debts were paid and he put everything in your mother's name? And she was in good health when he left. How could he have foreseen that she was going to get cancer and leave you alone?"

Images of the distant past flowed through Jo's mind—her father trying to put a barrette in her baby-fine red hair when her mother had been away for a few days, his bringing home a baby robin that had fallen out of its nest and letting her help him feed it with an eyedropper, his swinging her up into his arms when he came home from work at night. Tears welled up in her eyes. "I wish Mama had known."

"Jo," Aunt Becky said, "I'm sure she does and has for a long time. You remember her favorite verse?"

Jo nodded. "Love covers a multitude of sins." And it did. Her dad had made a poor decision, but he had been ill at the time. It explained so much. Love for her father had lain crushed and dormant all these years. But it hadn't died. Now it flowed through her warming her, quickening her. "Now," she whispered, "I understand, Daddy."

* * *

Much later that night, Jo's bedside phone rang. Her pulse racing, she picked up. "Yes?"

"Jo, it's Bram. Tassie's run away."

Chapter Ten

In Bram's pickup, Jo sat beside him as he turned onto the darkened old state highway. Flying down these back roads, they were trying to catch up with the Trailways Bus on its way to Little Rock. Jo stared straight ahead into the apron of brightness in front of the headlights.

"I just hope we can catch up with Tassie tonight," Bram said. "The world is much too dangerous a place for a fourteen-year-old girl."

"We'll find her, Bram. I know we will."

Under the cover of darkness, he took her hand in one of his.

The touch of his hand heartened her, sensitized her to him. "Why did Tassie run away?" Jo finally asked.

"I don't know." Bram sounded unhappy and distracted. "We'll have to ask her when we pick her up. Her note said she would write me when she reached Natasha's or I could call her there. I just don't get it." He slammed the steering wheel with his free palm.

"She's been doing so much better. I thought we were getting somewhere."

"I think you're right." She studied his profile by the scant green glow of the dashboard light. "Don't despair. It's a good sign that she left you a note telling you where she was going."

"I didn't think of that."

"What can I say—teens run amuck." For some reason, Jo thought of Johnny Harrison dying on prom night. She wouldn't bring that up now. "She'll be fine." She inched closer to him, either to comfort or to draw comfort. She didn't know which.

She caught herself again just as she was about to lift his hand to her cheek. She made herself release her hold on him. His hand lay on the seat just beneath hers.

He turned up his palm, caressing her hand. "I'm so glad you're with me, Jo. That I don't have to do this alone. You're so special."

Jo felt her traitorous lips tingle. *Kiss me, Bram.* But she must find out something important first. She recalled their conversation just a night ago. He'd said that this time was different. There would be no better opportunity than now to ask him what he meant by that. "Bram," she murmured, "who did you love before me?" She held her breath.

"Why are you asking me that?"

She blushed at the awkward way she'd phrased her question and drew back from him. "You said I was different, that this time was different." Uncertainty shivered through Jo. Had she asked too much? "What did you mean?"

He stared straight ahead for a few moments but didn't release her hand. "I was engaged to be married my last year in college." His voice hardened. "She was beautiful and I thought I'd made it. I was about to be drafted to the NFL."

"But you had an injury?" Jo ventured. The halo of city lights hovered ahead on the dark horizon.

"Then you've heard the gory details. I wrecked my knee and the draft offers vanished along with my fiancée. She married a teammate of mine that summer who went on to the NFL."

"I'm sorry." But Jo couldn't be completely sorry. She brought his hand close to her, cradling it.

"It was a definite learning experience for me." His voice became more normal. "I thought she wanted me and what she really wanted was a pro football player. It didn't do much for my self-esteem."

"She was a fool."

"Well, she put me off women for a long time." Bram slowed for a stop sign. "In fact, I'd pretty much stopped dating after that. I found that being a coach unfortunately drew the same kind of woman and I wasn't interested in women who were more interested in *what* I was than in who I was." Bram looked at her.

Jo smiled and laid a palm on his shoulder. The urge to rest her cheek there also taunted her. "You can't accuse me of that. I don't care a thing about football."

"Is that a fact?" Grinning broadly, he began to slow

as they drove into a Little Rock. "We're here." His tone became serious again and he put both hands on the wheel. "Let's hope we caught up with the bus."

Bereft of his touch, she moved closer to him, needing him. "Well, we should have."

They pulled up to the curb. The Trailways Bus was parked there, too. Relief flooded Jo. Now they just had to talk Tassie into going home with them.

Bram got out and so did Jo.

"Bram!" Tassie cried and ran toward him. "Oh, Bram! Miss Jo! Take me home!"

Jo and Bram sat at his kitchen table. During the ride home, Tassie had told them about overhearing girls talking about her dating Adam. They'd said several nasty things about Tassie. But by the time Jo and Bram had shown up, Tassie had already worked out the girls' motivation—jealousy. And she'd been more than ready to come home. Now after she'd inhaled two sandwiches and two glasses of milk, she'd gone up to bed. Peace had settled over Jo and Bram. The clock read a few minutes after two in the morning. "I'll drive you home," he said.

They both stood up. Bram opened his arms and Jo walked into them as if she'd always known them as a safe harbor. She rested her head on his shoulder, feeling his strong arms around her.

"I'm afraid I'm going to have to break a promise I made you," he said, his lips grazing her forehead.

"What promise was that?" she asked, completely unalarmed.

"To give you time. I want to marry you this June."

"June?" She was thrilled. She was aghast.

"Yes, if we marry in June, I'll have two months to focus every moment on you. You realize you'll be marrying a coach and my autumns are pretty much devoted to my team."

"I don't remember your proposing." Turning her head, she grinned at him, teasing.

"Will you marry me?"

"Yes." As the simple but binding word floated over her tongue, it had never felt more right.

"In June?"

"Yes." Her feeling of rightness doubled.

"I just won the Super Bowl."

Jo laughed out loud.

Epilogue

On the last day of June in the bride's room at Hannah's Mimosa Bed and Breakfast, Aunt Becky in her mauve aunt-of-the-bride outfit fussed with Jo's veil as the bride sat in front of a gilded vintage vanity. "I don't know how we pulled this all together in two months' time," Becky said with deep sincerity and fatigue.

After initial hesitance, Hannah and Elizabeth had accepted the fact that Jo was serious about marrying Bram. Both had agreed to be bridesmaids. Now, dressed in very simple sleeveless silk mauve gowns, they hovered behind her, all three of them peering over Jo's shoulder into the mirror. The door opened. "It's time," Elizabeth's mother told them. "Elizabeth, you're first." Elizabeth and Hannah both blew kisses to Jo and then swished out of the room.

Jo rose and turned. To Becky, she'd never looked lovelier. Near tears of joy, Becky pulled the veil down over Jo's lovely face. "I wish your mother could be here."

Jo's lips trembled into a smile. "Me, too."

Becky rested both hands on Jo's shoulders. "Honey, I want you to know something. I've prayed for your wedding ever since the day of Johnny Harrison's funeral. I overheard that pact you three girls swore to. But you and your friends deserve good, honest men. Bram is the perfect man for you. Now that you've regained your faith in men because of him, will you pray that God will bring Elizabeth and Hannah their true loves, too?"

Agreeing with a nod, Jo pressed her lips together, obviously holding back emotion.

Becky remembered that every good and perfect gift comes from the Father above. She closed her eyes and prayed, *Father, you've finally answered my prayers for Jo. Now please send two more good men for Elizabeth and Hannah. I'm not going to quit until all three have found the love they deserve. In Jesus' name, amen. And I mean it, Lord.*

* * * * *

THE DREAM MAN

Lenora Worth

To my husband, Don,
my very own dream man.

And if I have all faith, so as to remove
mountains, but do not have love, I am nothing.

—*I Corinthians* 13:2

Chapter One

He could tell she didn't want to do this.

Jake Clark watched, fascinated, as Elizabeth Sinclair shook her head and tried to hide behind the girth of a woman wearing a ridiculous cobalt-blue hat. He could barely see Elizabeth's golden-brown curls behind the dyed ostrich feathers fluttering out in the afternoon wind.

But he sure knew she was there.

Jake had taken a liking to Elizabeth the minute they'd met just before the ceremony. His best friend Bram Dixon had just married Elizabeth's friend Jo Woodward. This was a happy occasion for Jake. He was glad Bram had finally found someone to love. But he sure couldn't tell that by the little bundle of bridesmaid he'd watched coming up the aisle earlier. Elizabeth had done her bridesmaid duties with a look of solid fear plastered on her freckled face, her toes tapping nervously in her three-inch mauve-colored heels.

Apparently, hazel-eyed Elizabeth Sinclair equated

marriage right up there with executions and hog-killings. She didn't want any part of this and she sure wasn't about to try and catch the bouquet of spring flowers Jo was about to throw.

"Go," Jake heard someone saying. Then he watched, smiling, as Jo's Aunt Becky and her good friend and fellow bridesmaid Hannah West shoved Elizabeth toward the crowd of single women gathered just outside the church.

"I don't want to go," Elizabeth exclaimed, glancing back at the determined, laughing women urging her forward. "I'd rather stay back here, out of sight."

"Nonsense," Aunt Becky said, gently nudging Elizabeth. "You need to be right in the thick of things."

Elizabeth straightened her simple satin dress and glanced around, her gold-flecked eyes beaming in on Jake's grinning face as Aunt Becky marched her front and center. "What's so funny, cowboy?" she asked, tossing her head so fast her upswept curls lost a few pins.

Jake swept her an elaborate bow. "You, darlin'. I get the impression you'd rather be any other place on earth. What's the matter, Lizzie, allergic to weddings?"

She rewarded him with a cat-eyed mock smile. "Yes, weddings and long, tall Texans with lazy grins. They both give me the hives."

Jake let out a hoot of laughter that had everyone staring. "Need me to scratch that itch for you, Lizzie?"

She rolled her eyes as she hurried by, the brush of

lilac-colored satin from her gown teasing Jake like a breath of fresh air as she passed. "No, I don't, and my name is Elizabeth, not Lizzie."

"Yes, ma'am," Jake replied, waving her on with a hand out in the air. "I pity the man who gets you for a wife."

"Don't worry about me," Elizabeth said on a deliberately sweet note. "I don't intend to get married anytime soon."

Jake only nodded and grinned. "We'll see about that, Miss Lizzie."

"I don't like cowboys," Elizabeth said later as she shifted Jo's bouquet in her hands. Staring down at the beautiful grouping of white and burgundy-red roses mixed with babies' breath only made her want to hold on to the flowers forever, or sit down and cry. "And I wish I hadn't caught this bouquet."

Her friend Hannah patted her arm and gave her a mock pitying look. "Poor baby. Always the bridesmaid—"

"And I don't want to be the bride," Elizabeth interjected, her eyes scanning the crowd at the reception until they settled on Jake Clark. "I can't believe Jo turned traitor on us and got married."

While Elizabeth pouted and over-analyzed the handsome Texan who stood in the corner quietly watching the wedding celebration, Hannah buzzed around the table, making sure they still had plenty of chicken salad cream puffs and mixed nuts.

"She didn't betray us, Elizabeth," Hannah said. "She fell in love."

Elizabeth glared at the man across the way. He inclined his head and gave her a soft, knowing smile, which only aggravated her even more. "I know, and I'm truly happy for her, but we made a pact—"

"Yes, we did," Hannah said, coming to stand by her. "But, honey, we're not getting any younger. And life is short. I don't intend to get married either, but I can't begrudge Jo her chance. Bram is a good man and they make a wonderful couple. And look at her—she's beaming with joy."

"Yeah, I can see that," Elizabeth said, whirling to place the elaborate bouquet on a nearby table, her own hidden dreams too far away to imagine. "I need a glass of punch. My throat is so dry."

Hannah tugged at Elizabeth's arm. "We just made a fresh batch. I think one of the waiters put it over there on that table."

"Great," Elizabeth said, noting that the table with the fresh punch was in the vicinity of the Texan. She'd have to be polite to that offending man if she wanted to quench her thirst. Elizabeth strolled over toward the punch, intent on getting a drink and getting out of Jake Clark's way.

"Let me get that for you," he said as she approached the table and started to ladle some of the pink liquid.

"No, thanks. I'm fine. Got it," she said, hurrying so fast to pour herself a cup, she sloshed punch all over Hannah's white lace tablecloth.

"Oops," Jake said, quickly handing her a napkin.

"Thanks so much." She gave him her best fake smile and turned to beat a fast path to the other side of the garden.

"Hey, now, wait up," Jake said, his big hand roping her back around. "You move faster than a Texas twister."

Elizabeth glanced down at his tanned hand. His fingers felt warm against her bare skin, his grip sure and firm. "And you're kinda slow on the uptake."

"I don't get in any hurry, that's a fact," he replied, his gray eyes sweeping her face. "Life's too short to get all flustered."

"You're the second person who's said that to me today," Elizabeth replied, taking a quick sip of her punch for fortification. "If life is so short, why is this reception dragging on and on?"

"Maybe the Lord is trying to tell you something," Jake said, that slow, lazy smile slinking over her nerve endings like buttery-soft leather. "Maybe you need to slow down and enjoy your friend's happy occasion."

"Maybe," Elizabeth retorted, not in much of a hurry to get away now. "But I don't think the Lord is interested in dealing with the likes of me."

"Prickly, aren't we?"

"I'm not prickly," she said, gritting her teeth. "And besides, why are you so nosy and annoying, anyway?"

"Do I annoy you, Lizzie?"

"Yes, you do. I only just met you two hours ago, but I can safely say that out of those two hours, you've annoyed me pretty much the whole time." And she seemed to be enjoying it, inviting his flirtations, a little voice in her head pointed out. That was completely silly, but understandable. It had been a while since she'd had a decent date, after all.

"Just being friendly."

His shrug was as intoxicating as his killer smile. The man knew how to wear a well-cut suit, that was for sure. And with black cowboy boots, of course. Any pure-blooded Texan worth his salt always had a pair of dress boots in his closet.

Wanting to push matters, Elizabeth shook her head. "So you were just being friendly, the way you stared at me and kept winking at me during the entire ceremony?"

"So you *did* notice."

Hating the triumph in his glittering eyes, she tapped her foot and set down her drained punch glass. "How could I not notice? We were standing right across from each other."

He nodded, his eyes moving over her again. "I might say the same for you. How could I not notice an attractive woman standing right across from me? I tell you, Lizzie, I think I fell in love right then and there."

"Please," she said, spinning away with a wave of her hand and a hiss of satin. "Mr. Clark, you can save that good-ol'-boy routine for all those cowgirls back on the ranch. I'm not buying it." But she smiled, her first real smile all day, she decided. She could feel her jaw muscles actually relaxing.

"What a shame," he said, following her, his long strides outmatching her short, clipped steps. "Seeing as how I'm going to be in Prescott for a while, I could use a good tour guide."

"A tour guide? For Prescott! Just turn around at Elm Street and work your way back and you've just about seen the whole town."

"Right, but I'm gonna need to see more than just the main street through lovely downtown. I want to buy some land. Got my eye on a piece northwest of here, along the Caddo River. And rumor has it, you're the best Realtor this side of Texarkana."

"I'm flattered, but I deal in houses, not land, Mr. Clark."

"Jake. The name is Jake."

"Okay, Jake. I don't do land. But I can give you the name of another Realtor who does."

"But I want you."

The way he said it caused Elizabeth to look up into his eyes. A mistake. They looked as rich and mysterious as a moonlit mountain, all silvery and full of depth. "I'm really busy these days."

"I know. Top sales for the first quarter of the year, already. You must be a firecracker, since there's not a whole lot of property around here to sell in the first place."

Impressed that he knew her accomplishments, she said, "I work the entire region, not just this town."

"So work with me."

It was a challenge. And Elizabeth just loved a good

challenge. But working with Jake Clark, spending time with him? Elizabeth didn't think she was up to *that* particular challenge. The man had set her teeth on edge from the first minute he'd walked into the parlor of the church, too tall and way too good-looking to be a mere mortal. Maybe it was the way he'd looked at her, as if he knew her deepest, darkest secrets. Or maybe it was that smile that slid across his wide mouth and danced its way into those disturbing silver eyes until a girl couldn't breathe from the fascination and brilliance of it.

Mentally shaking herself, Elizabeth started to protest yet again. "I couldn't possibly—"

"I'd be mighty obliged," Jake said.

"You need to lose the hokey cowboy vocabulary," she said by way of an answer.

He straightened, his smile gone, his eyes turning the color of steel. "Sorry, Lizzie. This is who I am."

She could see she'd touched a nerve. It should have brought her some measure of satisfaction, but instead it left her unsettled and confused. She quickly covered that with a snappy comeback.

"Yeah, well, *this* is who I am. And I'm afraid I can't help you with your search for land, Jake."

He didn't back down. "Then how 'bout dinner sometime next week?"

Elizabeth actually laughed to hide the heavy tempo of her heart. "You're asking me out on a date?"

"Yeah. You do know what a date is, don't you, Lizzie?"

Elizabeth felt the blush all the way down her backbone. She hadn't been on an actual date in so long, she probably had forgotten what one was like. "My name is Elizabeth," she said, her jaws going so tight, she knew she'd get a migraine later. With a valiant effort at dignity, she tried to move past him. "I appreciate the offer, but no, thanks."

Jake headed her off at the pass. "Elizabeth," he said, his tone soft and full of exaggeration. "I'd like to get to know you, to take you out on the town. I'm going to be here for a good long while, and, well, I know I'll get downright lonely."

"It won't kill you."

"And it won't kill you to accept my invitation, will it?"

"Probably," she said.

Then against her better judgment, she nodded. "Call me next week, and we'll see. I'm in the book."

"Yes, ma'am," he said. He sauntered away, whistling the tune of some ridiculous country song.

Chapter Two

"The man doesn't waste time when he wants something," Elizabeth told Hannah two days later. She'd stopped by Hannah's bed and breakfast to have a quick lunch. And to complain about Jake Clark. The man who was renting a room in this very house, but she'd checked first to make sure he wasn't actually at Mimosa Manor right now.

"So that lazy attitude is just an act?" Hannah asked as she poured Elizabeth a fresh glass of mint ice tea.

"No, no. He told me it's real. And I believe him. But I think Jake is the kind of man who only gets in a hurry when he feels like it. And he seems in a mighty big hurry to take me to dinner."

"Maybe he just wants to talk about that land he came to look at," Hannah pointed out. "Bram convinced Jake it would be a good investment, and rumor has it Jake has lots of cash to invest. You might get a big commission out of this. He's certainly been tipping my help very nicely since he settled into the Library Suite."

"A big spender, huh?" That brought Elizabeth's head up. "I'd sure like that. A few more good, strong sales and I'll be up for Salesperson of the Year for the entire state of Arkansas. That surely wouldn't hurt."

"That's my Elizabeth, ever the ambitious career woman," Hannah said, her lips set in a firm line.

Elizabeth tapped her baby-pink-painted fingernails on the table. "I guess it wouldn't hurt just to talk to the man."

"No, not one bit."

"Oh, stop it," she said, seeing the teasing light in Hannah's eyes. "Okay, I'll admit he's a tall drink of water."

"Easy on the eye."

"Definitely that, but I'm only interested in his checkbook and how it can help me. And if that means having to spend time with the hunk, then I'll do it."

"You are ruthless to a fault."

Elizabeth looked across at her friend. Hannah seemed tired, but she'd never admit that. Running a bed and breakfast and catering weddings and other romantic events demanded Hannah's time almost twenty-four/seven, but Hannah loved it, just as Elizabeth loved selling houses and just as Jo loved creating beautiful flower arrangements.

They all loved their work, because they lived for their work, Elizabeth reckoned. Work was fulfilling, shutting out the loneliness and the bitterness that had held them all for so very long. But there was always that shard of hope mixed in with their longing, too.

Which was why Elizabeth couldn't begrudge Jo and Bram falling in love. She just prayed it would last.

There was always that hope in the back of Elizabeth's mind each time she sold a house, of course, that this one would take. But she'd seen too many houses around here going back on the market after a few months or a couple of years, because that happily-ever-after everyone dreamed about really didn't exist. And she'd sure seen that firsthand with her own parents.

"Do you miss Jo?" she asked Hannah now.

"Yes, I do." Hannah stopped folding the colorful linen napkins she'd washed earlier. "It's so amazing that one of us got married. After all we've been through."

"Yes, it sure is. And Jo, of all people. She's younger than us. That's a sad statement on you and me, isn't it, kiddo?"

Hannah nodded. "Well, we've made our bed—"

"Might as well lie in it, as Aunt Becky would say."

Hannah's smile was bittersweet. "Aunt Becky would also tell us to trust in the Lord and try different attitudes."

"Tried that, didn't work," Elizabeth said, getting up to go back to work. "We both know that we have two things to count on in this world—each other and our jobs. And speaking of that, I'd better get back to mine. I have a very important phone call to make."

"Are you sure about that?" Hannah asked, genuine concern clouding her eyes.

"Oh, now, don't go get all worried about me, honey. Jake Clark will be here and gone before the ink dries on his big, fat check. And I'll be laughing all the way to the bank."

"Sure," Hannah said, but she didn't seem convinced.

As Elizabeth backed her white convertible out of the long flower-bordered drive of Mimosa Manor, she had to wonder if she was doing the right thing, getting tied up with a man like Jake Clark.

A man who could easily cause her to take Aunt Becky's sage advice and change her attitude.

Completely.

He was completely smitten with her.

Jake watched as Elizabeth whirled her purring sportscar into the parking space in front of the Sinclair Realty Company. After taking off her dark sunshades, she tossed them in a black briefcase, then slid out of the car, her slender legs bare, her feet encased in high-heeled brown leather sandals that matched her brown-and-white floral dress.

She pranced toward the office door, then stopped like a deer caught in the headlights as she spotted him sitting on a wooden bench nearby.

"Hello there," Jake said, standing to meet her. "I've been waiting for you."

"Hi," she replied, nervous energy bouncing around her. "What are you doing here?"

Jake opened the door she'd just unlocked, and waited till she entered the storefront office. "I wanted to talk to you about that dinner I promised you and about the land I'm interested in."

"I'm not so sure I want to help you with your land deal," she said as she dropped her keys and her briefcase on an antique walnut desk centered in the big office.

Even as she said it, he could see the sparks of interest in her eyes. If she was the hotshot everyone said she was, she was interested. Very interested. Apparently, she just wasn't ready to admit that.

"And what about dinner?" he asked.

"Not real sure about that either."

"I don't bite."

She gave him a look that suggested he might do just that. "No, but you could strike. You're one of those kind, I think."

"Oh, and what kind might that be?"

"The kind that sits back and waits to make the right move at the right time. I think you like to throw people off guard."

He chuckled, thinking he'd been trying to do that very thing. He'd have to watch his step with this one. "You sure got me figured out, don't you?"

"Not really." She waved a hand around. "And I really don't have time to do a thorough study."

Jake waited for her to sit down, then leaned over her, his hands on the desk. "Well, I've got all the time in the world. And I'm not leaving here until you agree to at least have dinner with me, so we can get to know each other."

She became immediately flustered, her cheeks turning a becoming pink, her hazel eyes flashing golden fire. "Jake, I have so much to do. I have to meet with a client at two, and I have contracts to go over."

"Don't you have any help?"

She pointed to the small desk in the outer office, near the entrance. "Yes, but Brandy is out to lunch right now."

"I'll need a house, too, you know."

"What?"

"I need help with buying a house here."

"Here, in Prescott?"

Her voice had actually squeaked just a tad. She was as nervous as a cornered bobcat. But so adorable.

"Yes, here, in Prescott," he repeated, enjoying the flush that had now moved down her slender neck. "I don't want to wear out my welcome at Hannah's place. I was hoping you'd have some suggestions."

"Oh, I've got a few. But they don't really have anything to do with houses or land."

Jake let out a hoot of laughter, causing her to jump in her chair. "You don't mince words, do you?"

"I don't have time to beat around the bush." She sank back in her chair and stared up at him, her eyes so golden-green, he thought of deep lakes in high mountains. He saw so much in those eyes—doubt, regret, wonder, fear, and a sadness that made him think she'd been through some rough times. But then, hadn't everyone?

Not wanting to dwell in self-pity, Jake stood straight up. "I can always find someone else to help me, if I make you that uncomfortable."

She brushed a hand through her layered curls, her whole attitude changing. "Tell me your plans for this land by the river."

"It's a ways from here. It's a tract just north of where the Caddo empties into DeGray Lake." Jake relaxed, then settled into a floral-patterned chair across from her desk. "I want to build nice cabins out there. A nice, cozy neighborhood for family retreats and retirees."

"That land along the river could use some development," she said, nodding her head. Her gold earrings glistened, and so did her eyes. "It's pretty land. And the locals will want to keep it that way. It's a favorite for floating and rafting. You'd better have a solid plan that keeps nature in mind."

"Oh, believe me, I'm an outdoorsman. I intend to keep things scenic and environmentally sound. Do you know any of the property owners?"

"Mostly corporations, but some privately held tracts. Corporations use the land for hunting and fishing. And some might be interested in letting go, if the right offer is put on the table. So who's your seller?"

"Not a corporation. An individual I've met through business contacts. I deal in ranching and have other interests on the side, commercial real estate mostly. He's ready to deal and so am I," Jake said. "Bram's seen the land, but he wasn't sure how to go about arranging the negotiations. He suggested you."

"Remind me to thank him when he gets back from his honeymoon," she said, the sweet sarcasm in her tone belying the keen interest in her eyes.

"Okay, so…are you in?"

She stood up, extended her hand. "I'm in."

Jake stood, too. "And what about a house?"

"Rent or buy?"

"Buy, I think. I just might decide to settle here for a very long time."

The wariness came back into her eyes, in spite of her chirpy encouragement. "Prescott is always open to new business."

"That's good to hear."

She whirled, glancing at the pictures of houses located on a bulletin board behind her desk. "It's slim pickings right now, house-wise. But I might have something."

"Okay. When can I see it?"

"Tomorrow." She turned back around. "Tell you what. You come by here right after lunch tomorrow, and we'll ride up to the river. Then we should be able to make it by a house or two before dark."

Jake's heart did a dance. "And then you'll have dinner with me?"

"I'll probably be hungry by then, sure."

He grinned, tipped his hand to his head in a salute. "I'll see you tomorrow, then."

"It's a date." She stopped, shook her head. "Not a *real* date, understand. Just business."

"I understand completely," Jake replied. "I'll meet you here tomorrow afternoon."

"I'll be here," she said. Then she became very interested in some files on her desk.

Jake got the impression she wanted him gone.

But he'd be back. He was in no hurry. No hurry at all.

Chapter Three

"He's late."

Elizabeth glanced at the grandfather clock ticking away in the corner of her office, then ran a hand through the tousled bangs that constantly fluttered around her eyes.

"Maybe he got busy with something else," her assistant, Brandy Kendrick said.

"Yeah, right." Elizabeth flipped through her Rolodex to hide the disappointment coursing through her. "Well, I need to get busy, too. If the man's going to keep me waiting, I'll just move on to something else."

"You could just take a breath and relax," Brandy offered, grinning. "Want me to get us a soda or some of that flavored coffee you like?"

"No, I don't need any more caffeine," Elizabeth replied. Frowning, she listened to the ringing at the other end of the line, rolled her eyes at the answering machine, left a curt message, then hung up the phone.

"Apparently nobody in this town is working this afternoon but us."

"Well, it *is* a gorgeous day out there," Brandy replied, the wistful sound in her voice grating on Elizabeth's hyped-up nerve endings. "Hot, but a nice breeze. Good day to go to the lake."

"You can take the afternoon off," Elizabeth said, giving up. "If Mr. Clark isn't going to show up, I have plenty to keep me busy, but I don't think I'll need you."

"I wouldn't do that to you, boss. But you and I could go for a walk or something."

"A walk or something?" Elizabeth looked at her cute assistant as if she'd grown two heads. "I don't do walks, Brandy. You know that."

"Right. You do the treadmill—at five in the morning."

"It's the perfect time for me to listen to the stock reports and the news on the real estate market—you know, interest rates and the cost of housing, what's happening in the business world."

"I get it," Brandy said, shaking her head. "You eat, sleep and drink work. But you need to learn to relax, too."

"Thanks for the sage advice," Elizabeth said, her fingers tapping impatiently on the glass top of her desk. "But you know what they say—you snooze, you lose. And Mr. Jake Clark—"

"Is here," Brandy finished for her. "He just pulled up in the biggest, blackest truck I've ever seen. I bet that thing has a Hemi."

"I'm going to give Mr. Clark a Hemi," Elizabeth replied, wondering what in the world a Hemi was. But when Jake opened the door and walked in, his decidedly male presence filled the office and caused her to suck in the breath full of anger she'd planned on letting out.

He was wearing a black Stetson, to match the truck, no doubt. And he smelled like a fresh forest after a rain. How was she supposed to tell him off when he looked good enough to…the word *kiss* came to her mind. But Elizabeth quickly pushed it away, annoyed that she'd even thought such a thing.

Getting up, she grabbed her briefcase and hurried through the wide door to the reception area. "Let's go."

"And hello to you, too," Jake said, giving her an appraising look before grinning over at her gawking assistant. "You must be Brandy."

"Yes, I am." Brandy stood to offer him a timid handshake, clearly smitten with the tall, dark-haired Texan. "Nice to meet you, Mr. Clark."

"It's Jake," he replied, his amused eyes skimming over Elizabeth. "I think your boss is ready to get going."

"I've been ready for fifteen minutes," Elizabeth said as she adjusted the sleeves of her prim white cotton blouse. "The afternoon is half gone, and I've got miles to go before I sleep."

"Robert Frost," Jake said, nodding. "I didn't know you liked poetry, Lizzie."

Brandy let out a yelp of laughter. "Poetry? Her? Oh, that's a good one."

"I have no idea what on earth you two are talking

about," Elizabeth retorted as she breezed past him. "I only know that I've heard that particular quote somewhere, and I agree. I don't like wasting my time. Are we going to drive out to your land or not, Jake?"

"We are," he said, tipping his hat to Brandy. "Ornery little thing, isn't she?"

Brandy's grin was impish and full of innocence. Elizabeth would deal with her later. Giving Jake a smile, she said, "I'll be even more ornery if you don't get it in gear, cowboy."

"Yes, ma'am." Jake swept his hand toward her, then opened the door. "See you around, Brandy."

"You shouldn't flirt with her that way," Elizabeth said once they were outside. "She's young and impressionable."

"Not like her *mature* and *unimpressed* boss, huh?"

"Exactly." She turned to open the truck door, but Jake's hand over hers stopped her.

"Let me," he said, taking her hand away, the warmth from his strong fingers moving through her system. Warning bells, she told herself. And loud whistles— like a train coming too fast.

Elizabeth pulled her hand away and waited with a sigh for him to open the door. Then came her next problem. Her tight floral casual skirt wouldn't budge enough for her to put one leg inside the oversized vehicle. She tried a couple of times to be ladylike, then finally groaned and took a running hop.

Just in time for Jake to literally lift her by her waist up into the offending truck. He sat her down on the smooth, cool tan leather with a soft thud, then smiled down at her. "Don't forget to buckle up."

Mortified, Elizabeth childishly stuck out her tongue at his retreating back, then yanked the seat belt around and snapped it in place. She'd changed from her high-heeled sandals into sneakers and socks since they'd be traipsing around in the wilderness, so her feet barely touched the floor of the big Dodge.

"How does anybody actually drive one of these?" she asked after Jake got in and cranked the truck, his long, blue-jean-encased legs stretching comfortably. The big engine roared to life, causing her to put her hands over her ears.

"It's easy to maneuver," Jake said, that teasing light in his eyes. "Handles like a dream."

Elizabeth could believe that. And Jake was a dream, too. Stop that, she told herself as she pulled her eyes back inside her head. Think client. Think big commission. Don't think at all. Better that way.

"So what do you think?" Jake asked.

Gulping, she held on for dear life. "About what?"

"About this land? Did you get a chance to pull it up online?"

"I researched it some, yes. It's a good tract, prime and ready for development. The Caddo is surrounded by a lot of private property."

"I agree. That's why I want to get going on this. And a house since I'll be here for a while overseeing things."

"Right." She didn't know how she'd put up with him

being around all the time, but maybe once he got involved in his project, he'd steer clear of her. "Why don't you just rent a house?" she asked, curiosity making her cut her eyes toward him.

"I looked around. There's not much to rent around here. And I need to get away from Fort Worth for a while."

"Running from a trail of broken hearts, or just a bunch of mad women?"

"I've never left any woman mad, Lizzie. And the only broken heart I've known has been my own."

That direct, honest statement caused her to turn to face him. But Jake was staring straight ahead, a dark scowl making his usually jovial face look sad and forlorn for just a minute.

"Sorry I asked," she said, her low tone covering the intense need to know what had just gone through his mind.

"Oh, I don't mind. Just wanted to set the record straight. You know, you'd like me if you'd relax and get to know me."

"Who says I don't like you?"

He grinned then, making her heart rev just like the truck's motor. "Well, if you treat all your clients the way you've been treating me, I have to wonder how you win so many awards."

Embarrassed at the way she'd been acting, Elizabeth swallowed hard and cleared her throat. "I don't usually treat people so rudely, Jake. I'm sorry." She shrugged, hung on to the armrest on the door. "I've just been in a mood lately. One of my best friends getting married has left me, well…"

"Feeling left out?" He said, glancing over at her, his eyes full of understanding.

"Oh, no!" she exclaimed, shifting in her seat. "I don't intend to get married myself. It's just hard to let her go. Hannah and I—we've known Jo since high school. Even though she's a few years younger than us, we've all three been so close. We've been through a lot together, a whole lot."

"You can still have Jo as a friend," he pointed out. "Her getting married doesn't have to mean the end of your friendship, does it?"

She sat silent, then shook her head. "No, but it means the beginning of something else. Something we thought we'd never see."

He frowned, turned the truck off the interstate. "You want your friend to be happy, don't you?"

"Yes, I do," she said, meaning it with every breath she took. "But we've all had disappointments in that area. Enough to make all three of us decide marriage wasn't for us."

"That's a shame," Jake said, his eyes going dark and mysterious again. "Me, I kinda want a lifetime commitment. I rank it right up there with a good cup of coffee and a great-fitting pair of boots."

Elizabeth glanced down at his shiny custom-made boots. "Don't you think marriage is a bit more tricky than buying a pair of boots?"

"Yes, I do. But I also know that in both, you have

to find the right fit. Once you get that, everything else pretty much falls right into place."

"The right fit." She gave him a doubtful smile. "Well, I guess I've never looked at it that way. And so far, I haven't found the right fit. Marriage, unlike a pair of shoes, can't be ordered custom-made, Jake. It takes a lot of time and energy, a lot of compromise and caring. And a lot of love."

"I agree on all counts," he said. "It also takes faith, Lizzie. Faith in God, and faith in yourself and your chosen mate."

She slapped a hand on the seat. "Well, you see, that right there knocks me out. My mother was a churchgoing woman who put all of her faith into making a home for my philandering father. He left her and me high and dry in our perfect house on the hill. So I don't have any faith left. None at all. Not in marriage and certainly not in God."

A look of shock and compassion on his face, Jake stopped the truck on a bumpy dirt road near some trees, then looked over at her. "What if I told you I'm here to change your mind about all that?"

Chapter Four

"Okay, turn the truck around," Elizabeth said, seething with so much anger, her knuckles were turning white as she held on to the door handle. The anger felt good. It covered a multitude of sins.

"We just got here," Jake told her, concern marring his face. "What's wrong?"

"What's wrong?" She turned to him, lifted her chin a notch, waved her hands in the air. "Did you bring me out here to preach to me, Jake? 'Cause if you did, you can just find yourself another Realtor—"

"Whoa," he said, grabbing one of her flailing hands. "Settle down for just a minute, will you?"

Elizabeth took a deep breath then pulled her hand away from his. "Look, you don't need to redeem me or save me. Just show me the land."

Jake parked the truck on a wooded bluff, then came around to help her out. Elizabeth had no choice but to accept his hand, since the ground below her seemed far away.

"Thank you," she said, her tone clipped, her eyes straight ahead. "Let's go."

Jake just stood there, his big body blocking her from the open door. "Not until you hear me out."

"I don't need to hear you out. I just need to get on with the business of looking over this property."

"Yes, you do need to hear me," he responded, one hand on the truck door and the other on the cab. "I didn't mean to sound superior and sanctimonious back there. I was just trying to tell you that…well, Lizzie, I kinda like you. You intrigue me. I was hoping we might hit it off, that maybe I could bring that pretty smile to your face more often."

She stared up at him, her heart racing as her blood pressure shot up another notch. "So you brought me out here to preach to me *and* hit on me, too?"

Jake shook his head, groaned. "No, I don't plan to do either. My mama taught me to be a gentleman, and I don't intend to do anything to change that. She'd turn over in her grave if I did."

That brought Elizabeth's head up, and caused her to soften her stance. "Your mother's dead?"

He took off his hat and brushed a hand through his thick, dark hair. "She died about five years ago. My daddy's still alive, but he's in bad shape. I'm the youngest of six."

"Six?" She relaxed back against the truck, then glanced up at him, her anger simmering to a slow burn now. "Wow, a big family. That must have been fun growing up."

"It was at times," he said, his tone gentle with memories. "At other times, we barely had enough to eat. My parents went without just so all six of their children could go to college. My brothers and sisters are all successful, but they're scattered to the four winds. I live near my daddy, so now it's my turn to take care of him, and pay him back."

Elizabeth found herself fascinated and touched, in spite of being mad at him. Her own father had walked out on her mother and Elizabeth a long time ago, so it was hard for her to comprehend that type of family love and loyalty. "Is that why you want to build this rustic retreat? To make more money?"

"I don't need any more money," he said, his tone in no way proud nor braggish. "I just think it's a good investment and a good idea. And I hope to bring my father up here to live in a safe, pleasant environment."

Okay, that was noble, Elizabeth decided. But she had to find his weak spot, the one thing that would rank him in the same category with her wayward father. "How did you make all your money?"

He sighed, glanced out at the river beyond the hardwood trees. "I worked long and hard, and pretty much ignored everything and everyone around me."

"That's what hard work does," Elizabeth reasoned, feeling smug that he'd admitted that, at least. And a bit dejected. He didn't seem the type. "If you want to succeed, you have to sacrifice."

Jake backed away then, but not before she saw the dark sadness flaring in his eyes. "Yeah, well, I did sacrifice, a lot. If it hadn't been for my faith—"

"Oh, so we're back to that," she said, moving past him to stare out at the gurgling water below. "And here I thought the conversation was going so nicely."

"Look," he said, coming to stand beside her, "I'm here for one reason, to buy this land and get it developed. I'm not here to confirm you or to change you. I just need the best person for the job. I was told that person was you, but if you feel uncomfortable in any way—"

"I'm fine," she said, dollar signs zinging by on the wind. "I'll be fine, Jake, as long as we stick to business. I like business. I don't like all this talk about faith and fun."

"After what you just told me, I think you might could use a little of both."

"I shouldn't have told you about my father. Forget it. It's ancient history. My mother has managed to get on with her life, in spite of the fact that the man broke her heart." She didn't go into detail there. No need to tell him her mother lived for her church and charity work and stayed busy with both, now that she had retired from being a secretary. Her mother volunteered to fill the emptiness in her life. No husband and no grandchildren, as Phyllis Sinclair so often reminded her only daughter.

Jake brought her back with his next question. "And how about you, Lizzie? Have you gotten on with you life?"

Mercy, the man *sounded* just like her mother! Feeling defensive, Elizabeth held her hands in fists at her side. "I've managed just fine, yes."

"Then why do you seem so determined to put work ahead of everything else?"

Elizabeth thought about her bitter, angry mother, sitting in an empty, immaculate house, pretending that she was happy. She thought about how her mother had been forced to find work, any work, just to make ends meet. Elizabeth had worked most of her life, too, to help her mother and to pay for her own education.

Somehow, they had survived. But that survival had taught Elizabeth a valuable lesson. She would never live like that again. Even now, she worked to keep her mother from having to struggle in her golden years. Because Elizabeth had become so successful, Phyllis had at least been *able* to retire. A decision they both tended to regret sometimes.

Not ready to tell Jake that, she said, "Well, unlike you, I haven't made my *complete* fortune yet. So I don't have time for anything but work."

"That's a shame," he said, his eyes still rich with some unspoken emotion. "But if that's the way it has to be, then let's get right to it."

Elizabeth watched as he headed down a path toward the water's edge. Watched and fairly itched to know what he'd had to sacrifice. He looked healthy and happy, as if he didn't have a care in the world. She supposed when you had money to burn, everything was great and good.

Jake Clark could rely on his faith, because he'd never been through pain and heartache and disappointment, the way she had. What could he possibly know about those things?

But when she remembered that distinctive sadness in his quicksilver eyes, she had to wonder if maybe he had suffered at some point in his life.

And she longed to know just what had happened in his past to put that trace of regret and grief in his eyes.

Jake stared down at the clear water moving over the rock bed below, wondering how it was that the good Lord had seen fit to hook him up with such a feisty and determined woman. A woman who clearly needed to find her faith again.

Just stick to business, he told himself as he waited for Elizabeth to follow him. Jake didn't know why this particular little fireball seemed to be burning a path through his heart. He couldn't understand why, since Jo and Bram's wedding, when he'd watched Elizabeth trying so hard to avoid catching that bouquet—he couldn't get his mind off her. Maybe because she seemed so tough and cool, when inside she must be hurting just like the rest of humanity.

Just like him.

Jake refused to think about his own hurts right now. He had a major project to get on with. He wanted this to work, so he could bring his father here to rest and enjoy the beautiful views of the Ouachita Mountains, maybe do some bass fishing along the Caddo River.

And he wanted to find some sense of peace here in Arkansas, close to his college buddy, Bram Dixon.

Bram had encouraged Jake to come up and visit. He'd even suggested the land deal to him. But in his heart, Jake knew his friend was worried about him and only wanted to help him get over his grief and guilt.

Maybe he could heal here in these gentle, rolling hills. Maybe. But not if he got all tangled up with a curly-headed, pint-sized whirlwind of a woman.

A woman who wanted nothing to do with a man like him.

Lord, what's the plan? Jake silently prayed. What did God have in mind for him, he wondered, as he watched a lone hawk circling high out over the water.

"What's the plan, big guy?" Elizabeth asked from behind, causing Jake to start and turn around.

"Sorry," Elizabeth said, her eyes going soft with amusement and regret. "I didn't mean to sneak up on you."

"It's okay," Jake replied, glad to see her smiling again. "I was just imagining all the work I'll have to put into this place." He gave her a sheepish look. "And I was asking God to help me make the right decisions." At the skeptical lifting of her brows, he added, "You know, when you go into a project this size, and especially near a body of water, you have to deal with the environmentalists, the county, the state—a whole passel of people. It's going to take a lot of teamwork to get it right. I intend to protect the land and this river, but I also want to bring jobs to this area and its people, to boost the economy. Tourism is important to this state. I aim to help in that area, too."

"Sounds as if you've got it all figured out," Elizabeth said, her gaze moving over the water below.

Jake should have been proud of that spark of admiration he detected in her words. But he wasn't so proud. He'd learned to slow down, learned the hard way. He knew how to pace himself now. The work would be there, right where he left it. No rush. Just steady work, to make him tired at night, to banish the nightmares he still suffered through. Work to keep him sane.

But never again would he let work control his life. God did that now. God was in control.

With that thought in mind, Jake took a deep breath and smiled over at Elizabeth. She sure looked pretty, standing there in her cute little skirt and prim white blouse. Her golden, sun-kissed curls danced around her angular face with an artless beauty. Her skin was sparkling and freckle-dusted, her lips a pure peach color.

"I have to get this right," he told her, hoping she'd understand. "But I don't like to rush things, Lizzie."

"Then we're going to have to learn to work together, I guess," she said, her tone devoid of any confrontations or accusations. "Let's just get some things straight, okay?"

He nodded, tipped his head. "I'm listening."

"One, I am the best Realtor around, so you can depend on me to get the job done. Two, I might get in a hurry at times, but it's only because I like to be thorough and I like to get there first. Three, I think I like you, but I'm not ready for any romantic relationships, especially with a client." She looked out over the river, then glanced back at him, her smile causing his heart to bubble and gurgle like the water below them. "And four, I'm gonna have to buy some hiking boots, 'cause these pink canvas sneakers aren't cutting it out here in the duckweed and reeds."

"I'll buy you some boots," he said, relaxing when he saw that they'd reached a truce of sorts. "And I can agree to all your stipulations, except that part about getting romantic. But then, as I said, I don't want to hurry things. We'll just see where the road takes us."

"I guess I can live with that," she said. "Just watch yourself, Mr. Clark. Keep on being that gentleman your mama raised and we'll get along just fine."

"I'm sure we will."

She gave him an inquiring look, but Jake didn't feel the need to elaborate on his words. He figured this would all happen in God's own time. God had a plan for him. And if that plan included Elizabeth Sinclair, then so be it. Jake wouldn't rush that, either.

After all, he'd learned the hard way that some things couldn't be rushed.

And no amount of work could bring back the family he'd loved and lost. Ever.

Chapter Five

Summer settled over the tiny town of Prescott, Arkansas, like a damp blanket falling across a clothesline. It was humid and still, time moving with all the laziness of a ladybug crawling along a moist leaf.

Which only made Elizabeth want to move faster. She didn't particularly enjoy summer. Besides bringing back bad memories of sad times long ago, it was too hot for words, and it just required so much energy.

"Energy, I've got, at least for work," she said out loud as she mused over the contracts for Jake's land deal. Everything looked in order for the closing next month. She'd moved this one along pretty fast, since the buyer was anxious to sell. And, she had to admit, she'd moved it along fast because the quicker this deal went through, the sooner she'd be done with working so closely with Jake Clark.

She had no energy left for that particular man.

"I can't give in," she said, glancing around the cool

office to make sure Brandy was still out running er-
rands. True to his word, Jake had treated her to dinner that night a few weeks ago, after they'd looked
over the land and checked out a couple of houses.
Dinner at the nearest barbecue joint, at least. Not exactly romantic, but good food and an eclectic crowd.
That dinner had been fun, safe, interesting. And he
hadn't asked her out since.

But the man was sure up to something. She could
feel it in her bones.

Getting up, Elizabeth stared out the window to the
hot asphalt street. All she saw were the wilted white
and pink petunias Brandy had put in two planters by
the bench on the corner. She didn't see any signs of a
big black truck anywhere. Maybe Jake would actually
let a day pass without badgering her about finding
him a house. That was his excuse for showing up here
all the time, bearing flowers and candy for Elizabeth
(because she was doing such a fine job on helping
him to secure this property), bringing Brandy little
trinkets (for working so hard to help him get things
going on this development.)

Oh, you're a smooth one, Jake Clark, she thought,
the smell of the lilies and roses he'd brought only yesterday wafting toward her nose with a teasing fragrance.

Even though she was bored beyond words, she sure
hoped Jake didn't bother her today. After all, she'd
shown the man every available house in town and he
still hadn't settled on anything.

Every house except one, of course. Elizabeth

groaned, fell down in her leather desk chair, took a long swig of diet soda. "I won't show him that one," she said into the still afternoon air. "I won't do it. I can't let him have the one house I've always dreamed of restoring."

Feeling guilty, she searched inside the right desk drawer until she found the picture of "her" house. It was run-down, almost falling apart, but oh, how Elizabeth longed to make it her home. She sat staring at the turn-of-the- century Victorian structure, wishing she could make enough cold hard cash to renovate the charmer back to its original beautiful self. No one else would even consider looking at the house, not even Hannah, who loved to restore old houses. It looked haunted, rotten, old and forgotten, its turret sitting like a battered hat atop one side of the three-story stone-and-brick structure.

But Elizabeth couldn't forget it. If only…

Hearing the door jingle, she quickly dropped the picture on her desk and tried to look busy. Brandy breezed in, laughing. "Look who I found down at the diner."

Elizabeth looked up to find Jake standing there, holding a plastic container in each hand. "I brought you an ice cream sundae," he said by way of a greeting, his silver eyes laced with sparkling amusement. "Brandy says you'll do just about anything for pralines-and-cream ice cream with caramel syrup and whipped cream on top."

"Pity, I just ate," Elizabeth said, although her mouth watered with unabashed cravings.

"Oh, come on, it'll melt if you don't hurry and dig into it," Jake said, opening the container to reveal the creamy concoction. "I had them put extra nuts on top, just for you."

The way the man said things… Elizabeth's inside fairly shivered with anticipation. "Well, maybe a bite or two." Grabbing the spoon he so thoughtfully offered, she dipped it into the ice cream, then took a big bite. "Mmm, that *is* good."

Jake placed a hip on her desk, then started eating his own chocolate ice cream while Brandy finished off her milkshake with a great slurping gulp.

"Sorry," she said, giggling. "You know, Jake, you're spoiling us. We won't know how to act when the flowers and candy stop coming, and you quit buying us ice cream."

"Don't get used to it," Elizabeth said, her spoon returning again and again to the deep container in front of her. "We'll gain fifty pounds if he keeps this up."

Jake gave her a look that brought little chill bumps to her bare arms. "I think you could stand a few pounds."

"She works out on her treadmill," Brandy said, making a face. "Elizabeth isn't the outdoors type."

"Really, now?" Jake finished off his ice cream, then tossed his container in the nearby trash can. "You might be missing out on a lot there, Lizzie. Ever floated the river?"

"Excuse me?" Elizabeth said, her appetite suddenly dwindling. That's what she got for eating too fast.

"You know, you take an inner tube and float along the river, letting the current take you wherever it may lead."

"I know what it is, but I don't do rivers," Elizabeth said, shaking her head. "I'm not a water person."

"She almost drowned once," Brandy offered up, her big eyes wide with innocence.

"Did not."

"Did, too."

Jake looked from one to the other. "Well, did you, or didn't you?"

"I just fell off a raft. And everyone laughed at me. I thought I was drowning, so I kinda got all frazzled until someone pointed out I could stand up. The water was up to my waist." She tried to be solemn, but the glint in Jake's eyes was too much for her. Before she knew it, Elizabeth was laughing so hard tears were rolling down her eyes.

Jake and Brandy laughed right along with her.

"Okay, so I looked like a raving idiot, but I didn't like water then and I don't like water now."

"And she doesn't like to walk outside," Brandy informed Jake. "She just likes that expensive treadmill."

"Would you mind?" Elizabeth asked, her brow lifting. "I think there's some filing for you to do in the conference room."

"Oh, sure," Brandy said, grinning. "She also doesn't like to talk about her weaknesses," she threw over her shoulder in departing.

"Brat," Elizabeth said, smiling at Brandy's back.

"She's a sweetie pie," Jake said, grinning down at

Elizabeth with such a brilliance the air-conditioning couldn't cool the room enough. "And a hard worker, just like her boss."

"We aim to please."

"You are very pleasing, in every possible way." He gave her that slow, lazy look that kind of strolled its way down her face to her lips. Then he reached out a finger to her mouth. "You have a little dab of caramel, right there."

His touch was like a warm wisp of heat, just passing by. Their eyes met, held and then he dropped his finger as if he, too, had been burned by it. "It's gone now."

"Thanks," she said, her voice croaking out the word. She looked down at the papers on her desk, the typed words blurring in a heat of longing. Grabbing a stack, she pretended to be looking for something important. In her flurry of shuffling, the picture of her house fell out of the pile.

And landed right near Jake's lap.

"What's this?" Jake asked, picking up the picture, his eyes brightening with a flare of interest as he settled back against the desk.

"Oh, nothing." Mortified, Elizabeth tried to grab it away, but Jake had an iron-tight grip on the photo.

"Have I seen this one?"

"Uh, well, no."

"And why haven't I?"

"Uh, because, well, it's so old and rundown, I just thought—"

"Let's go see it right now."

"I have things to do—"

"Right now, Lizzie. I like this one."

Well, that just figured. Rolling her eyes to the heavens, Elizabeth placed her arms across her body in a stance of resistance. "You won't like it, Jake. It needs major renovations. It's falling down as we speak."

"I want to see it," he said, a stubborn glint coloring his eyes a steely gray. "I can see the potential and now I'd like to see the inside of this old house."

"I'm busy," she hedged, moving papers around on her desk.

"I'm not," he reminded her, his hand halting her. "And I am still your client, right?"

"Uh, right." She looked up at him, then sighed. "Oh, all right. I'll show you the Lockwood house, but just remember, I tried to warn you."

"I'll remember," he said as he pulled her out of her chair. "And I'll also remember that for some reason, you deliberately kept this house from me. That doesn't make very good business sense, Lizzie."

She grabbed her briefcase and cell phone. "Well, I haven't been thinking very clearly lately."

He stood over her, a big bear of a man with a frown on his face. "Is that because of me?" When she didn't answer right away, the frown turned to a triumphant smile. "I'll take that as a yes, and because that pleases me, I'll forgive you for holding out about this house."

"It's not because of you and I don't need any forgiveness," she said, the heat of his keen assumptions making her sweat in spite of the cold air coming out of the overhead vent. "I didn't show you this particular house because it just doesn't seem to be your style, if you get my drift."

"No, I don't get your drift," he said, his eyes skimming over her. "What exactly do you consider my style?"

She scooted past him toward the door, her cream linen trumpet skirt belling out around her legs. "All brawn and brash, all-consuming and very aggressive." Turning at the door, she said, "This house is old and historical, Jake. It has meaning and tradition. It's been around for a very long time, but the last Lockwood descendant moved his family to Little Rock. He just left the house and told me to keep it on the back burner unless I found a serious buyer, which I haven't. It needs someone who intends to live there for more than a few months or a couple of years."

It needs a happily-ever-after, Elizabeth thought. But then, that only happened in romance novels and fairy tales.

Jake studied her for a minute, his frown back. "Oh, I get it. You think I don't have staying power. You think I'll just whiz through town, build my resort village, then move on to the next project."

"Something like that."

He came toward her then, causing her to back into the door. "Maybe it's just that you don't think I have any good intentions at all—toward Prescott or toward you. Is that it, Lizzie? You don't want me to see that house because you think I'll abandon it, and...you?"

"*I'm* just the salesperson," she said, lifting her chin to stare him down. "So leave me out of this."

"I can't do that," he said, his hand on the door. "You are very much a part of this. Whether you like it or not."

"Let's just get this over with," she replied, whirling so fast she almost hit the door frame.

"You'd like that, wouldn't you? You'd like me to fall flat on my face, so you could say 'I told you so.'"

"Not my problem." She gave him a scowl, then called out to Brandy. "I'm going to show a house."

"Okay, boss," came the quick reply from the other room. No doubt her capable assistant had been eavesdropping.

"You sure *are* going to show a house," Jake told her as he followed her out the door. "You're going to show me every inch of that house. And then I'll show you that you're wrong about me."

"I'd love nothing better."

"Fine."

"Fine."

"It's at the corner of Hemlock and Spruce."

"Got it."

"Good."

They rode across town in silence.

A very loud silence.

Chapter Six

Jake broke the silence as they pulled up to the house. "Wow."

Elizabeth had to agree with him there. "Wow is right. It's just such an amazing house."

"When was it built?" he asked after they got out and stood on the cracked sidewalk near a cluster of old azaleas.

"Eighteen ninety-five," Elizabeth replied. She knew the entire history of the Lockwood house, but she stubbornly refused to tell Jake that. She didn't want to encourage him.

Jake lifted his dark head, his eyes brightening to a shimmering silvery-blue that reminded her of stars at night. "Look at those windows, and those rounded corners."

"Yes, there are round-windowed walls in the front parlor, the master bedroom above that, and of course, the turret tower," Elizabeth said, warming up to the house, if not the client interested in the house. "It could be turned into a showplace, the way it used to be. But it would take a small fortune."

"I have a small fortune," Jake said, unabashed and un-ashamed, from the sincere look on his face. "Let's go inside, Lizzie."

Elizabeth's heart did a beating protest, but her feet moved in spite of that. She'd never said no to a client. She couldn't do it now, but her mind was reeling with the possibility of losing this house to Jake. Elizabeth couldn't stomach the thought of him coming in and gutting the house, changing everything, rearranging things to suit his larger-than-life ideas.

Maybe he won't like it, she told herself as she un-locked the front-door lock-box. Yeah, and maybe cows really are purple.

Reluctantly, Elizabeth pushed at the huge stained-glass double doors, causing the aged wood to creak open like the lid to a treasure chest. They entered the front hallway, the smell of decay and neglect strong in the scorching heat, the swirls of dust balls dancing around their heads like invisible ballerinas.

"See, I told you it's in bad shape," she said, turning to bump into Jake's hard chest.

"I haven't seen the entire house, Lizzie," Jake pointed out, his breath warm on her hair. She couldn't see his eyes, but she had a great view of the dark chest hairs swirling just above his chambray shirt collar. "And I intend to see it, all of it. So stop stalling."

"Oh, all right," she said, pivoting to march into the

room to the right. "Here's the parlor. The other side was used for a formal dining room. There's a kitchen on the left and a study on the right through those doors. There's a half bath under the stairs."

Jake pushed her ahead of him as they moved through the rooms where a few pieces of furniture stood draped in dusty white sheets. "I'd put a nice den back here," he said as they entered the study. "Lots of dark paneling and lots of books. A big walnut desk over there." He pointed toward a spot by two tall windows.

"I always envisioned a den or study back here, too," Elizabeth said, forgetting she was supposed to be discouraging him.

They moved toward the long kitchen on the backside of the downstairs. "I can just see yellows and reds in here," she said. "Bright colors with lots of floral."

"That would be nice," Jake replied, his smile soft as he stared at her.

Elizabeth felt the intensity of his eyes on her like a spot of sunshine coming through a dark room. Moving to stand by the bay window in the breakfast room, she said, "It's hot in here." Unable to fathom having to sell her dream house to Jake, she could only stand there and stare out at the sloping backyard, visions of camellia bushes and magnolia trees playing through her head.

"You want this house, don't you?" Jake finally asked, coming to stand beside her. "Is that why you didn't want me to see it? Because you want it for yourself?"

Elizabeth couldn't look at him. She didn't want him to see the truth in her eyes. "Don't be silly. I just thought—"

"You thought I wouldn't understand," he said, his words full of some emotion she couldn't name. "You thought I'd come in here and change this house, but you already have plans for this house. Big plans."

"No, I don't," she said, turning at last to face him. "I can't afford to buy it and renovate it, and anyway, I have no illusions regarding this old house, Jake. Except this should be a happy house."

He nodded, his eyes moving over her face with a heated concentration. "And what exactly makes a happy house, Lizzie?"

She shrugged, shifted on her high-heeled mules. "I have this thing about houses. I guess it's why I became a Realtor. I can just tell when a house needs a family. Some houses are just too sad. They don't have that special feeling. I can sell those, but I always feel as if I haven't been quite honest with the buyers. But when I have a happy house to sell, I just know that the family is going to grow and thrive there. I so want this to be a happy house, the way it was over a hundred years ago. I want it to have a big family running up and down the stairway and halls, and I want it to have old rocking chairs on the wraparound porches and a big swing out there where the porch curves toward the carriage drive. I want it to have lace curtains and four-poster beds in every bedroom, and fat, drooping ferns and bright-red geraniums sitting in planters by the front doors. I want this house to be a good, solid house, Jake, a happy house, to make someone a happy home. It can be a good home again. It will be some-day, somehow. It's just waiting for the right family to come along."

Jake turned to her then, his gaze moving over her in that lazy, meandering way that seemed to stop time. "So you don't want me to live here? Because I'm not a family man, right? Is that why you didn't bother telling me about it?"

She thought she saw a trace of sadness and regret in his eyes, which only added to the mystery of him and made her want to apologize for deceiving him. "Something like that, I guess."

He inched closer, then touched a hand to her bangs, his fingers playing through her hair with an intimate disregard that left her baffled. "I like this house, Lizzie. I like it a lot." He leaned closer. "But I don't intend to live here alone."

Jake watched the play of emotions moving like changing clouds over Elizabeth's face as she stammered a response. "Oh, you…you have someone in mind? Someone back in Texas?"

He had to grin at that, even though memories of a *someone* came playing like an old movie through his head. Pushing the memories away, he concentrated in-stead on the woman in front of him. She was here and she was real.

And she looked downright disappointed at the

prospect of him settling down in this house with some-one else. That disappointment only fueled his hopes. "No, no one back in Texas. More like someone right here in Prescott."

"Oh, you're…seeing somebody then?"

"Yep, I sure am. Been seeing her for a while now."

She backed away, straightened and stood taller, her chin lifting out in that stubborn way he'd come to know and appreciate. "Funny, I had no idea. I mean, this is a small town and I haven't heard—"

"I'm looking at her right now," Jake said, advancing on her with one long stride, his pulse matching tempo with his need to hold her close.

She looked confused and flustered, a soft peachy blush moving down her face. "I don't understand."

"You will," he said as he curved a hand around her neck and hauled her close. "You will very soon, Lizzie."

Then he kissed her good and proper, with a firm branding that he hoped laid claim to her heart. Jake intended to buy this house, and he intended to move into it with his new bride.

But first, he had to convince the woman in his arms that she was the one, that she was his intended, and that he was the man for her. Because, after being around her for weeks now, after getting to know her and watching her and listening to her, working with her, and seeing what kind of person she really was un-derneath that business and bluster attitude, Jake couldn't imagine living in this great, rambling house with anyone but Elizabeth Sinclair.

And the amazing part, the part that had his heart beating to a new tune, was that he'd never thought to experience this kind of feeling again. He'd never thought he'd be able to love again. But Jake's instincts told him he'd be crazy to let this woman slip away.

So he kissed her to seal the deal. And when he was thoroughly and completely sure that she felt the same way, as indicated by her soft sighs and her hands around his neck, he stood back to stare down at her. "Let's negotiate," he said, his voice husky, his heart hopeful.

Elizabeth's eyes looked like newly fallen leaves in autumn sunshine. "About what?" she asked, her own voice just above a whisper.

"About the house, about us, about how we're going to be living here together one day."

She brought her head up, her eyes going wide as a little gasp escaped her lips. "What did you say?"

"You heard me," Jake told her, amused by the look of surprise on her face. "I want this house, Lizzie. But only on one condition. I want you in it with me. And I won't take no for an answer. Now, let's go see the upstairs."

Chapter Seven

"You sure are quiet."

Elizabeth glanced up to find Hannah, Jo and Aunt Becky staring at her with wide inquisitive eyes. She looked around the nearly empty Whistling Gofer, wondering when the lunch crowd had disappeared. Not sure which one had just spoken to her, she shook her head. "Just thinking of all the things I need to be doing. I've been very busy lately."

"With Jake Clark?" Aunt Becky asked, her smile as pleased as that on the cat that had swallowed the canary.

"With work," Elizabeth replied, bristling at the implications of her dear friend's pointed question. She'd certainly tried *working* with Jake, but that man had other things in mind. Such as the silly notion that she would one day live in the Lockwood house with him.

"But you're still working with Jake, right?" Hannah asked, worry and hope clashing in her blue eyes.

"Oh, yes." Elizabeth drummed her fingers on the

table and pushed away the remains of her half-eaten cheesecake. "He's a slow starter, but the man means business."

"Well, we're all just thrilled that he's restoring the Lockwood house," Jo said, pushing a hand through her red curls. "That place was turning into an eyesore."

Hannah's eyes met Elizabeth's in silent encouragement and complete understanding. "It *is* beginning to look like a dream home," she said.

"It was *my* dream house," Elizabeth retorted, the slow boil of her anger and frustration warring with the thrill of being able to watch the house being restored to its former beauty. And the thrill of Jake kissing her right there in the house. "Oh, well, I guess I should be glad someone can afford to overhaul the place."

"Jake seems to have money to burn," Aunt Becky stated, taking a quick sip of her spiced tea. "But he is such a nice, well-mannered man. The historical society is extremely pleased about how he's going to such pains to make sure the house is authentic in every detail." She paused to let that soak in, then added, "And he's always in church, each and every Sunday."

"He's a real saint," Elizabeth said, her bad mood turning to black about as fast as the wind was moving the clouds outside. "Looks like rain. Guess I'd better get back to work before that cloud burst hits."

"You work right next door," Jo pointed out.

"I might get wet," Elizabeth replied, trying to send her friend a message to drop the subject of Jake Clark.

"You work too hard."

Elizabeth glanced at Aunt Becky, but ignored the other woman's admonishment. Then she sent one to Jo, a teasing note in her tone of voice. "So glad you could join us. I guess marriage keeps a person extremely busy."

"She's very happy, but also very busy," Aunt Becky replied before Jo could retort. "She and Bram are doing great."

Elizabeth stared hard at Jo. "Well, you do look good. Your skin is glowing. You're even having a good hair day, in spite of this humidity."

"Love will do that," Jo replied. Then she touched a hand to Elizabeth's arm. "You ought to give it a try."

"Don't be silly," Elizabeth replied. But the dream of her house being remodeled by a man who just about fit the bill of good marriage material caused her to take in her breath and sigh. "Enough about my sad love life. What are you working on at the flower shop, Jo?"

"She's doing all the flowers for an anniversary party tonight," Aunt Becky said in her habitual way of answering for everyone else. "The Glanvilles—they've been married fifty years."

"Imagine that," Elizabeth responded, tears pricking her eyes in spite of her cynical words. It didn't help that every time she was forced to meet Jake at *his* house, she suddenly had visions of flowers and weddings and happy times. Just visions, nothing real, she reminded herself.

"Yes, imagine that," Hannah said, her eyes going a

dark blue that told Elizabeth she was remembering things neither one of them needed to remember.

"At least one marriage in this town has lasted."

Aunt Becky shot Elizabeth a disapproving look. "You girls need to quit trying to predict which marriages around here are going to last or fail. It's downright depressing."

"The truth is depressing," Elizabeth said. "And the truth is that half of all marriages in this country, and this town, for that matter, end in divorce." She stood up, grabbed her briefcase. "I'm going to work. It was nice having lunch with y'all." With that, she grabbed the check and hurried to pay it before any of them could argue with her.

"See you in church?" Aunt Becky asked, ever hopeful.

"Maybe," Elizabeth answered, thinking that one day dear Aunt Becky would take the hint and stop inviting her. Or maybe one day she'd just surprise them all and actually show up in church. Maybe the building wouldn't fall down around her. Telling herself this sudden urge to go to church had nothing to do with the fact that Jake attended, she thanked their waitress and offered her a nice tip.

"Bye, y'all." Waving a hand, she hurried to her own office just as big, fat drops of cool rain hit the streets with sizzling precision. Then Elizabeth thought some more about the little tidbit Aunt Becky had dropped at lunch. Jake Clark went to church, apparently on a regular basis.

Well, the man had never denied his faith in God.

Not the way you have, a small voice said in Elizabeth's head as she tossed her briefcase down and pulled up several of her current property listings on her computer screen.

It wasn't that she didn't like church. She did. Or rather, she had as a child. Back then, however, church had been part of that perfect illusion her parents had managed to cultivate. If she closed her eyes, Elizabeth could still see them there, the happy little Sinclair family, sitting in their favorite pew right up front and center.

Right there for God and everyone to see.

That is, until the day a few weeks after her sixteenth birthday when Milton Sinclair had come home from the office and started packing a suitcase.

Elizabeth shut her eyes tightly together to push away the tears that threatened to splatter down her face just like the rain now splattering against the sidewalk outside. She could still remember the calm way in which her father had announced he was leaving. She could still see the disbelief and shock on her mother's face as they'd both watched him walk down the stairs and out the door.

He was living in Hot Springs now, with his artistic younger wife. Almost fifteen years had passed by, and the man had yet to call or come and visit. Or give his daughter an explanation.

Elizabeth opened her eyes wide, blinking back the tears. *"So you explain it to me, God. You tell me why*

I should believe in You and why I should even hold out any hope that Jake Clark might actually be an honorable man?"

Elizabeth stared out at the falling rain, wishing that she could find the courage and strength to turn back to God, wishing that she had some sort of foundation on which to build her hopes and dreams. Her father hadn't bothered to give her any answers over the years and neither had God.

"You both turned away," she said, reasoning that she didn't need anyone's guidance or help. *"I can handle it from here on out, I reckon."*

But as she sat there in her plush office, with the dark clouds of a summer storm brewing all around her, in her secret heart Elizabeth prayed that God would turn His face back to her and give her a sign of hope.

At that precise moment, a clap of thunder boomed outside and the office door swung open with a clashing bang, causing Elizabeth to crane her neck to see who'd just entered the other room.

And there stood Jake Clark, big and bold, and larger than any fairy-tale prince she'd ever imagined.

"Trying to tell me something, Lord?" she said under her breath.

"I've been trying to call you," Jake said, taking off his Stetson so he could shake the rain off the soft felt.

"I've been out," Elizabeth said, getting up to walk out into the outer office. "And Brandy is home sick with a nasty summer cold."

Jake took in her smart navy-blue dress and matching pumps, and he also noticed that her eyes looked red-rimmed and full of worry and confusion. "Well, don't you ever check your cell phone messages or your office answering machine?"

Fingering the double strand of pearls at her neck, she gave him a smoldering look. "I said, I've been out. And last time I checked, I don't have to answer to you if I don't want to do so."

"What's got you in such a pickle?" he asked, genuine concern causing him to stare at her across the room.

"It's just been one of those days," she said, shrugging as she sent him a sheepish look. "What can I do for you?"

"I wanted to show you something at the house," he said, grinning. "Something we found in the attic."

"I don't have time to go traipsing through the Lockwood house with you."

"It's the Clark house now, sugar. Get used to it."

He could tell he'd struck a nerve. She bristled like a cornered bobcat.

"Oh, I'm well aware of that. Everybody in town is talking about how you're just so precious and precise, trying to renovate it to suit the historical society, the church women and everyone else from the town council to the governor up in Little Rock. Yes, we're all very much aware that Jake Clark is in Prescott, and here to stay a while." Running a hand through her curls, she laughed. "I declare, I've never seen anything like it.

You just ride in on that big old black horse of a truck and take over."

"I'm not taking over, Lizzie. I'm just trying to start over."

"And why are you starting over here, Jake? Why is it that you left the good life in Fort Worth to come to a small, out-of-the-way town like Prescott?"

He advanced toward her then, his own anger matching hers. "One day, I'll be glad to tell you the whole story, but right now, I think you need to tell me something instead."

"Oh, and what's that?"

"Why do you resent me so much? Why do you hate me being here, Lizzie? And why are you so all-fire mad because I bought that old house?" Before she could answer, he tugged her close. "I think I can figure it out for myself. You resent me because I am a contented, happy person, and you're so miserable you can't stand to see anybody else happy. That's number one. And you don't like the fact that I bought that house right out from under you, because you were sitting on it, hoping one day to claim it for your own." He stopped, saw the flare of pain in her eyes, but decided he'd gone this far. "That's number two. But you never got up the nerve to buy that house, because you're so afraid you might actually be able to live there and be happy, only you can't be happy because you're still so caught up in the mistakes and sins of your parents that you can't think straight. That's number three, and I think I just answered all my questions. Am I right?"

He watched as her expression changed from boiling mad to quietly resigned, and then, he watched as she pulled away from him and burst into tears.

Chapter Eight

Jake didn't know how to react to her tears. Elizabeth Sinclair wasn't the sort of woman to give in to tears on a whim. Something was terribly wrong.

"I'm sorry," he said as he came to her and pulled her into his arms. "I'm so sorry, Lizzie."

She hiccuped and pushed him away. "Don't be silly. I'm certainly not crying over you."

"That's the Lizzie I know," he said, almost grateful for her flippant attitude. "Why are you crying, then?"

Elizabeth shrugged, hugged herself with her arms, as if to ward off a chill. "I'm just in a blue mood. Summer rain always makes me sad."

Jake didn't want to be nosy, so he didn't try to pry anything out of her. Women were hard to figure out on a normal day, let along a rainy, dreary afternoon. Instead of asking more questions, he turned her toward the front window of the office. "Look at the rain, Elizabeth. It's exactly what we needed today. It's bringing water to the crops, to the flowers and trees, it's cleansing the streets and cooling down the heat."

"It's making a mess of everything," she said, sniffing. But she did look out the window, her eyes big and misty, her expression changing from dismay to acceptance. "It's not just the rain. It's everything. I guess I just don't like change and now I've had so much of it this summer."

"First Jo getting married and now me buying the Lockwood house," Jake said, suddenly understanding.

"Yes," she admitted, her gaze dismayed and ashamed. "Jake, I should be glad you're taking over that house. I've dreamed of doing the same thing. I don't want to resent you or be jealous, but I just—"

"You just wanted to do it yourself."

She nodded and held up a finger. "And don't go telling me that someday soon, I'll be occupying that house with you. That can't happen."

"And why not?"

She gave him a look full of disbelief and anger. "Because I won't be railroaded into falling in love with a man who doesn't take life seriously. You have this attitude that everything's going to be all right in God's own time. You never rush things or get in a hurry. I can't be that way, Jake. I've learned to depend on *my* time, not God's time. And I certainly can't sit around waiting for divine intervention."

He shook his head. "Sometimes, divine intervention happens pretty fast, Lizzie. I can see that each time I look at you."

"Now there you go again," she said, whirling around

the room. "You have to stop assuming that you and I are going to be together. We have a working relationship, but nothing more."

"There could be more if you'd quit being so sanctimonious and stubborn."

"Me, sanctimonious?" She jabbed a finger at his chest. "You're the one who thinks God is in control, Jake. You're the one who thinks everything will just fall into place around you. You're the one who has all the platitudes and prayers." She stopped, out of breath and apparently out of sarcastic things to throw in his face. "You have all the answers."

Jake had enough pain and hurt to last him a lifetime, but he refused to tell her that. "You don't know one thing about me, that's for sure," he said as he turned for the door. "But you will one day, Lizzie."

"Good. You're leaving. Maybe I'll find some peace," she said, though she didn't sound very convincing.

"You can't find peace if you don't give God a chance to give it to you." He stood with his hand on the door, watching the water washing over the streets outside. "If you want to see what I found at the house, come by later. I'll be there, waiting for you."

"I'll keep that in mind."

Jake left, steeling himself against the chill of her words. She was a tough one. Too tough to understand that she could be healed if she'd just turn to God and ask for that healing.

He should know. He'd had to do the very same thing not so long ago.

* * *

"Why did y'all call me here?"

Elizabeth stared at the four women sitting in the kitchen at Mimosa Manor. Surprised to find her mother amongst her friends, she shook her head. "This must be pretty serious if Mom's here."

Phyllis Sinclair looked at Elizabeth with wide eyes. "We're worried about you, darling."

"Why?" Elizabeth asked, suddenly feeling as if she'd been set up.

Hannah and Jo pulled her to a chair, then set a cup of hot tea in front of her. "You need to listen, Elizabeth."

Elizabeth looked from her two friends to Aunt Becky, then back to her mother. "Oh, no. Mama, are you sick?"

"No, honey," Phyllis said, her smile bittersweet. "But I have been going through a healing process."

Elizabeth fidgeted, drumming her fingers on the table as the others sat down. "What's going on?"

"An intervention," Jo said, her eyes big underneath the bangs of her spiky red hair. "You need to understand something, Elizabeth."

Hannah took Elizabeth's hand. "It's okay to fall in love, Elizabeth. Jo and I want you to be happy."

"Fall in love? What are you-all talking about?"

Aunt Becky took a sip of tea, then cleared her throat. "I've been praying for you—for all you girls. I was so thrilled when Jo fell in love with Bram. And now you have this wonderful man in your life—"

"You mean Jake Clark?"

They all nodded. Aunt Becky cleared her throat again. "He's perfect for you, honey. A dream man."

Oh, my, Elizabeth thought. Jake had said divine intervention could happen quickly. He'd really get a kick out of *friendly* intervention. Or how about *misguided* intervention?

"He's a nice man, true," Elizabeth said, pushing her chair back. "But I don't need you four telling me who to fall in love with. I don't love him. We have a working relationship."

"I've heard differently," her mother said, a hand on her arm. "Everyone knows you two have been spending a lot of time together, both during working hours and after hours. And I want you to know, darling, you can't miss out on life just because you think *I'm* miserable. I'm okay now, Elizabeth. I've accepted what happened with your father and frankly, I'm very content with my life and my church work."

Shocked, Elizabeth sank down on her chair. "Mom, you always seem so unhappy, so distant."

"I know, and I aim to change that," Phyllis said. "I was so wrapped up in my life, I didn't stop to think that my feelings might rub off on you. You can't give up on love, Elizabeth."

"Daddy did—at least with us."

"Your father was going through a tough time," Phyllis said. "It wasn't all his fault, honey. I shut him out. I turned away from him. He didn't think I loved him anymore."

More confused than ever, Elizabeth shook her head.

"That didn't give him the right to walk out on us. He hurt both of us, Mama."

"Yes, he did. But that doesn't mean you have to remain single and depressed all your life."

"I'm not depressed," Elizabeth said through a groan.

Jo grabbed her hand and forced her to look at her. "I'm happy now. I want the same for you and Hannah. Can't you give Jake a chance? He's a good man, and well, Bram says he's been through some heartache of his own."

"Not my problem," Elizabeth said, even though she longed to know the whole story. Thinking she probably sounded selfish and horrid, she added, "He does seem sad at times, when he thinks no one is looking. Or when I'm especially nasty to him." She glanced around, touched that they cared enough to talk to her, but wanting to get away from their smothering concern. "I'll try to be nicer, okay? But you've got it wrong. We're just friends, honestly."

"Are *you* being honest?" Hannah asked her, a look of resolve in her eyes.

Elizabeth could feel her defenses sinking. "But what about us, Hannah? What about our pact?" She glanced back at Jo, thinking she was the cause of all of this. But Elizabeth couldn't hold it against her friend. Jo glowed with joy and bliss, so it stood to reason she'd want that for her friends in spite of what had happened all those years ago.

"That was a silly adolescent promise," Hannah replied. "I can't ever forget what happened the night

Johnny died, but you can, Elizabeth. It's time to let it go."

"But what about you?" Elizabeth asked her. "Am I just supposed to abandon you, while I go in search of the perfect man?"

"There are no perfect men, darling," her mother said, her eyes warm with understanding. "But from what I've heard and seen, Jake Clark comes mighty close."

Hannah played with a doily in the center of the table. "You don't need to worry about me, Elizabeth. I'm going to be okay. And you don't have to hold back on your feelings for my sake."

Jo nodded. "I couldn't hold back from loving Bram, even when I tried. And while I regret breaking our pact, I don't regret marrying him. So now I'm praying that both of you find the same kind of love in your lives."

Elizabeth shook her head again. "So you-all called me here to give me your blessings?"

"Exactly," Hannah said. "Jake has been calling here all day. He really wants to see you tonight at the house." Her eyes held a secretive twinkle. "So I say, go for it."

"There's nothing to go for," Elizabeth replied. "I'm not going to rush into anything with Jake. I don't want any regrets."

"The regret would be in not trying," Aunt Becky said.

"Thanks for your concern," Elizabeth told them as she got up to leave. "But I'm fine, just fine." Seeing the tears in her mother's eyes, Elizabeth bent and hugged her mother close. "Thanks, Mama. I know it's been hard on you all these years, but I do appreciate that you care."

"We all care," Phyllis told her. "Now go and see that man before he gets away."

Curiosity killed the cat, Elizabeth kept telling herself as her sports car hugged the curve leading to the Lockwood house.

The Clark house now, she reminded herself.

Why did Jake need to see her? What had he found, and why did she care?

She cared, more than she wanted to admit. Maybe that's why she'd automatically headed toward the house after leaving Hannah's place. Maybe that's why the women's words kept ringing in her ears.

Divine intervention. It was rather strange that the very day Jake had talked about that, everyone she cared about had decided to give her some tough love.

As if she cared.

But she did care.

And she didn't just care about that old house. She cared a lot about Jake Clark. Why'd he have to go and be so nice? Why did he make her laugh, even when he made her so all-fire mad? Why did he seem to be a good, solid businessman who worked to make sure everything was done by the book and everyone had an equal piece of the pie?

"Why'd he have to come to my town?" she said out

loud as she pulled up in the driveway of the house. "And why did he buy this house? And why did I just have to go through prayer meeting with my friends and my mother?"

Glancing up at the house, she had to admit it looked better already. The house stood sturdy now, its foundation firm. It no longer listed to one side as if it might topple over onto the sidewalk. The many scaffolds surrounding it told the tale of how much work the crew was doing.

And made Elizabeth cringe with a jealous pang of regret.

"I'll just go see what the man found," she said, gritting her teeth against the way of things. "I'll just smile and say how nice it looks. I'll make small talk, and then I'm out of here. I am not here to conquer the conquering hero."

Since it was still drizzling, she ran up the stone steps toward the wraparound porch, then nearly tripped on some old lumber lying across the rickety steps. Mortified, she managed to right herself just as the front door opened.

"You came."

Elizabeth lifted her brows. "I'm standing here, yes. But I don't have much time."

"Always in a hurry," Jake said as he guided her around old furniture and piles of torn carpet.

If he looked disappointed, Elizabeth chose to ignore it. What did the man expect? That she'd sit down and have a full-course romantic dinner with him?

Apparently, that's exactly what he expected.

Standing in the entranceway, Elizabeth gasped as she looked into the parlor off to the right. The big empty room was drenched in candlelight from a multitude of white candles. They sat on covered furniture. They perched on the mantel and in the big open bay window. And in the center of the room sat a small bistro table, complete with fresh flowers and its own burning candle.

"Oh, my," she managed to say.

He shrugged, stared down at his boots. "I thought you could use a nice, quiet dinner. What with you being so blue and all."

"You did all of this? For me?"

"I had some help."

"I'll just bet."

"You're mad."

"No," she said, her heart heavy, her mind reeling as she tried to find her next breath. "It's just that…I feel like I did that day I fell off my raft and into the river. In over my head."

Jake took her hand, then smiled. "But you can stand up here, Elizabeth. See? I've got you. And I won't ever let you fall."

Swallowing the hot burning in her throat, Elizabeth took it all in, and knew she'd been set up bigtime. By this man.

And by her friends and her mother.

Chapter Nine

"Guess I'm staying a while after all," Elizabeth said, the smell of something wonderful drifting to her nose from the covered dishes on the table.

He seemed pleased with that. A grin split his face, making her heart ache with longing. He really was a good man. In fact, Elizabeth couldn't think of much bad about him. He was polite, smart, considerate of others, a nature lover—he'd probably been a Boy Scout. He was fair in his dealings, and he was pretty to look at. Maybe he was a dream man, after all.

But dreams didn't always come true, and this man was too good to be true. To countermine the treacherous thoughts slinking through her head, she whirled to stare at him. "Just what exactly are you trying to do?"

He shrugged, held up one of the silver lids covering the dishes on the table. "I'm trying to have dinner with a very attractive, very interesting woman."

Elizabeth glanced down at the food. "Is that by any chance Hannah's famous chicken enchiladas?"

"You have a good nose."

He lifted the lid off the next dish.

"And is that praline cheesecake?"

"Hannah's special recipe."

"You certainly pulled out all the stops."

He motioned for her to sit down. "Just like you told me once—I aim to please."

Elizabeth allowed him to help her with her chair, then waited for him to join her. "This is nice. I'm starving."

"I've noticed you don't always take the time to eat right."

"Really? What else have you noticed about me?"

"Your eyes. I really like the way they light up when you're working a deal."

"Thanks, I think."

"And I like your hair, the way it goes here and there and everywhere."

"Terminally curly."

"And I like how hard you work, how much you care about things, how you try to hide your heart behind all that bluff. I like all those different high-heeled shoes you wear. I just plain like *you*, Lizzie."

She stabbed at the creamy chicken and cheese concoction he'd placed on her plate. "Is this the part where I tell you what all I like about you?"

"Could be. But then, what do you really know about me?"

It was an odd question, but the sincerity in his eyes

made her stop and think. "I know a little. I like that you, too, are a hard worker, even though you take your own sweet time, which, by the way, drives me crazy."

He grinned, tipped his head. "Go on."

"I like how you take control and go for what you want, except for your constant pestering of me, of course."

"I'm listening."

"I like that you're friends with Bram. Because he's a nice person and he's crazy in love with my best friend."

"Uh-oh. Don't go getting sad on me again."

"I'm okay with it, really. Maybe a bit wistful and jealous, but happy for Bram and Jo. She's just gushing with love and happiness."

"Love can do that to a person."

Elizabeth remembered Jo saying almost the same thing. "Have you ever been in love?" she asked, realizing she really didn't know a thing about his personal life.

"I was." He went silent, his fork of food clattering to his plate. "Want some more iced tea?"

"No, I'm good. When were you in love?"

"You first. I bet you had boys all around you in high school."

"And grammar school," she said, quirking her brows as she nibbled her food. "Practically had to beat 'em off with a stick."

"I hear that."

His grin was gone, replaced by a serious expression that was both hopeful and regretful. This look was very appealing and very dangerous. And he'd somehow managed to avoid her question.

"I've had boyfriends," she said. "But nothing serious for a while now. I dated a biker once. My mother did not approve of him, let me tell you. Then it was the used-car salesman. He was nice, but he wanted a stay-at-home wife who could bake cookies. Hannah would be better suited to him, but she refuses to even consider it."

"Well, all that's about to change," he said, his eyes so deep and mysterious, Elizabeth had to swallow a gulp of tea.

"Hannah, you mean? Do you know something I don't know?"

"I'm not too worried about Miss Hannah. I'm talking about you, Lizzie. You and me. Things are going to change between us."

Disappointment surging through her like a current of electricity, she nodded. "Good. At last you understand that we can never have anything between us beyond a working relationship, a friendship of mutual respect and admiration."

"You didn't hear me right."

"Oh? What'd I miss?"

"Things are about to get serious between us, real serious."

Her heart was beating against the thick cotton of her sleeveless turtleneck. She could feel it fluttering there, trapped and trying to escape. "I told you—"

"I know what you told me. But I'm telling you that I'm falling for you. And that's that."

She got up to spin around the candlelit room. Her shadow danced along the walls like a ballerina trying to find an exit. "I don't even know about you, Jake. You haven't told me anything about Fort Worth and your former life. You're like some dream that just popped into my head. A dream that I can't accept."

He got up, came to stand behind her as she stared out the big bay window. The rain was still falling, a gentle, slow shower that caused light-pink crape myrtle blossoms to drift down around the porch.

"I'm not a dream, Lizzie. I'm flesh and blood, and I'm not perfect by any means. You asked me if I'd ever been in love and I have. I've loved so deeply, that even now it hurts me to think about it."

She pivoted to stare up at him. "What are you saying?"

The raw pain in his eyes told her that this was very real. He turned away to stare at a grouping of candles sitting on an old table. "I was married."

Elizabeth gasped and sank back down on her chair. "Why didn't you say something? Bram never—"

"I asked Bram not to tell anyone."

"What's the big secret? You're ashamed of being divorced?" She wanted to shout See, you're not so perfect, after all. But the wounded look in his eyes told her to keep that thought to herself.

"I didn't get a divorce." He sighed, ran a hand down his face. "I'm a widower."

Elizabeth was glad she was sitting. She might have dropped to the floor, her knees felt so weak. "What? You mean—"

"I mean my wife died a few years ago. My wife and my little girl."

Elizabeth felt physically ill. Her hands were shaking, her skin felt clammy. Hot moisture blurred her eyes. "Oh, Jake." She swallowed the lump in her throat. "What happened?"

"I killed them," he said, the sharp-edged tone of his voice cutting like stone.

Elizabeth blinked back tears. "You…I don't believe that. What are you talking about?"

He stood looking out at the darkening night. "I grew up in a big family. We didn't have much. I had to scrape and save for everything. I had to fight for money, an education, a good job. I got all that and more by working hard, day and night."

She didn't speak. She just sat waiting to hear the rest, her heart shifting and falling away from that wall she'd built up around it.

"I fell in love with Trisha the minute I saw her. We got married and after I started making good money, we decided to have a baby. A couple of years later, Melissa came along. Everything was great, except that I worked such long hours, I didn't get to see them very much. I missed out on Melissa's first time to sit up, the first time she crawled. I missed out on her first steps. But I was too blinded by ambition and the need to make more money to worry about that. After all, we had it all on tape, right?"

He turned then to look down at her. "So you ask me how I can be so laid back and unconcerned now? Well, I learned that lesson the hard way. The night they died, I was running late for a meeting. It was Melissa's fifth birthday and I had promised I'd have dinner with them. We had an early dinner, then I insisted that I had to get to my meeting. Trisha got so mad at me, but she didn't argue with me. I hustled them in the car to get them home. We were about two blocks from our house and I was going way over the speed limit. I didn't see the other car—"

"Jake, please." Elizabeth jumped up. She rushed to him, tried to hold him, but he pushed her away. So she stood staring at him, her mind whirling with memories of another accident on another night long ago. The night Johnny Harrison had died. "Stop, Jake. Don't talk about it any more."

"I don't talk about it, don't you see? I don't allow anyone ever to talk about it. It just hurts so much."

"It wasn't your fault."

He glared at her, his eyes full of memories and guilt. "Yes, it was. It was all my fault." He sank down on the window seat. "The day I buried them, I made a promise to God that I would never get in a hurry like that again. I made a vow that I wouldn't let ambition or money make me so blind that I couldn't see what was really important. So you have to understand, Lizzie, I don't rush things now because

I've learned that nothing, I mean nothing, is as important as having someone to love. I still get the job done, but I will never again sacrifice my time or my heart to work, to a career." He turned to stare over at her then, tears misting in his eyes. "I had it all, everything a man could ever hope for, and in one split second, I lost it all. A man never forgets that kind of hurt, Elizabeth."

Elizabeth went to him, falling down on her knees in front of him. "Jake, oh, Jake. And here I thought—"

"You thought the worst, that I was just some good ol' boy out for fun, a man who didn't take life seriously. Well, I take life very seriously, let me tell you."

"You called me Elizabeth," she said, tears trailing down her face while the rain fell outside. "You called me that earlier, when you told me you wouldn't let me fall. I think it's my turn to hold you up."

He looked down at her, then reached his hands down to cover her face. "Elizabeth, such a pretty name. But you'll always be Lizzie to me." He ran his hands over her face, his eyes drenching her with a need that left her open and exposed, but also washed clean.

"Jake, I'm so sorry."

He nodded. "It's hard to talk about it."

She touched a hand to his face. "One day, I want to hear all about them. Promise me that?"

"One day," he said. "But not tonight."

"No, not tonight," she replied as she lifted her face to his kiss.

He held her there while the candlelight flickered a sweet, steady fire and the rain echoed a pure, cleansing drizzle that seemed to be telling them both to hold tight.

Chapter Ten

Somehow they managed to slide down to sit on the floor, Elizabeth curled in Jake's arms as they leaned back against the old window seat. He held her there as the rain continued to fall like a soft and steady song outside.

"Are you cold?" he asked, his voice husky against her ear.

"No. I'm fine." She wanted to stay right here forever, but she still had questions, lots of questions. And she knew she needed to tell him something. Lifting up, she looked into his eyes. "Do you know why I vowed never to fall in love?"

He gave her a twisted smile. "I think I've pretty much figured it out. Only because Bram's filled me in on some stuff." He shrugged. "I guess now is a good time to tell you the rest."

"The rest? What are you talking about?"

"I know a lot more than I've let on—about that night."

"Then you know about Johnny Harrison?"

He nodded. "I know he was Hannah's boyfriend and that he died the night of the prom. I know that his older brother, Griff, was driving the car. And that after he died, you three decided you'd never find the perfect man. So you made this pact—"

"Never to fall in love, never to marry." She sat up, her hand on his chest. "But it was more than just Johnny's death. We'd all seen the worst of love and marriage with our parents. I think that's the main reason we felt so determined to honor our pact."

"You didn't want to be hurt," he said, his hand stroking her hair, his eyes soft with understanding.

She nodded. "But now, I see that you've suffered through the worst kind of hurt. How did you survive that, Jake?"

He let out a breath. "At first, I didn't think I would survive. I just about went insane. I shut down to the point that I became physically drained. Then my daddy sat me down and gave me a good talking to. That man's seen both good and bad in his day, but he always held fast to his faith. He reminded me that love endures all things."

"But you lost everything you loved," Elizabeth said, unable to grasp how anyone could endure that.

"But God's love endures loss," Jake explained, his

tone gentle and full of hope. "God's love can see us through the worst of times."

"So that's how you coped, by turning to God?"

He nodded, tugged her back into his arms. "I prayed for the pain to end, I asked God to give me a second chance. That and finding a good counselor to help me through it. Surprisingly, that person had been through the loss of a loved one, too." He stopped, ran a hand through his hair. "That man was Griff Harrison, Lizzie. I met him through Bram." At her gasp, he hurried on. "He really understood what I was going through. And he's suffered just about as much guilt and self-condemnation as I have."

She frowned, then sighed. "I never knew what became of him. We can't tell Hannah about this. She hates him."

"I know. But he's my friend. And he's been wronged."

Elizabeth doubted that, and right now, she didn't want to discuss it. "I don't want to hear about Griff Harrison. Just tell me how you came to be the man you are today."

He shook his head. "It wasn't easy, but after the initial grief, I felt as if I had two special angels watching over me." He stopped, his voice cracking. "And I couldn't let them down."

Elizabeth felt the hot sting of tears in her eyes. "I've never looked at it that way. I guess we've let Johnny down all these years by denying the love he felt for

Hannah. Instead of celebrating that love, we turned away from it."

"Johnny wouldn't want that," Jake said. "I mean, I didn't know the fellow, but nobody would want the burden of misery you three placed on yourselves and on his memory."

Elizabeth snuggled close in his arms. "So you think Johnny wants us to be happy?"

"Absolutely. And so does God. It took me a long time to see that, but once I came out of my grief, I decided to take life slow and easy, but never, ever to take one single minute for granted ever again."

She turned her face up to his. "I've wasted so much time wallowing in grief and self-pity. Why did it take me so long to let go?"

He grinned, then touched a finger to her nose. "Maybe you were waiting for me."

Elizabeth sighed, then offered him a quick peck on the cheek. "Well, if all that suffering and waiting had to bring me to this moment, then I say it was worth the wait."

His eyes light up. "Do you mean that?"

She nodded. "Sure. I get praline cheesecake out of the deal." At his groan, she added, "I'm getting soft in my old age."

"You're not old. But I want to be right here with you when you do grow old."

The familiar fears came back to haunt her. "But what if—"

"Love endures all," he reminded her, his finger on her lips. Then he kissed her again. "I can't speak for all those hurt souls out there who've loved and lost, Lizzie. But I can tell you this—if I make a commitment to you, I will do my best to honor that commitment, because I have faith that God will be showing me the way."

"Do you think God will allow me back into his fold?" she asked, her smile bittersweet. "I haven't exactly been a card-carrying member of His fan club, you know."

"You don't have to carry a card to get back in," Jake said. "You just have to turn everything over to Him."

"That might be hard. I'm used to doing things my way."

"And how's that been working for you?"

She slapped him lightly on the arm. "Not so great."

"We're going to be okay, Elizabeth."

Jake kissed her again, holding her tightly to him there in the candlelight. Then he remembered he hadn't even shown her what he'd found in the attic.

"Okay, this had better be good," Elizabeth told him a few minutes later. She polished off her slice of cheesecake, then turned away from the table.

He watched as she paced around the roomy parlor,

her eyes still misty with unshed tears, her bravado back in place. He watched her and his heart surged with a joy that he hadn't experienced in a very long time.

Is this it, Lord? Is this why you brought me here?

Jake thanked God for Elizabeth Sinclair. And he thanked God for the opportunity to share his faith with her, to help her find her way back to the Lord. But mostly, he thanked God for allowing him to find love again.

"I told you, you'll be glad you stuck around, trust me," he said as he urged her to sit down on the window seat. "Here, let me bring one of the candles so you can see."

"What do you have there, anyway?" she asked, fluffing her skirts as she waited for him.

"Hold your horses. You'll see."

"Okay, I'm still learning that patience is a virtue."

"And I'm going to have fun teaching you all about that," he replied, a surge of longing making him feel as if he had indeed been reborn.

Then he sat down beside her and opened the worn, tattered book he'd found in an old trunk. "This, my dear Lizzie, is proof positive that you were right about this house all along." He handed it to her. "Just take a look."

She opened the book, then gasped as she turned the pages. "Oh, my goodness. It's a scrapbook—it's a history of the Lockwood family."

"That's right. And as you can plainly see, there

were many happy memories in this house. Birthdays, weddings, christenings, holiday get-togethers." He squeezed her shoulder as she continued to turn the pages. "Newspaper clippings, announcements, and oh, I saved the best part for last."

"What?"

He took the book and turned to a page where a yellowed family tree had been pasted. "Look right up there in the far corner. You see that name?"

He pointed, his finger on the page, and watched as her face split into a beautiful smile. "Serena Sinclair. She married a Lockwood around the turn of the century. Anybody you know?"

"I'm not sure."

Jake traced his finger down the page. "If I'm not mistaken, I think dear Serena was your great-aunt."

"What?" She stared down at the page. "Are you telling me that one of my relatives married into the Lockwood family?"

"Yep. And had six children. And lived happily ever after with her husband for over sixty years. In this very house."

"Oh, wow. My wayward father never had much to do with his distant relatives." Then she dropped the book on the window seat and leapt onto Jake's lap. "It's a sign."

He steadied her, then grinned. "A good sign, I hope."

She was crying again. "It's more of that divine intervention you've told me about."

"How do you feel about that, Lizzie?"

She grinned, then touched a hand to his face. "I think it's…simply divine."

"You look so beautiful, honey," Aunt Becky told Elizabeth a few weeks later as they stood in front of an antique mirror at Mimosa Manor. "You are a lovely bride."

"I'm a nervous bride," Elizabeth responded, checking her hair and dress for the tenth time. After making sure her pearls were straight and her hair was in place, she whirled in a flurry of white satin and lace to hug her dear friend. "Oh, Aunt Becky, what if I mess up?"

"You're not going to mess up," Hannah said from the doorway. She was wearing a shimmering bridesmaid gown of amber shot with gold. "Besides, how can you go wrong with a man like Jake?"

Elizabeth rushed to hug Hannah close. "Are you sure you're okay with this?"

"I'll be just fine," Hannah replied, but Elizabeth didn't miss the worry and determination in her friend's eyes. Hannah's worry was fueled with a trace of anger that shimmered just as brightly as her gown. Elizabeth knew the anger wasn't directed at her, though.

Jo came bustling in then, her matching amber-and-gold dress falling around her trim waist. "Everyone's here. It's about time to get started."

"Is *he* here?" Hannah asked, her fingers gripping her bouquet of fall mums and baby's breath.

"If you mean the best man, Griff Harrison, yes, he's here," Jo said as she shot Elizabeth a confused look. "I still can't believe Jake asked that man to stand up for him."

"I'm sorry," Elizabeth said. "I didn't even know they were friends until that night in the house, when Jake told me. He was Jake's counselor in Fort Worth, and both Bram and Jake wanted him to be here. I was fit to be tied when Jake told me Griff was going to be his best man, but I didn't want to have a fight with Jake right before our marriage."

"It's not your fault," Hannah said, going to the window to stare down into the garden where the ceremony was about to take place. "I'm sure Jake means well. I'm sure he hopes that I'll forgive Griff for what he did, but that can't happen."

Elizabeth touched a hand to Hannah's shoulder. "Jake said Griff helped him through the bad times after he lost his family. Maybe he's changed, Hannah."

"Some people can't change," Hannah replied. Then she turned, took a breath, smiled. "Now, hush up about Griff Harrison. This is your day. Let's go get you married, before Jake storms the gates and kidnaps you."

Elizabeth nodded, gathered her bouquet of mums

and roses, then waited as her mother greeted her at the top of the stairs. "This is it, Mama."

"I'm so proud of you, honey," Phyllis said, her eyes misting with tears. "And I want you to be happy." She glanced down at Hannah and Jo. "I want all of you to be happy."

Hannah sent them a wistful smile. "Well, two out of three ain't bad."

Elizabeth waited to hear "The Wedding March," and while she waited she said a prayer for her friend.

"Lord, you brought Jake to me, and I thank you. You've made Jo so happy with Bram, and I thank you. Now please help our friend, Hannah. She deserves someone special, Lord. She deserves a good man."

As she passed the window in the hallway, Elizabeth glanced down to find Griff Harrison staring with open interest as Hannah took her spot in the wedding procession.

"Hmmm," Elizabeth said, her head spinning with what ifs and maybes.

"Are you all right, Elizabeth?" her mother asked.

"I'm great," she replied. "I've found my dream man and we're going to live in my dream house. I could just burst with joy." She kissed her mother on the cheek. "Thank you, Mama, for agreeing to give me away."

Then they reached the back steps and saw Jake standing there in his suit and tie in the golden-hued garden, the fall leaves glistening with sunshine and breathtaking beauty all around him. He smiled at her. Elizabeth smiled back and accepted the blessings God had given her.

As Jake opened his arms to her, she opened her heart to God's promise of enduring love—and made her own promise. Somehow, she'd see Hannah happily married very soon, too.

* * * * *

SMALL-TOWN WEDDING

Penny Richards

This book is for Billie and Barbara,
wonderful Christians, wonderful friends.
I'm blessed to have you in my life.

Be ye kind one to another, tenderhearted,
forgiving one another, even as God for
Christ's sake hath forgiven you.
—*Ephesians* 4:32

Chapter One

~❧~

"Fancy meeting you here."

The words, spoken in a deep, familiar voice, stopped Hannah West where she stood, directly in front of the A&P's tomato display, smack dab between the lettuce and the bell peppers. Her hand tightened involuntarily around the tomato in her hand.

Griff Harrison. A quicksilver river of emotions washed through her. Disbelief. Pain. Fury. And something else, something she couldn't name. She gripped the tomato tighter to still the sudden trembling in her hands and pressed her lips together to stop the torrent of angry words threatening to spew out. How dare he act as if everything were all right? How dare he even have the nerve to speak to her?

Don't make a scene, Hannah. Just say something polite and leave. Oh, but she wanted to make a scene. She wanted to tell Griff Harrison exactly what she thought of him. Wanted to scream out her fury and frustration and heartache at him. Instead, she carefully laid the bruised tomato back on the pile, lowered her clenched hand to her side and turned to face the man who had destroyed her dreams, robbed her of her youth and broken her heart beyond repair.

Seeing him face-to-face for the first time since her friend Elizabeth had gotten married two months earlier, Hannah couldn't stifle the little gasp of surprise that escaped her. At thirty-four, Griff was even better looking than he had been in their youth, more handsome than she remembered as he'd stood up as best man to Jake Clark. His looks were the rugged, masculine type, with something that shouted Danger to any woman with her wits about her.

The problem was, most girls had been all too willing to throw caution to the wind when it came to Griff Harrison. She'd been tempted once, herself. Lean and broad-shouldered, he had a square jaw, a nose that had been broken a time or two, a shock of thick coffee-brown hair, cut stylishly short and left slightly messy, and eyes so deeply blue you could drown in them. He wore faded jeans and a shirt that matched his eyes beneath a brown leather jacket, a devastating combination.

Hannah took his stock in seconds, registered her reaction and hated herself for finding anything attractive about him. Her voice was as cold as a December day as she said, "I suppose in a town of four thousand people, it was inevitable that we run into each other sooner or later."

"I was beginning to think it would be later," he told her. "I've been in town almost five weeks and haven't seen you around, except at a distance."

"I've been very busy," she said in a prim voice as she shoved a head of lettuce into a plastic bag.

"So I hear. You do showers and parties and things in the old Carmichael house, don't you?"

Hannah moved to the green beans without looking up. "Yes."

"I haven't seen you at church much."

That made her look at him. "I've been there," she said, defending herself. "But I haven't been sticking around to visit when the service is over. I've—"

"—been busy," he interrupted. "So you said." Their gazes clashed for a few seconds longer. "You're looking extremely well."

For a thirty-year-old spinster. Hannah added the words in her mind while she resisted the urge to swipe back a tendril of her dark hair that refused to be tamed by her hair clasp.

"I didn't have a chance to tell you at the wedding."

How like him to bring up the wedding, something Hannah didn't like to think about. To her mixed joy and dismay, her friend, Elizabeth, had been married in mid-September. As the caterer, Hannah had been too busy refilling the hors d'oeuvre trays to mix much with the wedding party, and she had avoided all contact with Griff…until the moment Elizabeth had singled her out to catch the bridal bouquet.

"Hannah? Are you all right?"

"I'm fine," she snapped. "But I'm catering a birthday dinner tonight, and I don't have time for idle chitchat."

"Especially not with me."

The words were softly spoken, and Hannah thought she heard a hint of resignation in them. "That's right," she told him, punctuating the statement with a short nod. She shoved a couple of handfuls of green beans into another plastic bag and turned to put them in her buggy. She'd taken no more than two steps when she felt hard fingers close around her upper arm. Griff spun her around to face him.

"When are you going to let me tell you what really happened that night?"

"I know what happened," she said, her voice low and vibrating with intensity. "Johnny was in the truck with you. You were drunk, and you lost control and hit a tree. Johnny was killed and you walked away with a cut on your forehead. That about sums it up, doesn't it?"

Griff didn't speak for several seconds. Though she tried, she couldn't read his expression. There was nothing in his eyes but emptiness. Finally, he nodded. "Yeah. That about sums it up."

She turned and started to walk away, but his voice stopped her.

"Do you think I don't still hurt, too, Hannah?"

She turned to face him, steeling her heart to the anguish she heard in his voice and saw in his eyes. Hindsight was always twenty-twenty, and remorse was easy enough to feel after the fact.

"Do you think I don't regret what happened?" he asked. "Do you think there's a single day that passes that I don't remember how Johnny looked when they loaded him into the ambulance? That I don't wish it had been me instead of him?"

"Then that makes two of us."

Before she turned her back on him again, she saw him close his eyes and scrub a hand down his lean cheek. Keeping her back ramrod straight, she began to push her buggy away from him. She was near the end of the aisle when he asked, "When are you going to forgive me, Hannah?"

Hannah stopped short. She refused to turn and look at him. "Never." The finality in her voice sounded harsh, even to her own ears.

"That's too bad," he told her. "It's been twelve years, and you're too beautiful a woman to let bitterness eat you up."

"Believe me, I haven't forgotten how long it's been."

"Have you forgotten that we're supposed to forgive one another?"

Furious, Hannah spun around to face him. "Don't you dare preach to me!"

"I'm not preaching. Just reminding you what the Bible says. It also says we're to love our enemies, doesn't it?" Without waiting for her to reply, he turned and left her standing there. Only when he made a right turn at the end of the aisle did she realize she could hardly see him for her angry tears.

"Jake says he's going to die of exhaustion if we don't get the house finished soon," Elizabeth said the following afternoon as the three friends were having a cup of tea at Hannah's. Ever since they'd returned from their honeymoon, Elizabeth and her new husband, Jake Clark, had been working at restoring the old house that had brought them together.

"I know it's a lot of work," Jo said, "but it'll be worth it."

"That's what Jake says. And it really is a labor of love."

Hannah sipped her tea and let the conversation drift on around her.

"—really hard to adjust to sharing a house with someone else—not to mention a bathroom…"

"—bought me a new nightie…"

"—wants to have a baby as soon as possible…"

"—us, too…"

Hannah stifled the urge to walk out of the room. She was sick and tired of the intimate hopes, dreams and plans as well as the good-natured ribbing and recipe-swapping. It was irritating and downright disgusting to see them so smug and happy…like two cats who'd just licked up a bowl of spilt cream.

Face it, Hannah. You're jealous.

Jealous? Ridiculous! She was really happy for them, wasn't she? She sighed. If she were honest, she'd admit that her feelings fell somewhere between. She *was* happy for them. They were both wonderful people and deserved the joy they'd found. The problem was, Hannah no longer fit into their lives. She knew they didn't mean to make her feel left out; in fact, they went out of their way to include her whenever possible. They both called every day and they still saw each other several times a week. It was simply that she had little in common with them anymore.

"—says Griff is doing really well since he opened his office. I guess there are a lot of people who need counseling, even in a small town."

The comment about Griff snagged Hannah's wandering attention.

"I hear he's very good," Elizabeth said before asking Hannah, "Aren't Susan, Lane and Kim seeing him?"

Hannah reached for the delicate Haviland teapot and topped off their cups. "I think they've been once or twice," she said, careful to keep any animosity out of her voice.

"And?"

"I really haven't talked to her about it," Hannah said.

"Do I detect a little frost in your voice?" Elizabeth asked.

"You know how I feel about Griff Harrison," Hannah said, getting up so abruptly she bumped the table and set the tea to sloshing in the cups.

"I know you think he's responsible for what happened to Johnny, and—"

"He *was* responsible."

Jo gave a slow nod. "I guess he was. I know you loved Johnny, but you were just kids, Hannah, and it was a long time ago," Jo said in a gentle voice. "It's time you let it go. Time to forgive and forget."

Hannah's laughter rang with bitterness. "Forget? Never. And forgive? That's what Griff told me I should do the other day."

"You spoke to him?" Elizabeth asked, flashing another look at Jo.

"I ran into him at the store," Hannah said. "First he tried to act as if nothing had happened, and when I wouldn't play his little game, he let me know I should practice forgiveness."

"He has a point," Jo said. "You know it's the Christian thing to do, Hannah. And the forgiveness is more for you than for him."

"Whatever that means," Hannah grumbled, knowing her friends—and Griff—were right but unable to get past the pain and anger that were stuck in the place her heart should be.

"You know what it means," Elizabeth said.

Hannah pinned her friend with a hard stare. "Do you think I'm filled with bitterness, too?"

"I'm afraid so," Elizabeth said. "Not that you let it

show to anyone but us," she hastened to add. "It's just that Jo and I know how special you are, and we want you to be happy."

"I'm content."

"Happy," Elizabeth reiterated.

The expression in her eyes brought a lump to Hannah's throat. "The holidays are coming. I'm always happy during the holidays."

"You're always busy during the holidays," Jo said. "There is a difference. And speaking of the holidays, are you having Thanksgiving at Susan's?"

"Always the diplomat," Hannah said, knowing her friend had changed the subject on purpose. "But yes, I'm having Thanksgiving at Susan's. Since I have something booked for almost every day in December, Susan said I had enough cooking to do without making Thanksgiving dinner."

Jo smacked her forehead with the palm of her hand. "Oh! I meant to ask. Elizabeth and Jake are coming over for dinner tomorrow night. Why don't you join us?"

Hannah forced a laugh. "Thanks, but no thanks. I'd just be in the way."

She noticed the look that passed between her friends before Elizabeth said, "Don't be ridiculous. You'd never be in the way."

"Spoken like a true friend," Hannah quipped.

"I hope so," Elizabeth said, sincerity in her voice and eyes.

"You are," Hannah said, looking from one to the

other. "Both of you. But I really do have things to do tomorrow night."

They accepted her excuse, but when they left, Hannah couldn't shake the fact that her friends were worried about her. In truth, she was worried about herself.

Chapter Two

"All done setting the tables." The announcement came from Susan, Hannah's older sister, who always came when Hannah needed help, which was almost daily. The arrangement worked out well for them both, since Hannah knew she could count on Susan, and Susan, a single mom, appreciated the extra money her three part-time jobs brought in.

Hannah dipped the last chicken breast in egg white and then in the fresh garlic-Parmesan breadcrumbs. "Thanks, sis. I don't know what I'd do without you."

"Me, either," Susan said with a half smile. She glanced at her watch. "I have time for a quick cup of coffee before I have to pick up Kim from school. Want some?"

"I'd love a cup," Hannah said, placing the last piece of chicken with the others and going to wash her hands.

"How are the kids doing?" she asked, sitting down

at the oak table that had belonged to their mother. "It's always so crazy around here, I forget to ask."

"It's been some easier the last week or so. You know we've all been going to see Griff once a week?" It came out a question and was delivered in a tone of apology.

"I know," Hannah said with a nod.

"He said to tell you hello."

Hannah grimaced. "So, is he working miracles?"

"Of sorts," Susan said. "At least the three of us aren't at each other's throats the way we were. I'm trying to lighten up, and the kids are trying to be more responsible, but I still don't like that boy Kim has a crush on. He's a little too wild from what I hear, not to mention he's Lane's age. Luckily he hasn't shown much interest in Kim so far."

"Well, Griff should be able to give you all sorts of advice on dealing with bad boys. After all, he was one."

"Actually, he's said as much to Lane."

"Really?" Hannah couldn't hide her surprise.

"I think he's helping both the kids to see that teenagers all go through similar experiences. He's trying to give them the ammunition to make the right choices when temptations come along."

"Is he preachy?" Hannah asked, knowing Griff was classified as a Christian counselor.

"Not really. Mostly, he listens. He isn't judgmental, which the kids appreciate, since they claim I am. Griff just tosses the ball back in their court when they make some outrageous statement. He's forcing them both to look ahead and imagine what the possible fall-out might be if they choose a certain course."

Whether or not she liked who gave the advice, Hannah was glad it was helping and told her sister so. Lane had been a handful since his dad had walked out two years earlier for another woman, and Kim had recently begun to show signs of following in his footsteps, now that she was approaching high-school age.

"Griff's been a blessing, that's for sure," Susan said. She laughed. "I think Kim has a crush on him. He's certainly a hunk." She gave Hannah a sly smile. "If I remember correctly, you used to think so, too, little sister."

Hannah's heart gave a little lurch. "Wrong brother," she quipped.

"I don't think so," Susan said with a shake of her finger. "I may be older than you, but I'm not senile yet. As I remember, you had a crush on Griff before you started dating Johnny. I even remember him coming to the house a few times."

The crush was something Hannah had done her best to forget, but she knew there was no use arguing with her sister. Right or wrong, Susan always won. "Okay, okay," Hannah said. "Guilty as charged. Thank goodness I realized he was way too old for me."

"Four years!" Susan scoffed. "That's nothing."

"But back then, in experience alone, it was more like ten."

"You have a point," Susan conceded with a laugh. "I remember every mother in town got the shivers if they saw their daughters even look at Griff. Mama was no exception."

"I know." The expression in Hannah's eyes softened at the memory of her mother and father, who had died in a car crash when she was just twenty-five. "She used to say she didn't know how Margaret and Harold could have raised boys that were so different. Griff was a wild one, and Johnny was so good-hearted and polite."

"The perfect man," Susan said jokingly.

"He was!"

"Honey," Susan said, reaching out and patting Hannah's hand. "No one will argue that Johnny Harrison was a good person. But believe me, he wasn't perfect, as you'd have no doubt found out if he'd lived."

"But he didn't live, did he?" Hannah snapped. "Thanks to your miracle worker."

Susan's brown eyes were troubled. "Hannah, honey, it's way past time for you to get over this…this hatred you feel for Griff. You aren't a child anymore. Most things aren't black and white. You need to take a hard look at the past from an adult's perspective."

"So you think I'm behaving like a child?"

"To put it bluntly, I think your judgment is stunted in this particular area. You condemned him twelve years ago, and in your mind that's the end of it. But people change. Griff certainly has. He made some bad choices when he was younger, and he knows it. Besides being responsible for his brother's death, he made a bad marriage, went through a divorce and lost custody of his child. Don't you think he's lived with the heartache of his mistakes every day, the same way we all do?" Susan gave a little shrug. "Well, everyone but you."

Hannah remembered Griff claiming to suffer daily pain the day she'd run into him at the grocery store, but it was her sister's last comment that gave her pause. "What do you mean, everyone but me?"

"You don't have to grieve over your mistakes, because you never made any. Saint Hannah. No wild nights, no stolen kisses, no undesirable men."

"You make it sound as if I've done something wrong, as if trying to live a Christian life is a bad thing."

"In some ways you have done something wrong. You've shut yourself off from anything but the most superficial relationships. Whenever someone gets too close, you shy away. If the status quo changes, you retreat to your comfort zone."

Shocked at what she was hearing, Hannah could only ask, "Meaning?"

"Jo and Elizabeth both say you're holding them at arm's length since they got married."

"I don't! I just don't have anything in common with them, anymore." Hannah denied, but she knew it was the truth.

"They're your friends, honey. You have almost thirty years of things in common, and don't forget it. And don't forget that Christian life you claim to lead includes forgiveness."

Hannah thought about what her sister had said long after she left. Was she emotionally stunted? Did she shy away from anyone who wanted to get close? She hadn't had three dates in that many years and told herself she liked it that way, but truthfully, even before Jo and Elizabeth got married, she'd felt a yearning for a close relationship, for children, for someone to come through the door at the end of the day, someone who loved her beyond reason.

Without warning, an image of Griff striding through her kitchen door flashed through her mind. It was Susan's fault for making her remember her old crush on Griff, especially since she'd tried so hard to forget it.

She'd been seventeen, a junior, and watching the service station while her dad went to make a bank deposit when Griff had pulled up in his restored 1957 Chevy. She'd known it was him when she heard the rumble of the glass-packed mufflers and the low roar of the Corvette engine….

Hannah had been standing behind the counter looking through a teen magazine when Griff came strolling through the door. "Hey, pretty girl," he said with a smile that made her heart stumble. "What are you doing here?"

"Dad had to go to the bank," she told him. "He'll be back in a few minutes."

"I'll wait. He was supposed to see about some new tires for the Chevy." Without waiting for her to reply, he took some change from the pocket of his jeans and put it in the soda machine. He held out a can. "Want one?"

"I have one, thanks."

He popped the top, sauntered over to the counter and, resting an elbow on it, leaned toward her. Griff looked her straight in the eyes and smiled. The smile hit Hannah with a wallop, and she knew without a doubt that the man before her—and he was a man— was dangerous. She forced herself not to back up.

"I haven't seen you at church in ages," she said.

"I work Sundays now," he told her, taking a sip of the cola.

"Couldn't you come at night?" she asked, risking a glance.

He regarded her with narrowed eyes, then smiled. "Maybe. If there was a really good reason to."

"What about because you're supposed to?"

"My parents have been making me do what I'm supposed to all my life. Now that I've moved out, I do what I want." He took another drink of the soda and said, "So, are you dating anyone?"

Embarrassed, Hannah shrugged. "No one seems interested."

"What's wrong with those bozos? Are they blind?"

Hannah forced herself to look at him before letting

her eyelashes flutter down again. She was flirting with the most dangerous guy in town. Throwing caution to the wind, she lifted her lashes and smiled. "Maybe I don't appeal to them."

"Then they must be crazy." His voice sounded like a low growl. Before she realized what he was going to do, he leaned forward and kissed her. Startled, thrilled, scared, all she could do was stand there, her elbows resting on the counter while the kiss worked its particular brand of magic. And then, just as suddenly as he'd touched his lips to hers, he jerked away.

Feeling bemused and strangely bereft, Hannah just stood staring at him. Griff looked as dazed as she felt.

Griff pointed a finger at her. "You are flat-out dangerous, Hannah West."

Without another word, he turned and left her standing there, thanksgiving and fear in her heart. She was no match for Griff Harrison, and that was a fact.

Though she usually shared everything with Elizabeth and Jo, she'd never told them about the kiss or the feelings it generated. Two days later, Johnny had asked her to go out with him.

Physically, Johnny looked a lot like his brother, but he was nothing like Griff. Where Griff was tough, Johnny was gentle. Where Griff was bad, Johnny was good. Johnny had no problem doing what he was supposed to do. They were inseparable their senior year. They sat together at church, went to devotionals together, double-dated with their friends and made plans for their future together when they graduated. She would be a teacher; he would become a cop. They would have three children and live in the big Carmichael house.

Their dreams and plans never had a chance to come to fruition.

It was funny, she sometimes thought, that even though she loved Johnny and even though—as perfect as he was—he sometimes pressured her to go farther than she knew was right, she never had a problem saying no, and he always respected her wishes. Luckily, she'd learned a valuable lesson the day Griff had kissed her. Desire was a strange emotion. It could be found where you least expected it, and resisting it was much harder than she'd ever imagined.

Griff. She hadn't seen much of him her last year of high school, which suited her just fine. If he'd pursued her, she feared she would have given in…with no pressuring at all. Griff Harrison was too much of a temptation, and Hannah was afraid she wouldn't have had the strength to flee.

Chapter Three

"So you'll need the parlor for at least two hours, right, Mrs. McCallum?" Hannah asked, wedging the phone between her cheek and shoulder as she started a page for the upcoming lingerie shower Clara McCallum was giving her niece—Griff's former wife.

"That's right, dear," Clara said. "I know it's a hectic time for everyone, and I can't believe you have an opening, but since Josie is coming in for Christmas, we thought we'd kill two birds with one stone and save her a trip later." She gave a heartfelt sigh. "The whole family is just so happy for her. She and Griff tried, but he was all wrong for her. Still, they've both turned out well, though we did wonder about them both back when they were young—"

Knowing Clara's penchant for gossip and with a clear memory of Josie Jones's slightly naughty past, Hannah cut off the older woman. "It's no problem,

Mrs. McCallum. I'm catering a party that night, but I'll be taking the food to the Bickhams', so the house will be all ready for you."

"You're an angel," Clara gushed. "Always willing to work things out."

"I try, Mrs. McCallum. After all, hospitality is my business." Hannah spent the next few minutes firming up the details of the shower, which included theme and color scheme and quoting and negotiating prices for various finger foods. Satisfied that she had enough information, she was preparing to end the conversation, when Clara said, "Did you hear about Harold Harrison?"

Hannah paused in writing down how many and what kind of finger sandwiches she needed to make. Harold was Johnny and Griff's dad. He'd been diagnosed with Alzheimer's more than a year ago, which, according to the local grapevine, was one of the reasons Griff had moved back. No matter how she felt about Griff, she'd always liked his parents, who'd attended her church all her life. "No, ma'am. Is he worse?"

"Effie Poteet said he wandered off yesterday afternoon while Margaret was taking a shower. She thought he was asleep, so she didn't go in to check on him for a couple of hours. By that time, he'd gone off and she couldn't find hide nor hair of him. She called Griff, and he notified the sheriff's department. They didn't find him until after midnight."

Poor Margaret. "Is he all right?"

"He's scratched and bruised up and has a broken leg

from tumbling down a creek bank. He'll be in the hospital a day or two." Clara gave a little sigh. "Griffin was right there all night with the rescue workers. You know, for all his wild ways, I never thought he was as bad as he was made out to be."

Talking about Griff was the last thing Hannah wanted to do. Thankfully, her other line rang. "I'd love to visit with you more, Mrs. McCallum, but my other line is ringing."

"You go right ahead and get it," Clara said. "I'll stop by and look through your cake book one day this week. Bye now."

Hannah hung up and answered the other line. "Mimosa Manor. This is Hannah."

"Hey, it's me," Elizabeth said. "Did you hear about Mr. Harold?"

"Mrs. McCallum was just telling me about it. How is he?"

"Fair. They're hoping he doesn't develop pneumonia from being out in the cold and damp so long. They said Griff sent his mother home, and he's staying at the hospital. Jo and I were going to take dinner over to Miss Margaret's tonight and we were wondering if you'd like to send something."

"Of course. I always have something in the freezer."

"Great! How about dragging out a cake? I'm picking up a box of chicken and some bread, and Jo is doing a couple of vegetables. If you have dessert, we'll be set." She paused, then asked, "I don't suppose you'd have time to pick up our stuff and drive it out there, would you?"

Hannah raked a hand through her dark hair. "Oh, Elizabeth, I have a million things to do before tomorrow night."

"I was afraid of that. Jo has two funerals tomorrow and said she'd probably be at the shop until late. Bram is out of town, I'm showing a house way out in the country at five, and Jake is up at the river property without his cell phone."

"I guess I don't have much choice, then," Hannah said with a sigh.

"If it will help, I'll bring our food to your place."

"That would help tremendously."

"Good," Elizabeth said. "I'll see you about four-thirty."

Hannah hung up and went to get one of her famous banana cakes out of the freezer. If Elizabeth brought the food to her, it shouldn't take over thirty minutes to run it out to the Harrisons'. She'd be fine.

As she began filling mini puff pastries with almond chicken salad, her mind wandered back to her conversation with Clara McCallum. It sounded as if even the Joneses had a favorable opinion of Griff despite the fact that his and Josie's marriage had failed. Was she the only one whose life Griff had wrecked who hadn't forgiven him? The thought was unsettling.

Josie and her daughter, Callie—Griff's daughter— came to visit three or four times a year and always went to see Harold and Margaret. What did Josie think about Griff moving home? Would it make a difference? Was their divorce amic-able, for their child's sake? Would he try to see her while she was in town?

Why do you care, Hannah?

She knew it was none of her affair, but it was impossible not to wonder about him, not to think about him, since—like it or not—he seemed to be invading her life from various avenues. One of the pitfalls of living in a small town, and something she'd have to get used to.

Elizabeth showed up early and helped Hannah load the food into the van she used to transport her catered items. After dragging a brush through her hair, adding another swipe of mascara to her brown eyes and freshening her lipstick, she was on her way to the Harrisons' home, which was located five miles north of town, down a gravel road. Weak western sunshine, the last remnants of the November day, shimmered off the red and deep purple of the black gum and sweet gum trees that bordered the road. Shadows gathered beneath them. As she approached the Harrison place, a pristine white two-story farm house, she noticed two vehicles in the driveway. One, she knew was Margaret's. The other no doubt belonged to a well-meaning neighbor.

She picked up the cake from the seat, carried it to the door and knocked. In a matter of minutes it swung open to reveal a disheveled Griff. Hannah couldn't stifle her gasp of surprise. Why wasn't he at the hospital? Then she noticed he was as surprised as she. Surprised and…weary.

"Were you sleeping?" she asked, as he smothered a yawn.

He offered her a sheepish smile and ran a hand through his already tousled hair. "Yeah. I was asleep on the sofa. What have we here?" he said, gesturing toward the cake in her hands.

"Jo, Elizabeth and I decided to bring your mother dinner. I thought you were at the hospital."

"Which is why you volunteered to make the delivery."

"Actually," she said, shoving the cake toward him, "I was the only one free, and I need to get back ASAP."

"Party?" he asked, relieving her of her burden.

"Yes. City officials and their wives." Without waiting for him to reply, she turned and headed for the van.

She was taking the chicken from the insulated container when a voice from behind her asked, "You stay pretty busy, I guess."

"Very," she said, without turning. "Considering the size of the town." She handed him the chicken and a package of rolls. She picked up two containers of vegetables and pushed the van doors closed with her hip. "That's it."

"Ladies first."

Hannah preceded him into the house and went

straight to the kitchen. Things hadn't changed much since the days she'd visited with Johnny. New paint, new curtains, new flooring. Other than that, things in the house were the same. But she knew they weren't. The house was older, as were its inhabitants. Harold wasn't the same gentle man who'd teased her unmercifully and kept a pocket full of candy for the kids at church. Now he was often violent, contrary. And the wear and tear was showing on Margaret, Hannah thought as she set the bowls on the counter and gave the older woman a hug.

"What's all this?"

"Elizabeth, Jo and I fixed your dinner."

"That's just like you," Margaret said, a fond smile crinkling her plump cheeks.

"How's Mr. Harold?" Hannah asked.

"Doc Mayfield says he'll be all right barring complications of some sort. They gave him something to calm him down and help him sleep and told me and Griff to come home and get some rest."

"If he's stable and sleeping, there's no use wearing yourself out by staying there," Hannah said.

"I suppose not." Margaret gestured toward the food. "It's almost suppertime. Won't you stay and have a bite with us?"

"Thank you, but I have a houseful of people coming at seven-thirty." She glanced at her watch. "And I won't be ready for them if I don't get back."

"I understand." Margaret gave Hannah another hug

and said, "Griff, walk Hannah out. I'll start warming up supper."

"That's all right. I can see myself out," Hannah said.

"Nonsense. He'll just be in my way if he hangs around here."

Hannah forced a smile and headed for the front door, Griff tagging along behind. "I hear Clara's having Josie's shower at your place," he said.

Hannah paused in the doorway and turned. "Yes. December fourteenth."

"From everything I can tell, Josie is getting a great guy this time." Implying that he wasn't, Hannah thought.

"Clara seems happy for her," Hannah said. "But she was quick to say that the two of you had really tried."

"Clara always did like me," Griff said, one corner of his mouth lifting in a wry smile.

Hannah wound her fingers together and forced her brown gaze to his. "So you'll be seeing your daughter soon. Do you get to spend much time with her?"

Griff smiled again. "We see one another as often as we can."

"That's good."

"Yes," he said, "it is. Especially for me and my family. Callie is very much a Harrison."

He looked extremely satisfied about that. Hannah wasn't sure why the idea of Griff being proud of his daughter's genes filled her with such sadness. "You're close, then?"

"As close as we can be under the circumstances." He smiled, a full-fledged, thousand-watt smile that made Hannah all too aware that he was a handsome man. "Well, now, this hasn't been too hard, has it?" he asked.

"What?" she asked, bewildered.

"Carrying on a conversation with me without cutting me to ribbons with that sharp tongue of yours or throwing my sordid past in my face."

Hannah felt the heat of a blush creep into her cheeks, making her even more uncomfortable. "As I said the other day, it's a small town. We're bound to run into each other every now and then."

"Bound to," he agreed, solemnly as he plunged his fingertips into his jeans pockets.

"It would be a little immature of me to resort to insults whenever we do cross paths."

Griff gave a slow nod. "Well," he said, "it isn't forgiveness, but it's progress of a sort, I suppose."

Despite what she'd just said, Hannah felt her ire rise at the mockery she heard in his voice. "What do you want from me, Griff?" she snapped. "Absolution for your sins?"

"No," he said. "I already have that from Who it counts the most. As for what I want from you…" His voice trailed away. "You aren't ready for that." He gave her a sad smile. "And I'm beginning to wonder if you ever will be."

Chapter Four

On Sunday morning, Hannah slept through the alarm and had to rush to get ready for church. Since there was no time for a proper breakfast, she grabbed a muffin and poured herself a cup of freshly brewed coffee. Though she knew what day it was, habit made her glance at the calendar. Five weeks to go until Christmas Eve and the end of the annual madness that paid her bills. She took a sip of her coffee, hoping the strong brew would perk her up. She was already exhausted.

After washing down the last of the muffin, Hannah grabbed her purse and her Bible from the countertop and headed for the door. She was going to be late.

The bell that signaled the beginning of Sunday-school class was ringing as Hannah stepped through the door of the educational building. She heard doors closing as she hurried down the hallway to the adult class she attended. She waved at Elizabeth and Jake, as they stepped through the doors of the young married class, no doubt joining Jo and Bram. Fighting the sting of tears, Hannah quickened her pace. She took a pen from her purse and added one more to the attendance slip hanging outside the door. As she stepped through the aperture, every eye in the room turned toward her.

"Sorry I'm late," she mumbled, letting her apologetic smile move from face to face until she found the front of the small room. Stunned to see Griff instead of the usual teacher standing at the podium, she stopped dead in her tracks. The smile melted from her face.

"No problem," he said, smiling.

Recalling that the regular teacher was away for the weekend, Hannah gathered her scattered wits and found a seat near the back of the room. She opened her Bible to the text, Matthew 6:14, and read the familiar words. *For if ye forgive men their trespasses, your heavenly Father will also forgive you...*

A flash of anger shot through her and she slapped the pages shut. Had Griff deliberately chosen the passage to rub in her unwillingness to forgive him? Had he moved to Prescott just to make her life unbearable? On the heels of that uncharitable thought, she remembered that the class had been studying forgiveness for several weeks. Her anger dissipated, and shame settled over her. Why was she so quick to think the worst of Griff? Why was she so unwilling to forgive him? And how was she going to make it through the next forty minutes?

For the remainder of the class, Hannah kept her gaze focused on the Bible in her lap and her mind firmly on the study so no more ugly thoughts could work their way into her head. To her relief, she wasn't called to take part in any of the discussion, probably because she never once made eye contact with Griff. When the bell rang, signaling the end of study, she escaped the room before anyone could speak to her. She made a beeline for the auditorium, determined to put as much distance as possible between her and Griffin Harrison.

As she took her regular pew, she saw Bram and Jo following Elizabeth and Jake down the far aisle. Elizabeth smiled and waved; Hannah waved back. The foursome settled in next to a distinguished man who sat with his arm encircling Elizabeth's mother's shoulders. Hannah's mouth fell open in surprise. Jake's dad and Phyllis Sinclair, Elizabeth's mother? Was there something in the water? The envious thought slipped into her mind before she could stop it and again, she was overwhelmed by an immediate sense of shame.

What was wrong with her that she couldn't be happy for her friends and their happiness? And what about Elizabeth's mother? After Phyllis had been so hurt and suffered so many years of being alone, Hannah knew she should be thrilled that the older woman had met a good and decent man she might spend the rest of her life with. And she was thrilled, but...she was sad, too, and maybe just the tiniest bit jealous. Not a very noble attitude, but she was at least being honest with herself.

Why don't you try being honest with yourself about Griff? the small voice inside her nagged. She was, wasn't she? After all, she'd admitted to Susan and herself that she'd once been attracted to him, dangerously attracted. Thank goodness she'd come to her senses. Men like Griff Harrison had no staying power. They were only out for a few laughs and a good time.

Everyone said Griff had changed. Were they right? Had he turned into the upright, devoted and caring person they claimed? If so, where did that leave her and the anger that filled her every time she thought of him and how his recklessness had robbed her of Johnny, her perfect man?

After the service was over, Hannah agreed to go with her friends to the Broadway Café for lunch. Truth to tell, she was starving for some good country cooking, something she didn't have to fix herself.

They had just placed their order when Griff walked in, accompanied by the preacher and his family. He gave the table's occupants a smile and a little wave and followed the Kendalls to a room usually set aside for club meetings and opened up to handle the Sunday lunch crowd. Hannah was glad she wouldn't have to look at him throughout the meal.

She pushed her chair away from the table. "If you'll excuse me, I'm going to the ladies' room before my lunch gets here," she said to her friends.

Turning, she crossed the narrow room and went up the steps that led to the lobby of the historic hotel. The hall was empty—no doubt everyone was in the dining room—and the sound of her suede heels echoed hollowly on the mosaic tile floor. She saw by the movable sign on the door that the unisex bathroom was occupied and leaned against the wall to wait.

In a matter of seconds, the knob turned and the door swung open. To her surprise and horror, none other than Griff stood before her. He looked as surprised to see her standing there as she felt.

"Hi, there," he said, recovering first.

In spite of herself, Hannah wondered if her hair was straggling around her face and if she still had on any lipstick. Then, realizing the turn of her thoughts, she felt her anger rise.

"Hello." She tried to step past him toward the door, but he moved the slightest bit, blocking her.

"How are Lane and Kim doing? They haven't had an appointment in a couple of weeks."

Hannah stared at him, her eyes wide with disbelief. He really did expect her to act as if there were no bad blood between them. Unfortunately, as much as she knew she should make the effort, she was unable. Without answering, she took another sideways step and tried to brush past him, but before she realized his intent, she found herself once again against the wall. This time it was Griff's hands that held her, though not so hard as to cause pain. She wasn't sure, but thought she gasped in surprise. Blood pounded in her ears as she stared at the angular, masculine face so close to hers.

"For the life of me, sometimes I'm not sure why I bother," he murmured, his brooding blue gaze boring into hers.

"Then why do you?" she asked, her voice sounding breathless, reedy.

"Maybe because we all want to be liked and accepted."

"Liked?" she echoed. "I can't believe you expect me just to forget what happened the way you have and like you."

He shook his head. "Believe me, I haven't forgotten. As much as I might like to, I'll never forget anything that happened between me and Johnny. Or between me and you."

She didn't have to ask what he meant. As clearly as if it had happened yesterday, the memory of the day he'd kissed her rose up between them.

"You remember, too."

Unable to face the demand she saw in his eyes, she closed hers and shook her head.

"Of course you do. I even think you liked it. I know I did. I liked it too much."

The admission that he'd been as moved by that kiss as she had been robbed her of breath. She opened her eyes, needing to see the verification in his.

He released his hold on her and smiled, a crooked, derisive smile. Though she was free, she couldn't have moved if her life depended on it.

"Does that surprise you, Hannah? Why? You were a beautiful girl, and you're even more beautiful as a full-grown woman, with that thick dark hair and those big brown eyes…"

"No…" She shook her head, uncertain if it was because she didn't believe him or because she didn't want to know.

"So now you know the truth…or at least part of it."

"What do you mean, part of it?"

"You told me that day at the grocery store that you knew what happened the night Johnny was killed, and you were right, as far as you went. If the day ever comes when you're ready to take Johnny off his pedestal and want to know the whole truth, give me a call. The truth will set you free, you know."

"How dare you—"

"What?" he interrupted. "Speak evil of the dead? Slander Johnny when he isn't here to take up for himself? He was my brother, and I loved him as much as you did. But he was just a man, Hannah, with weaknesses and faults and sins…just like you and me. It just seems like a crying shame that another life had to end when he died."

Hannah didn't have to ask what he meant. She knew. Neither of them spoke for long seconds. Then, Griff's mood seemed to mutate, the expression of sorrow and helplessness in his eyes fading. He smiled again, another bittersweet, lopsided smile.

"At least I've had the memory of that one kiss to hold on to all these years. I've thought about it thousands of times, and every time I do, I wonder if it could really have been all I remember, or if I've built it up in my mind."

He raised his hands and placed them against the wall on either side of her face. "I guess there's only one way to find out."

Before she could object, before she could move, she felt his lips on hers, warm, mobile, softly persuasive.

Like Griff, she'd spent far too much time thinking about their other kiss, even when she was dating Johnny. Like Griff, she'd wondered through the years if she'd made it something more than what it was. She felt herself responding to the pressure of his lips and had actually started to reach out and touch his cheek when he pushed away from her.

Confused, trembling, she stood staring up at him with wide, questioning eyes, her hands curled into tight fists at her sides. There was no smile on his face now. He looked solemn, almost sad.

"Well, now we know, don't we," he said. And without another word, he turned and left her standing there.

Yes. Now she knew. The kiss had been everything

she remembered. And more. She watched him go, her heart beating with uncertainty, filled with a curious sorrow and an aching regret she didn't understand.

Chapter Five

"What happened to you?" Jo asked when Hannah returned to the table and saw that the waitress had brought their meal while she was away.

"Long line," she said, following the fib with a silent prayer that begged forgiveness. When Griff had left her, she'd gone into the rest room and held a wet paper towel to her hot cheeks while she tried to rationalize her response to his kiss and let her heart settle into a more sedate rhythm. A quick glance at her friends told her she wasn't fooling them, even though their spouses might have fallen for her story.

Hannah ignored the considering gleam in Jo's eyes and the question in Elizabeth's steady gaze. "I hope your food didn't get cold while you were waiting on me."

"They just brought it," Jake told her. "You timed it just right."

"Good." She took a bite of her meat loaf, thankful

for the reprieve. The meal passed pleasantly, and the conversation was easy, even though Hannah intercepted a couple of considering glances that passed between Jo and Elizabeth. When they'd all finished their dessert, Hannah said her goodbyes and left, hoping she wouldn't have to see Griff again, eager to get home and escape…at least for the moment.

As luck would have it, Elizabeth scheduled a last-minute appointment the next morning and was unable to drive out to check on Griff's parents. Once again, Hannah was the one she called to take up the slack.

"I hate to ask you," Elizabeth said. "I know you're as busy—if not busier—as anyone in town, especially with Thanksgiving tomorrow."

"I'm not cooking for tomorrow, remember?" Hannah said. "But I can't go out to the Harrisons' until after lunch. I have several people coming by to pick up their Thanksgiving pies and things this morning, but I should be free by eleven-thirty, and the next batch won't be picked up until after five."

"If it's too much for you, we can just call Miss Margaret to check on her."

"If I phone her, she'll say she's all right. If I drive out, I can look her in the eye and see for myself."

"Good point," Elizabeth said. "And Hannah, I really appreciate this. You're an angel."

"Right."

"Oh," Elizabeth said, the tone of her voice muting

slightly. "I wanted to ask what happened between you and Griff when you went to the rest room yesterday."

How on earth had Elizabeth come to the conclusion that Griff had been anywhere in the vicinity? Hannah wondered. She voiced the question aloud, not even bothering to deny it.

"Elementary, my dear Hannah," Elizabeth said with a laugh. "At first I couldn't figure it out, but you were definitely flustered, and when Jo and I started kicking around theories, that's what we came up with. Are we good or what?"

"Too good," Hannah said. "And you obviously know me too well."

"So what happened to make you all flitterpated?"

"The man upsets me," Hannah snapped, avoiding the question.

"Well, duh. What happened?"

"He told me that when I wanted to know what happened the night Johnny died to give him a call."

"We know what happened," Elizabeth said.

"Well, according to Griff I don't know the whole story, and he doesn't think I'm ready to hear it."

"I can't imagine…" Elizabeth said, letting her voice trail away. "Do you think you could get it out of Miss Margaret?"

"Maybe, if she knows. But I wouldn't dare bring it up under the circumstances. The last thing she needs with Harold under the weather is to unearth all that old pain."

"You're right," Elizabeth agreed. "So, is that all?"

"Isn't that enough?"

"Not if something else happened," Elizabeth said. Hannah sighed.

"Aha! I knew there was something else."

"All right! All right! He—" Hannah drew a deep breath "—admitted that he thought I was pretty and that he was sort of interested in me back in high school." Saying the words out loud to her friend didn't make them any easier to believe. In fact, Griff's confession sounded even more absurd coming from her own lips.

"What!" Elizabeth cried. "*Griff* was smitten with you back then, and you didn't know it?"

"Well," Hannah said, "I...he...had been flirty with me once."

"You never told me about it. Jo, either."

Hannah gave a snort of exasperation. "Where is it written that I have to tell the two of you everything that goes on in my life?"

"Nowhere, I suppose," Elizabeth said. "But we've always told you everything."

"I'll bet."

"Come on, Hannah. Tell me about the flirting."

Hannah knew Elizabeth well enough to know she might as well 'fess up. She'd know no peace until she did. "It was one day when I was at the station. Dad had gone to the bank, I think. Griff stopped by to see him about some tires. We started talking, and I admit that I...I might have flirted a bit myself."

"You? Miss Prim and Proper?"

"Just hush and listen," Hannah said in exasperation.

"Okay, okay."

"Anyway, somewhere along the way he kissed me."

"No!" The denial dripped disbelief.

"Yeah. And it was scary, Lizzie." Even now, Hannah recalled exactly the way the kiss made her feel. The way yesterday's kiss made her feel…

"Scary?" Elizabeth said with a laugh. "A kiss from the hottest guy in town?"

"Yes, scary. He made me feel things I'd never felt before, things I knew were dangerous…and wrong."

"Oh, Hannah!"

"If he hadn't broken off the kiss, I'm not sure I could have. Then he had the gall to tell me I was the dangerous one."

"Which means, Ms. Naïveté, that he felt the same things you felt and knew he was on dangerous ground."

"I can't believe that," Hannah said.

"The man admitted to being interested. You know, you don't give yourself enough credit."

"For what?"

"Anything," Elizabeth said. "Look, I gotta go. Give me a call and let me know about Miss Margaret and Mr. Harold."

"I will." Hannah hung up and stared out the window at the chill November day. The thought that she could ever make a man like Griff experience the dangerous emotions he'd ignited in her was too far-fetched. Still, he had kissed her.

In spite of herself, hating herself for harboring any thoughts about the man who was her enemy, Hannah wondered what—if anything—Griff felt for her now…and what he could possibly tell her about the night Johnny died she didn't already know.

All the pies and ready-to-pop-in-the-oven pans of Hannah's special cornbread dressing and sweet potato casseroles had been picked up by eleven-thirty as expected. Freshening her makeup and donning an emerald-green sweater, she carried the casserole and bread she'd baked for the Harrisons to the van and drove to the country.

She pulled to a stop in front of the white frame house fifteen minutes later and got out with her gifts in hand. She knocked on the front door and, within a matter of seconds, it swung open. Hannah was surprised to see a dark-haired, adolescent girl with vivid cobalt-blue eyes standing in the doorway. She had no idea who the child was, but there was something familiar about her.

"Hi," she said, smiling at the child. "Is Miss Margaret here?"

"Yeah," the girl said. "Come on in." Closing the door behind Hannah, she yelled, "Grandma! You have a visitor."

Margaret emerged from the kitchen, a finger to her

lips. "Shush, child. You'll wake the dead. Or worse, your grandfather."

Grandma. Grandfather. Hannah's mind came to the only possible conclusion. This pretty child was Griff's daughter. Griff and Josie's daughter. That's why she looked so familiar. She had the Harrisons' dark-haired, blue-eyed good looks. She looked like Griff.

"Hello, Hannah," Margaret said, pulling Hannah's thoughts away from the proof of Griff's misspent youth.

"Hello, Margaret." Hannah held out her offerings. "I wanted to bring you a casserole and a loaf of fresh bread and see how you're doing."

Griff's mother took the proffered gift. "Why thank you, child. You didn't have to bake for me. You have enough on you, cooking for half the town."

"I know I didn't have to," Hannah said, pulling the scarf from around her neck. "I wanted to, and I thought it might help with your dinner tomorrow. How are you? Really?"

"Doing as well as can be expected," Margaret said. She turned to her granddaughter. "Callie, take Hannah's coat and hang it on the hall tree, please."

"Oh, I can't stay," Hannah objected.

"Nonsense. It's lunch time, and I have a nice pot of vegetable soup on the stove. Even you have to eat. And rest."

Hannah realized that she was hungry. And tired. She was caught up with her cooking. There was no reason she couldn't stay long enough to have some soup.

Even as a teenager, she'd always enjoyed Margaret Harrison's company. "Thank you, Miss Margaret. Soup sounds delicious."

"That's settled, then. Callie, you can set the table after you've hung up Hannah's coat."

"Yes, ma'am."

Margaret looked from one to the other. "Did you two meet?"

"No ma'am," Callie Harrison said.

"Callie, this is Hannah West, an old friend. She used to date my Johnny, back a long time ago. Hannah, this is Callie, my granddaughter. She and her mother have come from Dallas to be with her family for Thanksgiving, and they're letting Callie spend some time with me and Griff while they're in town."

The young girl held out her hand. "Pleased to meet you, Ms. West," she said.

"It's nice to meet you, too, Callie," Hannah said, shaking the girl's hand, impressed with her manners and wondering how Griff could bear being away from her.

"Come on into the kitchen," Caroline said. "We'll eat in there."

Hannah followed Caroline. "Callie looks like her dad," she said to her hostess's back.

Margaret paused for the briefest second, mid-stride. "Yes," she said, continuing through the doorway, "she does."

"Is there anything I can do to help?" Hannah asked.

"Just keep me company while the corn bread finishes baking. Callie, you can set the table for us."

"Sure." Callie smiled, a smile so like Johnny's, Hannah's breath caught in her throat. Of course, the smile was like Johnny's. Callie was a Harrison.

"Is it okay if I go watch TV until lunch is ready?" Callie asked, when the table was set to her grandmother's satisfaction.

"You may," Margaret said. "I'll call you when lunch is ready."

Hannah sighed as the eleven-year-old left the room. If things had been different, if Johnny had lived, they might have had a child by now, maybe even one as old as Callie. Hannah fought back the sudden sting of tears for all she'd been denied by that senseless accident.

"What is it, child?" Caroline asked.

Hannah's voice was thick with unshed tears when she spoke. "I was thinking that if Johnny hadn't died, we'd have had children by now."

"Maybe. And maybe you'd have gone your separate ways and married someone else, too."

Hannah stared at her hostess, surprise in her eyes. "Why would you say that? I loved Johnny."

"I know you did, but it was a young girl's love, and sometimes young love doesn't last." Margaret shrugged. "Who knows? You might have gone off to college and found someone else." For just an instant there was a faraway look in her eyes. "Or…Johnny might have." She smiled, but it looked forced. "A lot of things might have happened."

Hannah's intellect told her Margaret was right, but her heart didn't want to believe it. No, right or wrong, her heart would rather cling to her conviction that her life had been ruined by Griff's actions that night. After all, that philosophy was all she had to live for. That, and the anger that still consumed her when she contemplated her loss.

"You're right," she said, nodding, meeting Margaret Harrison's steady gaze. "I know that, but it's so hard. Johnny was so good, so perfect. We were so perfect together."

"No relationship, no marriage, no person is perfect, Hannah. You know that. Johnny was a good boy, a good son, but far from perfect, as you'd have found out."

"I'm sure you're right," Hannah admitted, albeit reluctantly.

"I know I am. And while we're on the subject of Johnny, I want to say that I know you still blame Griff for what happened."

"I—"

Margaret held up her hand to stay whatever Hannah was about to say. "No. I need to say this, and you need to hear it." Hannah nodded. "For all his wild ways, deep down, Griff was a good boy, too. Oh, I know he drank and I know there were… girls. I'm not condoning what he did. It was wrong, and he knows that. Knew it even back then. Harold and I were always thankful he never got into drugs."

Hannah could see the lingering aftermath of old pain in Margaret Harrison's eyes.

She reached out and took one of Hannah's hands. "We always knew he'd come back to God someday, and he has. I want you to know that he's paid dearly for his sins…for Johnny. Paid more than you know. I hope you'll give him a chance, that you'll set aside your feelings and open your eyes to what he's become, not what he was. And I hope you'll find it in your heart to forgive him."

The pain and pleading in Margaret Harrison's eyes made Hannah feel small. Small and judgmental. She'd made no secret of her feelings. How must Margaret and Harold have felt seeing her at church every Sunday, knowing she despised their only living son. Yet never once had they given the impression that they felt anything toward her but love, practicing the Christianity they professed.

For the first time, Hannah saw herself as others must see her. For the first time, she realized her friends, Margaret and even Griff were right. She had to rid herself of the hate and bitterness. The scripture they'd studied the day before in class slipped into her mind. If she didn't forgive Griff, God wouldn't forgive her. A frightening, sobering thought.

Chapter Six

Thanksgiving with her sister and her two children was a pleasant, uneventful day. Hannah arrived at Susan's house at mid-morning to help with the last-minute details, only to find everything under control.

"I haven't worked with you the past two years without learning something," Susan said, sliding the roasting pan full of corn bread dressing into the oven.

"Thank goodness," Hannah said. "I don't mind telling you I'm worn out, and there's still more than a month to go until it's all over."

"You work too hard," Susan said.

"I agree, but do you have any idea what it costs to heat that house I live in?"

"I don't even want to think about it." Susan reached into the cabinet for a cup. "How about some spiced cider?"

"Sounds good." Hannah watched as her sister took

two sturdy mugs from the cabinet and filled them from a pan warming on the stove.

"Where are the kids?"

Susan's lips twisted into a semblance of a smile. "Like all boys his age, Lane is taking advantage of a day to sleep in. Kim is upstairs listening to music and probably talking to Callie Harrison on the telephone."

"Callie Harrison?" Hannah asked, taking the cup her sister offered. "How does Kim know Callie?"

"Well, the Joneses live just down the street, and you know there isn't a shy bone in Kim's body. She introduced herself to Callie a year or so ago, and they hang out together when she comes to town to visit her grandparents."

Hannah wondered why she hadn't heard that bit of news before and concluded that her sister probably hadn't wanted to stir up Hannah's memories of Griff.

"I met Callie the other day when I took some food out to the Harrisons," Hannah said. "She certainly looks like her dad, doesn't she?" Though she tried to make the statement sound casual, she heard the tension in her voice.

"She's a Harrison, no doubt about it," Susan agreed. "You know," she said thoughtfully, "I still remember how that marriage shocked the whole town."

"So do I," Hannah said. "The preacher's daughter and the town's baddest boy sneaking off and getting married just days after they buried Johnny."

"It wasn't that so much," Susan said. "Everyone

knew Josie was a little on the wild side, so her coming up pregnant wasn't the bombshell it might have been if it had been someone like, say...you. The strange thing was that no one had a clue who she was seeing. I guess she and Griff kept it so hush-hush because her dad would have had a fit, not only because Griff had a reputation but because he was way too old for her."

"Probably," Hannah concurred.

"It's too bad the marriage didn't work out," Susan added. "Divorce is tough on everyone, especially the kids."

"You'd know all about that."

"Yeah," Susan said, "I would."

"You do know I'm doing Josie's bridal shower the fourteenth of December, don't you?" Hannah said.

"Really? And how do you feel about playing hostess to a party honoring Griff's ex?"

"I don't have anything against Josie Harrison. She's just one of many who made a mistake and has had to live with it. I certainly don't blame her or Griff for their marriage not working. According to Clara Mc-Callum, they did their best, and at least they tried to make their wrong right."

"Well, well," Susan said with a lift of her eyebrows. "I've never known you to be so magnanimous toward Griff Harrison."

"Maybe I'm finally getting things into perspective," Hannah told her.

"Wouldn't that be nice?"

Ready to ditch the topic of conversation for something less volatile, Hannah asked, "How are your kids doing? When I saw Griff on Sunday, he said he hadn't seen them in a while."

"Matt was late sending my child support, so I've had a bit of a cash flow problem this month. I told him he'd better be on time next month with Christmas and all."

"I'm sorry it's so hard for you," Hannah said.

"There are a lot of people in town who have it rougher than I do." Susan smiled. "I'm just thankful to have two healthy kids…even if they are driving me crazy right now."

"The counseling isn't helping then?"

"Actually, it's helping a lot, but Lane is sixteen, and Kim is almost thirteen. Apparently they feel the need to challenge everything I say and every decision I make."

Hannah's smile was reminiscent. "Every child's God-given duty," she said.

"So all my friends say. At least you've been spared that."

The smile on Hannah's face faded. "Yeah. I've been spared that."

"I'm sorry."

"Don't apologize. I've gotten used to being the town's resident old maid, moreso now that Jo and Elizabeth have married."

"You'll find someone," Susan said, her voice filled with conviction. "And so will I."

"Really? Who, in this town?"

"Maybe no one from this town," Susan said. "Elizabeth and Jo both married men who moved here. And you did catch Elizabeth's bouquet," she added with a teasing smile. "You can't discount that."

Knowing it was no use arguing with her ever-optimistic sister, Hannah just nodded and said, "True." Hoping to change the subject, Hannah said, "Are you helping out with Breakfast with Santa this year?"

The event, sponsored by the Chamber of Commerce, was a popular one. Children gained entry to the event by bringing canned food for the needy. There were various Christmas crafts, a breakfast of sausage biscuits, juice and doughnuts and photos snapped with Mr. and Mrs. Claus. Hannah helped every year. This year it fell on the day after Josie Harrison's shower.

"I have to skip this year. Kim and I are going to do some Christmas shopping."

"I'm in charge of the cookie decorating," Hannah said.

Susan rolled her eyes. "Food. It looks like they'd at least promote you to Christmas cards."

"I don't mind."

"You might when you hear who's helping you."

Hannah felt her heart sink. "Three guesses, first two don't count?" she hazarded. "Uh…let's see. Griff Harrison?"

"Right the first time."

"Well," Hannah said with far more confidence than

she felt, "there's no reason I can't get along with the man for a few hours." She only hoped she felt as certain as she sounded.

As usual, Thanksgiving dinner was served at noon. Susan had invited two of her octogenarian neighbors, who had no relatives living nearby, to join them. Lane led their pre-meal prayer, thanking God for their food, their family and their friends. At the mention of friends, Hannah felt a tightening in her chest and a stinging beneath her eyelids. Friends. She was so blessed to have Susan not only as a sister but also as a friend, not to mention how grateful she was for the love and caring of Elizabeth and Jo.

She knew she had backed away from their friendship since they had both married, but she now realized the distance wasn't jealousy. It was a way to hold her own heartache at bay because she didn't foresee the same happiness they had in her own future. The realization left her with a resolve to do better, to reestablish the closeness they'd always shared.

After the dishes were cleared, Hannah and her family spent the afternoon playing board games, a tradition started when Susan and Hannah were kids. It was a low-key, relaxing, fun day, and Hannah left her sister's at six-thirty after indulging in leftovers everyone claimed they were still too full to eat.

She drove home, replete with satisfaction and good will toward her fellow man and filled with a true sense of thanksgiving. She fixed herself a cup of Darjeeling tea and sat down to familiarize herself with her schedule for the next few days. She soon realized she couldn't concentrate with the memory of her conversation with Susan running through her mind. Today was a milestone, of sorts. She had actually discussed the man she considered to be her enemy in a rational way.

True, she hadn't felt comfortable talking about him, but at least she was making strides. She was closer to forgiving him than she'd ever been, partly because of the change she saw in him that everyone felt was genuine, partly because she knew it was the Christian thing to do and her conscience was smarting, and partly because it was hard to hold a grudge against a man who had done the right thing when he had been caught in his sin, something she hadn't done.

She knew there were no small sins, and her unwillingness to let go of her anger for what had happened when Johnny was killed was no less a sin than the things Griff had done in the wildness of his youth. As he had then, she needed forgiveness now.

With tears smarting in her eyes, she bowed her head to ask for that forgiveness. The first words had barely been thought with the doorbell rang, jolting her from her repentance. She was halfway to the front door when the telephone rang. Uncertain which to get first, she headed for the living-room extension, yelling "Come in!" to the visitor.

"Hi!" Susan said when Hannah picked up the receiver.

"Hey, what's up?" Hannah asked, turning toward the doorway that led to the front hallway just as a man stepped into view. Not just any man. Griff Harrison. Griff, looking extremely attractive in a pair of worn jeans, a dark turtleneck sweater and black leather jacket. He gave a little wave, and Hannah's heart skipped a beat. She forced a small smile and tried to concentrate on what her sister was saying.

"I wanted to let you know that Griff is stopping by for that movie Kim left when she spent the night last month. She's staying overnight with Callie, and they wanted to watch it."

"No problem," Hannah assured her. "I know exactly where it is."

"Thanks, sis."

"Sure thing. 'Bye." She hung up, turned off the phone and lifted her gaze to Griff's. "That was Susan," she said, tugging at the bottom of her sweater in a nervous gesture. She crossed the room to join him in the spacious front hall. The fire blazing in the oak-flanked fireplace cast dancing shadows on the staircase and the hard angles of Griff's face. "She wanted to let me know you were coming."

Griff smiled, but the action didn't reach his eyes. "Sorry she didn't give you enough time to bolster your defenses."

"Do I need them bolstered?" she asked, tipping back her head in a small, defiant gesture.

"You tell me."

What was he thinking? She wondered. Did he expect her to attack him? And why wouldn't he? Isn't that exactly what she'd done every time they'd been together? All the good feelings Hannah had been feeling toward him, all her sorrow for her behavior and her resolve to make her actions right not only with God but with him, evaporated in the face of his inscrutability. Unable to say the words she knew he wanted to hear, her gaze slid from his. "I'll get the movie."

She returned in a matter of minutes and handed him the DVD. "How was your Thanksgiving?" he asked.

"Good. Yours?"

"Quiet. It was just me, Mom and Dad. Callie was with Josie and her parents, but I get to have her for the next couple of days, which is plenty to be thankful for."

"It must be hard on you, not seeing much of her since you left Dallas."

"It is, but Josie and I have an amicable relationship, and I know she and David will never keep Callie from me."

"So you approve of the husband-to-be?"

"David is a good man. He loves Josie and Callie, and they both love him. A man can't ask for much more than that."

"No," Hannah said, as the horn honked from outside, "he can't."

Griff smiled, a genuine smile. "I'd better go before those two take off without me."

"Yeah," Hannah said. "You'd better."

They said their goodbyes and she closed the door behind him. Then she watched the glow of his taillights until they disappeared across the railroad tracks. And all the while, she fought back her tears along with feelings of hopelessness and regret.

Chapter Seven

November passed, and December blew in, cold and blustery. Hannah barely noticed, she was so busy with dinners at the house, catering parties and baking specially ordered goodies for gifts. By the time the shower for Josie Harrison rolled around, Hannah was certain she'd never make it until the new year.

For the shower, the ten-foot pocket doors that separated the dining room from the parlor had been slid into the wall, opening up the two rooms into one large space. A selection of teatime goodies, both savory and sweet, was set out on Hannah's grandmother's kidney-shaped buffet. An antique lace tablecloth graced the dining-room table under an arrangement of bare branches, pine boughs and pyracantha berries, bounty harvested from the backyard.

As Hannah lit the candle beneath the silver coffee carafe and placed the Swedish wedding cakes just so on a crystal platter, she couldn't help but hear some of the comments coming from the living room.

"Gorgeous, Josie!"

"Wow, that one's really pretty!"

Hannah felt a shaft of something between sorrow and envy pierce her heart. She turned, but her gaze swept right past the sheer confection Josie Harrison held up for the guests to see to the woman herself. Josie had always been attractive with her blond hair, blue eyes, petite body and an outgoing personality that drew people, both male and female, like ants to a picnic.

Hannah stared at the other woman, wondering what had driven Josie and Griff apart. To her surprise, Josie's bright blue gaze found hers. Feeling like a Peeping Tom, Hannah turned her attention back to the buffet table, but in the instant before she turned away, Hannah could have sworn Josie Harrison's eyes held apology. For the life of her, she couldn't imagine what Josie could have done that she needed to feel sorry for.

That evening, Hannah agreed to watch Kim while Susan finished up her Christmas shopping. Lane's team was playing an out-of-town basketball game. Thank goodness Kim was almost thirteen; Hannah wouldn't have had the energy to keep up with a toddler, especially since she had to get up and spend the morning at Breakfast with Santa.

Kim came over after school and helped clean up after the shower, which, of course, Hannah paid her for doing. Then Hannah checked her calendar to make certain she did the necessary things to stay on top of her cooking schedule before collapsing in her recliner while Kim walked to the video store to pick out some sappy movie for them to watch. When she returned, they decided on pizza for dinner. Hannah ordered a meat lovers, extra cheese—clogged arteries be hanged—and they ate it in the den in front of the television from paper plates.

As they ate and watched the movie, Hannah couldn't help noticing that Kim wasn't her usual self. Something was wrong, and Hannah had a way of getting out of her niece information she would never tell her mother.

"What's wrong, Kim?" Hannah asked, turning off the video and setting her soda on the table. "And don't say nothing, because I know better than that."

Kim lowered the piece of pizza she was holding to her paper plate. "Does every kid in the world have some sort of problem growing up?"

Hannah smiled. "All of them I've ever known have. Of course some have worse things than others to deal with. What's wrong, honey? Are you still upset about your dad?"

"No. Not so much anymore. Mr. Harrison has made me see that there's nothing any of us could have done to stop him, and that we didn't do anything wrong.

Dad's the one who did wrong." She dropped her gaze from Hannah's. "You know he's marrying Brenda, don't you?"

"Yes. Your mom told me. Are you worried about having a stepmother?"

"Some, I guess," Kim said with a grudging shrug. "Brenda's such a twit. Mom says I'm more mature than she is." Kim sighed. "At least Callie likes the guy her mom is marrying."

"I hear he's a nice man."

"Yeah. And Mr. Harrison likes him, so that's good." She sighed. "Why is it that kids are the ones who have to take the fallout from their parents' mistakes."

"What do you mean?"

"Well, Callie says her mom and Mr. Harrison have different ideas about how she should be treated. Her mom is too strict because she made so many mistakes when she was young, and she doesn't want Callie to follow in her footsteps. Mr. Harrison says Callie has been brought up right and they have to trust her, that if they keep too tight a rein on her she will do something stupid."

"It sounds to me as if her mother has a genuine concern, but I've known cases where exactly what Callie's dad says has happened, so that's a valid argument, too."

"He isn't, you know."

Hannah frowned. "He isn't what?"

"Mr. Harrison isn't Callie's dad."

Hannah felt as if the bottom had just fallen out of her world. What on earth was Kim saying? "Of course he is," Hannah said, striving to keep the tension she felt from her voice. "Callie looks just like the Harrisons. Why would you think otherwise?"

"She told me. She overheard her mom and Mr. Harrison talking yesterday about her real dad, Mr. Harrison's brother."

Hannah's stomach clenched in sudden nausea, and the blood drained from her head so swiftly she felt faint. Very carefully, she set her plate of pizza on her TV tray. "Callie must have misunderstood. Johnny Harrison was my boyfriend back then, not Josie Jones's."

"It's no mistake," Kim said. Her eyes grew wide. "Oh, gosh! That means he cheated on you with Mrs. Harrison like Dad cheated on Mom with Brenda."

Johnny and Josie? It wasn't possible. It was a lie! Johnny would never, never have done such a thing... would he? Certain that her heart was breaking all over again, positive she was going to be sick, Hannah leapt to her feet, sending her TV tray crashing to the floor. "I can't believe the two of you were talking about such a thing!" she said in a harsh voice.

"Callie is my friend," Kim said, her own eyes flashing with anger. "She was upset about what she overheard and what her mom had done. She needed someone to talk to."

Hannah set the tray upright and paced the length of

the room, regretting the burst of temper, knowing it was unfair to take out her uncertainty and heartache on her niece. "I'm sure she did," she said in a calmer voice. "And I'm sorry I yelled at you. Being there for Callie is a good thing," she added, "but in my opinion, you're both too young to be discussing such things." Besides, I don't want to hear these lies! "When I was your and Callie's age I was still playing with my Barbie dolls."

"Times have changed, Aunt Hannah," Kim said, sounding very grown up. "If adults don't talk to their kids about this stuff, they'll find someone who will."

"Well, obviously Callie is mistaken. And neither of you has any business repeating hurtful lies."

"She wasn't mistaken," Kim said. "Callie confronted her mom and Mr. Harrison about what she overheard. They sat down and told her the whole story, about how her mom got pregnant and then Johnny got killed. Callie said she cried and her mom cried, and Mr. Harrison cried, too."

Hannah barely heard. All she could think of was Josie and Johnny…together in ways he'd pressured her to be. A sudden memory flashed into Hannah's mind. The memory of Josie's eyes meeting hers during the shower, those blue eyes holding an apology Hannah hadn't understood. If what Kim was telling her was true—and it seemed it was—that look made sense. With the confrontation with her daughter so fresh on her mind, Josie's conscience must have been bothering her.

Hannah tipped her head back and stared at the ceiling through a film of tears. She wanted to scream out her misery. Wanted to tell Kim to be quiet, to stop repeating such hurtful things about Johnny, to leave her memories of him pure and beautiful the way things between them had been.

But she couldn't do that. Wouldn't. Deep in her heart, the heart that refused to believe what Kim was saying, Hannah knew it was true. No one would confess to something so damaging unless it were the truth. And clearly, things between her and Johnny hadn't been as perfect as she'd believed. She buried her face in her hands.

"I'm sorry, Aunt Hannah."

The sound of Kim's voice pulled Hannah's attention from the past to the painful present. She lowered her hands—clenched into hard fists—to her sides. Kim's amber-colored eyes were sad. "I know how bad it must hurt to find out what your boyfriend did, just like it hurt Callie to find out what her mom did." Kim gave a rueful smile. "At least Callie can get professional counseling about her feelings."

Leave it to kids, Hannah thought. They had a way of not sugar-coating things, a way of cutting to the chase.

"Yes," Hannah said in a numb voice. "At least she has Griff to help her work through things." The question was, who would help Hannah with her problems?

Long after Kim had gone home, Hannah sat in the darkness of the den, wrapped tightly in an afghan, with no illumination but the fireplace. She needed the cocoon of darkness to hide her tears. Needed the tightly wound blanket to keep her from flying into a million irreparable pieces.

Johnny and Josie. She'd never once suspected there was anything between them. Never once suspected anything was wrong with her and Johnny's relationship. In her naïveté, she'd assumed that Johnny would happily accept her decision not to engage in premarital sex. Well, he'd accepted it, but evidently not too happily. Her eyes filled with tears that ran down her cheeks in silent rivers. There was only one explanation for what had happened. Johnny hadn't loved her the way she'd loved him. Hannah blew her nose and tossed the tissue in the general direction of the wastebasket. What a fool she'd been to think any man was perfect!

Numb now, recovered somewhat from the initial shock of the news she'd heard, her mind wandered to other questions. If Johnny was the father of Josie's baby, why had Griff married her? Did the Harrisons know the truth? And is this what Griff meant when he'd told her she didn't know the whole truth about the night Johnny died?

There was only one way to find out. She knew she had to confront Griff with what Kim had told her. As the woman Johnny had professed to love, the woman he'd said he wanted to marry, she felt Griff owed her some answers, and from past conversations, she knew he would be happy to give them to her. The problem was, did she really want to hear what he had to say, and could she humble her stiff-necked pride and ask?

Chapter Eight

Hannah woke the next morning and pulled her dark hair into a severe knot at the nape of her neck. The austerity of the style fit her mood. She had no way of knowing it emphasized the pure lines of her oval face, the size of her dark eyes and the elegant sweep of her cheekbones. Even the paleness she felt made her look like death warmed over was attractive, giving her a haunted, ethereal look.

She donned jeans and an off-white sweater whose turtleneck made her feel protected somehow. She drove to the fair grounds, her heart still bruised, its load no lighter, but with her determination to get to the bottom of things firmly in place. She would fulfill her morning duties and then ask Griff if he could spare some time to talk to her. She was ready for the truth. Finally.

She spoke to several people as she entered the building, got herself a cup of coffee and set out the cookies, candy sprinkles and plastic knives for the frosting. It wasn't long before children began to arrive and she was bombarded with little ones who smeared frosting and dumped far too much colored sugar on top of their cookies. She was wiping icing from a chubby little boy's hands, smiling at the mess he'd made when she heard a masculine voice from behind her.

"Hi."

Griff. Hannah swiped at a smear of frosting on the child's face, handed him a paper towel and forced herself to face Griff with a smile. "Hi."

"I'm sorry I'm late. I was literally walking out the door when I got this frantic call from a parent."

"No problem," Hannah assured him. "I have things as under control as they can be when you mix kids and messy stuff."

"They're having a blast, though," he said, pulling up a folding chair and sitting next to her. "What do I do?"

Hannah gave him the simple instructions and they sat and watched as half a dozen children coated their cookies with the gooey frosting.

"Just think. In a few years some of these kids will be hiding drugs in their rooms."

Hannah turned to look at him. "That's a terribly depressing thought."

"Believe me, I know. It's a fact, though." He sighed. "I wish there were some way we could know beforehand which ones were the ones who'd grow up with problems. Maybe we could intervene before things reach the boiling point."

"Do you really think knowing what the future holds would make us behave any differently?" she asked, fearful that the pain she felt was mirrored in her eyes.

There was an unnerving directness in his gaze. "I'd like to think it would, but the reality is that even knowing what the consequences of our behavior might be, we sometimes make the wrong choices."

"I'd like to talk to you about that," she said, her voice quivering the slightest bit.

"What?"

"My behavior."

"I'd be glad to talk to you about anything you'd like, Hannah. Any time."

Something in his eyes—tenderness—made her swallow hard. She knew she had to forge ahead before she lost her courage. "Is after we get through here okay?"

"Sure," he said with a shrug. "We can go to my house."

Hannah had hoped they could talk in a café, somewhere where there would be people around and she wouldn't feel so vulnerable. On the other hand, her curiosity was definitely piqued. A person's home said a lot about his personality. "That's fine."

"Good. It's a date." He smiled again, and her heart did a little tap dance. "Uh-oh," he said, the smile fading as a group of about ten children headed their way. "We're about to be besieged."

"You're right," she said, grateful for the brief reprieve. As she doled out cookies and sprinkles, her mind replayed his words. *It's a date…a date…a date…*

"How about a cup of coffee?" he asked two hours later, when she was settled in an armchair next to his fireplace. "Or are you a tea drinker?"

"I like them both," she said. "Whatever's easiest."

"Good. I'll be back in a few minutes."

Left alone, she made a visual tour of the room. The house was one of the historic homes on Elm Street. Somehow she hadn't thought of him as an antiques lover, but he evidently was. The room was tastefully and classically decorated with an abundance of green plants.

"This is a beautiful room," she said when he returned a few moments later with a tray bearing two cups of steaming coffee, a matching sugar bowl and creamer and a small plate with several cookies.

"Thank you." He set the tray down. "I'll bet you never thought of me as a traditional sort of guy, did you?"

"Actually no," she confessed. "Or a plant lover."

"If I hadn't chosen family counseling as a life's work, I'd have gone into horticulture."

Her eyebrows lifted in amazement. She accepted the cup and saucer he offered. "That was fast."

"I cheated. This is the leftover breakfast coffee. I poured it into one of those insulated carafes. But the cookies are homemade," he hastened to add. "Mom."

She watched as Griff added a spoonful of sugar to his coffee. Seeing the surprise in her eyes, he said, "I'm sure you'd be the first to agree that I need a little something to sweeten me up."

Since he was obviously teasing her, Hannah made no reply. Instead, she asked the question that had plagued her since their earlier conversation. "What sort of problem did you have growing up? Your parents were the best."

He had no difficulty making the leap in conversational topics to what had caused him to go bad as a teen. If he was offended by the very personal question, he didn't let it show. One corner of his mouth hiked up in that familiar wry smile. "What is this, Hannah? Genuine interest about my wild youth or morbid curiosity?"

"A little of both, maybe."

"Well, well. An honest woman. Something of a rare bird these days."

"Really?"

"Really." He took a swallow of his coffee and set his cup back on the saucer. "I guess you could say that my parents' genuine decency was part of my problem. They seemed so perfect, so inherently *good* that I felt I'd never measure up. Johnny was the good son. He did as he was told—at least it appeared he did. It was always 'Yes, ma'am' and 'no, sir.' I never seemed to do anything right."

"So you took out your frustrations by rebelling?"

"That's the road I chose, yes. And believe me, it was

a deliberate choice, the way all our actions are. But I was born to the role. I was always the mouthy one, the one who questioned and challenged everything, pushing the boundaries. And I had more than my share of impure thoughts.

"In retrospect, I was a fairly normal teenage boy, but Mom and Dad had no idea how to handle me, which eventually underscored the fact that they had feet of clay, just like everyone else."

"How?"

"Well, I found out that they did have tempers and they weren't always fair if it meant punishing me, and Dad was even known to let loose with a cuss word every now and then."

"And did it make you happy to knock them off their ped-estals?" Hannah asked, fascinated by this intimate glimpse into the thinking of this man who'd set the small town on its ear and caused his share of gossip and scandal.

"Happy, no. At first I felt this sort of gloating satisfaction that they weren't all they seemed, weren't what I thought they were. Then all those years of Bible study started nagging at me, and I felt bad that I'd pushed them so hard. I knew I needed to clean up my act, but I wasn't sure how. And then Johnny died."

His off-hand comment about Johnny hit a raw and bleeding nerve. Hannah glanced away for a moment, then forced her gaze back to his. "That's what I wanted to talk to you about."

"Johnny?"

"Johnny and the fact that my behavior toward you hasn't been very exemplary."

Griff didn't press. He just sat down in a chair across from her and waited for her to continue.

Hannah took a deep breath, met his eyes with sheer effort of will and made the plunge. "Callie told Kim about overhearing you and Josie talking about…Johnny and the fact that he…he's her real father, not you."

Griff's eyes drifted closed, as if, she thought, he wanted to block out the pain he heard in her voice, the pain that must be mirrored in her eyes.

"I know it must be true," she stated when he opened his eyes again. "You wouldn't tell something like that to a child if it weren't."

"It's true." His voice was emotionless, flat.

"Does…did…that have anything to do with the accident?"

"It had everything to do with the accident."

Another shaft of pain sliced her heart. "Tell me, Griff," she said simply. "Tell me everything. I'm ready to hear it."

Nodding, Griff exhaled a noisy breath and scraped a hand through his hair. "After Johnny took you home from the prom, he came looking for me. I was down at the creek drinking beer and playing poker with some of the guys. Johnny had a bottle of Jim Beam and he'd been hitting it pretty hard. He said he needed to talk to me, so we got in my truck and took a drive.

"He told me he had a problem, a bad problem. He said he'd been seeing Josie on the sly." Griff glanced at Hannah.

"Go ahead," she said.

"I told him he was a jerk, that if he wanted to see someone else, he should have the guts to break up with you first. He said he didn't really want to break up with you, that he loved you, not Josie, but that he'd started seeing her because—as he put it—he couldn't get past first base with you."

Hannah pressed her trembling lips tightly together.

"I told him to dump Josie, then, but he said he couldn't do that because she was pregnant. He was crying."

Hannah's own eyes filled with tears. Hearing the story in Griff's cold, unemotional tones did nothing to lessen the pain of the truth.

"I told him a lot of things," Griff said, his voice laced with the remnants of an old anger. "And I called him a lot of things. He asked me what he should do. I told him there was only one thing he could do. The right thing, the honorable thing for Josie and his baby. I told him he should marry her."

Griff's mouth twisted into the familiar mocking smile. "I'm not proud of it now, but as upset as I was, a part of me relished his misery. Perfect Johnny had finally messed up and messed up big-time." Griff slumped back in his chair and pinned her with that unnerving, penetrating gaze. "He told me he didn't want

to marry Josie and accused me of wanting you for myself. I didn't deny it."

A soft gasp escaped Hannah's lips, and her eyes
widened in surprise.

"I found a place and turned around, so we could go
to your house and he could tell you what was going
on. He asked me what I was doing. I told him that if
he were going to abandon Josie, if he wanted a future
with you, he should be a man and tell you what was
going on and let you decide if you wanted him under
those conditions. I told him he should know that good
marriages weren't based on lies and deceit."

Griff leaned forward and rested his elbows on his
knees, staring at the floor. "He started yelling at me
to stop—to turn around. I wouldn't. Then, before I realized what he was doing, he grabbed the steering
wheel. We wrestled with it for a few seconds and the
next thing I knew we were headed for the ditch and
this big pine tree…. When I woke up I was in the hospital with a bump and a cut on my forehead, and
Johnny was dead."

Hannah wanted to cry. She even felt tears prickling
beneath her eyelids, but they didn't fall, maybe because the soul-deep chill that had seeped into her
bones had frozen them. The cup and saucer in her
hands began to rattle.

"Hannah…" Griff's voice held concern and wariness.

Instead of answering, she set the cup on the tray
with extreme care. Then she stood. As she reached for

the coat that lay on the back of a nearby chair and headed for the door, Griff stood, too.

She was at the front door when his hands closed over her shoulders. "Hannah…" he said again.

The pain in his voice was almost her undoing. In an effort to escape before she made a complete fool of herself, she shook her head and wrenched free of his hold. She couldn't talk about it right now, couldn't take anymore. She might have other questions later, but for the moment, her mind had absorbed all the pain it could bear.

The next thing she knew she was running down the sidewalk toward her car, the bright December sunshine making mockery of the agony in her heart.

Chapter Nine

Later that afternoon, when she thought she'd gained control of her emotions enough to talk, Hannah asked her friends over.

Jo and Elizabeth divested themselves of their coats and settled at Hannah's kitchen table where cups of hot tea and cream scones sat before them.

"What's up?" Jo asked. The look in her eyes was as sharp as her short spikes of red hair.

"Yeah," Elizabeth said, frowning. "What's happened? You look like you've been crying your eyes out."

"I have," Hannah said in a voice that quavered the slightest bit.

Elizabeth patted the tabletop with her palm. "Sit," she commanded. Hannah obeyed, without a word. "Now spit it out."

Hannah looked from one of her friends to the other.

"It's a couple of things, actually. First, I owe the two of you an apology."

"For what?" Jo asked.

"For pushing you both away since you got married. For being so standoffish and aloof."

"Standoffish?" Elizabeth said. "You? I never noticed."

"Me, either," Jo said. "I just thought you were tired from being overworked and upset about Griff coming back to town."

Hannah's eyes filled with tears. She realized thankfully that these weren't the kind of women who looked for slights. She stretched across the table and offered a hand to each of her friends. Each was taken in a warm clasp. "You two are far too good to me," she said with a sniff. "I've been such a fool."

"You aren't a fool," Elizabeth said. Then she grinned. "Well, not much of one, anyway."

Hannah laughed, gave her friends' hands a squeeze and released them to swipe her fingertips across her damp eyes. "I really have been happy for you both finding the right men, but I see now that I've been feeling sorry for myself. Ever since Jo got married I've been holding my own private little pity party. I'm sorry for that. I love you both so much, it would kill me if anything really came between us."

"Nothing could," Jo told her.

"Never," Elizabeth said with a shake of her head. "Friends forever, remember?"

Hannah remembered all too well. *No men, but*

friends forever. The sound of their young defiant voices echoed through her mind. It was the pact they'd made the day Johnny was buried. "I remember," she said now. She heaved a heavy sigh. "It was a silly, youthful promise."

"We *will* be friends forever," Jo said.

"I know, but the part about no men was ridiculous."

"Yeah," Elizabeth said with another smile. "But remember we had very limited possibilities back then. Who'd have ever thought Prescott would wind up with three new hunky single men?"

"Three?" Jo said.

"Yeah. Bram, Jake and Griff."

She cast an apologetic look at Hannah as she spoke Griff's name, almost, Hannah thought, as if she knew Hannah would take offense. Instead, she said, "That's the other things I want to talk to you about."

"Hunky guys?" Elizabeth said with a lift of her eyebrows.

"No. Griff."

Elizabeth and Jo exchanged speculative glances.

"What about Griff?" Elizabeth asked.

"It seems we've misjudged him all these years."

"How can you say that?" Jo said in an indignant voice. "Everyone in town knew what he was up to. He never tried to hide it."

"I'm not talking about his wild escapades," Hannah said. "I'm talking about what he's really like…inside."

"So you're finally convinced that he's changed,"

Elizabeth stated with a satisfied smile. "Good. Now maybe you can forgive him and put all that old bitterness behind you."

"I already have," Hannah told her. "I've spent a lot of time this afternoon thinking about things and taking a good look at myself." She gave a short laugh that ended on a little sob. "I didn't much like what I saw."

Her friends exchanged another glance, this time one of concern.

Sensing that they were about to speak, Hannah gave a wave of her hand. "No. Don't say there's nothing wrong with me. I know exactly what I'd become. Oh, maybe I hid it from everyone except the two of you, but that doesn't change the truth, which is that I had become bitter and cynical about men and marriage."

Jo looked away and a dull red flushed Elizabeth's cheeks. "I wouldn't say you had the market cornered on those feelings. I believe all three of us were guilty of that."

"Elizabeth's right," Jo agreed.

A slight smile curved Hannah's lips. "Thank you for sharing the blame like the friends you are, but I can only speak for myself and my feelings and actions." She sighed. "I've done a lot of crying and a lot of praying since last night. I asked God to help me set aside my anger and prejudice, so I could see and accept the truth about what happened twelve years ago."

"But we know what happened," Jo said looking from one friend to the other. "Don't we?"

"We knew part of it," Hannah said. "But we didn't have all the truth until I spoke with Griff earlier today."

"Griff!" Elizabeth said. "You've lost me. I'm glad you've had a change of heart, but other than your deciding to forgive him, I guess I don't see where Griff fits into all this."

"Yeah. What happened last night?" Jo asked.

Hannah told them about her conversation with Kim when she'd confessed the truth of Callie's paternity. Elizabeth and Jo's faces wore similar looks of shock.

"I cornered Griff this morning after Breakfast with Santa. We went to his place and talked. Really talked. There was no finger-pointing, no accusations. I wanted to hear what had happened from him. I needed to know the truth, finally, not just what I perceived as the truth. What Callie told Kim is true."

"I can't believe it," Jo said with a shake of her head. "Johnny and Josie Jones. And no one suspected a thing! You didn't, did you, Hannah?"

"I didn't have a clue. I guess I was so blinded by Johnny's charm that I couldn't see the forest for the trees. Looking back, though, I can think of a few instances when I should have been more suspicious."

"And to think we thought he was such a perfect guy," Jo said in disgust. "And he was just another two-timer. Aren't you just furious, Hannah?"

Hannah shook her head. "Being mad at a dead person serves no purpose. Besides, I've wasted enough of my life on anger. I was mad at Johnny for dying, Griff for being the cause of it and God for letting it happen. If I'm furious at anyone now it's myself."

"Why would you be angry at yourself?" Elizabeth asked.

"Because I put Johnny on a pedestal. I should have known he'd fall off. For the past twelve years I've compared every man I've met to him, and they've all come up short. Who knows? I may have pushed away some men—imperfect but good men—because they didn't measure up to my selective memories of Johnny Harrison. I set him up as my god, and all these years I've worshiped at the altar of his memory, instead of letting God work in my life to heal me." She drew in a steadying breath. "And I've unfairly blamed Griff for Johnny's death."

"But he was driving that night," Jo said.

"Yes, he was driving, and he'd been drinking. But so had Johnny." She told them the story of the accident Griff had related earlier in the day.

"Unbelievable," Jo murmured.

"I had no idea Johnny ever drank," Elizabeth said.

"Me, neither," Hannah said. "But I'm learning there were a lot of things I didn't know about Johnny."

"Do the Harrisons know the truth about the accident?"

"I'm not sure," Hannah told them. "I was too upset to ask many questions."

"Not many guys would take the blame for their brother's death when he had a major part in it," Jo said.

"Not many guys would marry the girl their brother got pregnant and raise the child as their own," Elizabeth pointed out.

"I know." Hannah's voice was heavy with sorrow. "You know, Margaret told me the other day that Griff wasn't as bad as people believed he was, and she said that I'd have eventually found out Johnny wasn't as perfect as I thought."

No one spoke for long seconds. Finally, Elizabeth broke the silence. "Wow! What an emotionally draining conversation. I need another cup of tea."

"Me, too," Jo said.

Hannah summoned a half smile and the teapot. She poured them each another cup of the fragrant brew and said, "I realized something else last night."

"What's that?" Jo asked.

"That all my success here has been for nothing, because I wasn't doing it for God. I worked myself half to death to try to forget, to prove I didn't need a man to take care of me and that I could do it all on my own. I did it for me. But the truth is, I couldn't have been the success I've become without God's help, without Johnny dying. I know that now. The past several hours have made me realize that God really is in control if we'll only trust him. It's still hard for me to comprehend the kind of patience He must have to sit back and wait for us to come to our senses."

"I think about that more and more every day," Elizabeth said. "More so since I met Jake." Her smiling gaze moved from Jo to Elizabeth. "As Aunt Becky would say 'What a piece of work we've been.' So smug and self-righteous, thinking we had all the answers, letting our parents' hurts and disappointments poison us. I just thank God we've all come to our senses."

"Me, too," Hannah said.

"What's next?" Jo asked.

"What do you mean?" Hannah asked.

"What's going to happen between you and Griff?"

"I don't know what you're talking about."

"Don't give me that," Jo said with a warning look. "Elizabeth told me about that kiss at the Broadway, which didn't surprise me much. I always did think he liked you back then."

Hannah felt her face flame but couldn't help the little frisson of pleasure that danced through her. "Why on earth would you think that?"

"I caught him looking at you a time or two when he happened to be around for some reason or another. Sometimes there was a sort of yearning in his eyes. Sometimes there was sadness, especially when you were with Johnny. I didn't understand it, but now I do."

"You're just imagining things."

"I don't think so," Jo said. "I saw that same look this morning at Breakfast with Santa. Personally, I think you ought to test it."

Chapter Ten

By the time her friends left, Hannah's heart felt lighter than it had in years, maybe since the night of her senior prom. Why did people doubt that the truth really did set a person free? Unfettered from the bitterness that had ensnared her emotions for so many years and tentatively hopeful that Griff had been and still was interested in her as a woman, she felt almost giddy with happiness.

All the praying and pondering of the past had led her to the conviction that her utter devotion to Johnny had been a transference of the fragile, forbidden feelings she'd harbored for Griff. She faced the truth that she'd suppressed for so many years, the truth she'd suspected since Griff had first come back to town. It was Griff who'd made her heart race that last year of high school, not Johnny. It was Griff she thought about when she'd dressed for her dates, Griff she looked for when she and Johnny were in the midst of a crowd of friends. But, knowing Griff was off-limits, she'd contented herself by settling for second best—Johnny.

Oh, she'd cared for Johnny. What girl in her right mind wouldn't have? He was fun and funny. Good-looking. Smart. And his reputation was impeccable, unlike his rebellious brother's. Caring for Griff, she'd convinced herself that what she felt for Johnny was the real thing.

She suspected something else, too, now. She had a sneaking suspicion that her overreaction to Johnny's death, her refusal to let his memory go and her subsequent bitterness toward Griff were all steeped in her own guilt for caring for one brother while planning a future with the other. Even her treatment of Griff since he'd moved home was the by-product of an unconscious guilt for feelings she refused to recognize.

She wasn't a girl anymore. She was a woman who'd suffered because of her own stubborn will. A woman who had learned hard lessons. The past had been laid to rest. There was no need to deny her feelings for Griff, as she had at seventeen.

The question was, did Griff care for her as her friends thought? She recalled him saying Johnny had accused him of wanting her for himself. He hadn't denied it. She thought of the kiss in her dad's gas station and recalled Griff's words about her being dangerous. And she thought of the kiss in the hallway of the Broadway and how it had made her feel. She remembered the sound of his voice as he'd spoken her name earlier in the day when she'd run outside to escape the painful truth of her past. There had been tenderness and concern in his voice and in the touch of his hands on her shoulders.

Were those small things enough to build a relationship on? Would Griff want to have a future with her? She knew there was no way to find out but to put them to the test as Jo had suggested. Never mind that she'd treated him badly since he'd come home. The next move was up to her, and she had to make it. This might be her last chance to find fulfillment, and she had to take it or spend the rest of her life making memories for others.

Griff's lights were on when Hannah pulled into his driveway an hour later. She'd showered away the fatigue that seemed to drag at her and used all her skill to hide the rav-ages of the tears and sleeplessness. She'd left her long, slightly curly, hair down and donned a new pair of wool slacks and a beaded vintage angora sweater, hoping for what? That Griff would be impressed? Yes. That's exactly what she was hoping for. Nerves fluttered in her stomach as she turned off the engine. It was hard to believe that her life and her goals had changed so drastically in a scant twenty-four hours.

Hannah got out of the car and went to the door. It swung open as she reached to press the doorbell. Griff stood there, looking strong and steady and incredibly handsome in his jeans and plaid flannel shirt.

There must have been a question in her eyes, because his first words were, "I was in the living room and saw you pulling into the driveway."

"Oh," she said in a breathless voice.

He stepped aside. "Come in. We're letting all the warm air out."

"I guess we are," she said, following him inside.

"Let me take your coat."

Griff stepped behind her and eased the jacket from her shoulders. Hannah unwound the wool scarf from around her neck and watched as he hung both on a mahogany hall tree.

"Come sit down. Would you like a cup of coffee?"

"No, thank you." Hannah followed him into the living room, tugging at the hem of her sweater in a gesture that betrayed the nerves screaming inside her. "You haven't asked why I've come," she said, sitting on the edge of the camel-back sofa.

An unreadable expression flitted into his eyes. "All that matters is that you did."

The unexpected sentiment took her by surprise. "I came for a couple of reasons, actually."

"You have questions." It was a statement.

"Yes. Once the shock wore off, I realized there were things I didn't know or understand."

Griff went to stand next to the fireplace. "Ask me anything you want."

"Why did you decide to take responsibility for the accident?"

She watched him prop one foot on the hearth and rest his elbow on the mantel, the better to stare into the flickering flames. "Several reasons, I guess. For the first time in my life I fully understood how our decisions affect other people. My image was already tarnished, so taking sole blame seemed like the best thing for everyone concerned. There was no sense in everyone knowing Johnny had been drinking and sending his reputation down the drain, too."

Griff raised his head and looked at her. "My parents had lost a son. I didn't want them to suffer any more pain. So, when I got out of the hospital, I went to the coroner and swore him to secrecy. I guess that was a lie in a way, but I hoped it wouldn't count since I was doing it for a good reason. Mom and Dad didn't want me to do it, but I think they were relieved, deep down."

His smile more resembled a grimace. "That was the easy part. Once I got that squared away, I had to tell them about Josie. It was the hardest thing I've ever done. Mom and Dad called the Joneses but Josie had already told them. While they were all talking about what they were going to do and how they were going to face people, I told them I'd marry Josie and give the baby the Harrison name."

"That was very honorable of you."

"Honorable? I doubt it. I had this twisted idea that

righting Johnny's wrong could somehow atone for my own sins."

"You married Josie as a sort of penance?" Hannah asked.

"I guess I did, and Josie was grateful the baby would have a name. It's too bad hindsight is twenty-twenty. I know now it doesn't work that way, just like I know that if Johnny had married Josie while loving you, the marriage would never have lasted. Gratitude, the need to right a wrong, duty. None is reason enough to go into a lifelong commitment.

"When I counsel people in the same situation, I tell the parents not to press for marriage unless both parties are sure it's what they want to do, because two wrongs don't make a right. Never have. Never will."

"So you regret marrying Josie?" Hannah asked, trying to understand, wanting and needing to know how he thought, how he felt, as much as she needed to draw her next breath.

"I regret that we couldn't make it work and that it cost me the chance to pursue my own happiness, but I don't regret the load of worry it took from two sets of parents or the pleasure I've had from being Callie's father."

Hearing how he felt, Hannah's certainty that she was standing in the presence of a changed man grew. Here was a man who could advise people with true understanding and compassion because he'd stood where many of them were standing.

"What happened?" Hannah asked.

"After Callie was born, Josie and I tried to make our marriage real. We even thought about having a baby of our own—another wrong move—but thankfully she never got pregnant, and a few years ago, we both just sort of gave up on things. We loved each other, but we were never able to fall in love, no matter how much we wanted to. She met David at a friend's house, and when she realized she was falling in love with him, she asked me for a divorce. It seemed senseless not to give her one."

"And you're still friends?" Hannah asked, knowing that state of affairs between divorced people was rare.

"The best of friends, and I thank God for that. The hardest part about coming back here is that I don't get to spend as much time as I'd like with Callie."

Neither of them spoke for long moments. "No more questions?" Griff asked at last.

"Not at the moment. I'm just sitting here feeling like the world's biggest fool." She managed a weak smile. "I can't believe I was so gullible, that I never once suspected a thing."

"Never be sorry for trusting in love, Hannah, and don't be afraid to trust your heart to another man. You're too special a woman to waste away in that big old house doing for other people."

She gave a soft, embarrassed laugh. "I thought I was providing a needed service, making happy memories for folks in town."

"You are. But you were made to love and be loved by someone."

You, Griff? Was I made for you to love? Hannah didn't speak but knew the question must be in her eyes.

"Back when we were kids, I really had it bad for you," he said.

"You did?" she said in a soft voice.

"Bad," he reiterated. "Surely you knew I felt something for you after I kissed you at your dad's gas station that day."

She gave a little shrug. "I thought you did it because you could. You could have any girl in town you wanted, why should I be any different? I never suspected it meant anything to you."

Griff smiled his mocking smile. "It meant more than you'll ever know. Every time I thought about you kissing Johnny, every time I saw him walk out the door to pick you up, every time he came home grinning and telling me about something you'd said or done, it was like someone ripped out my heart."

"Are you saying you were…" Her voice was so low she could barely hear it.

"Jealous? Yeah. I was crazy about you. But I knew I wasn't good enough for you. You were the town's sweetheart. Homecoming Queen. Most Likely to Succeed. I was too old, too jaded, too bad, so I deliberately stayed away and let Johnny move in on you. I guess my not pursuing you was my one stab at decency."

Hannah stared at him, unable to believe what he was saying. He left his spot at the fireplace and came to sit on the sofa, close to her.

"What about you?" he asked. He reached out and took one of the hands clasped tightly in her lap and laced his fingers through hers. "Did the kiss make you feel anything special?"

The warmth of his hand gave her comfort and hope. "It scared me to death."

Griff smiled, but his eyes looked troubled. "You really know how to boost a guy's ego."

In for a penny, in for a pound. "It scared me because I liked it so much. I knew you were too old and worldly for me. I knew you were dangerous and that I'd never be able to tame you."

"Funny," Griff said in a husky voice. "I always knew you were the only one who could." Seeing the disbelief on her face, he said, "It's true. I loved you then, and I love you now."

Hannah's eyes filled with tears. "How can you love me when I've been so terrible to you?"

"I can't answer that. I guess that's how real love works. All I know is that when I saw you this morning at Breakfast with Santa, wiping the frosting off that little boy's face, it was all I could do not to cry."

"Why?"

"You were so beautiful. You looked like a Pre-Raphaelite portrait of the Madonna with your hair pulled back and that soft smile in your eyes. All I could think of was that that's the way you'd be with children of your own."

With her heart filled with gratitude, love and thanksgiving, Hannah threw caution to the wind and herself into Griff's arms. His kiss was everything and more than she remembered from their two previous kisses. When they had tasted and tested themselves long enough, Hannah leaned back in Griff's arms and smiled up at him. "I do have one more question."

"Shoot."

"Will you marry me and be the father of my children?"

Griff smiled at her. This time there was no derision in his smile. "It would be my pleasure Ms. West. I only have one stipulation."

"What's that?"

"That we keep it small and simple and soon?"

"Of course we can." She offered him a serene smile and tilted back her head for his kiss. She had no illusions about her marriage to Griff. He wasn't perfect, but then neither was she. As his lips found hers, she knew that perfect or not, he was the best man for her, and with God as the center of their marriage, however many years they had left would be as close to heaven as she could ever hope for on earth.

Epilogue

The church auditorium and fellowship hall might have passed for a florist's shop they were so full of flowers. White roses, stargazer lilies, alstromeria, ferns of every sort and delicate swathes of tulle festooned every nook and cranny.

To say the wedding was well-attended would be an understatement, since it seemed half the town was in attendance. Hannah and Griff had said their "I dos" eaten cake, drunk punch and opened wedding gifts. Now, wearing a going-away suit of winter white, Hannah joined her new husband, who, looking just a tad harried, was surrounded by a roomful of friends and well-wishers.

"Did I tell you how gorgeous you are?" Griff said under his breath as they stood at the top of the steps.

"Only a dozen or so times," Hannah said, "but in this case I don't mind redundancy."

"I hate being redundant," Griff said. "So how about my telling you how lucky I am instead?"

Hannah felt her eyes fill with tears. No. She was the lucky one. Standing on tiptoe, she gave him a quick, hard kiss.

"Stop smooching and throw the bouquet!" Someone in the crowd yelled.

Blushing, Hannah turned her back to the crowd and tossed the posy of roses and rosemary and thyme over her head. She heard several groans of dismay and a squeal of happiness followed by a roar of laughter. When she turned around, she saw Phyllis Sinclair holding the bridal bouquet. Nearby, red-faced but smiling, stood Jake's dad. Hannah found Elizabeth in the throng. Her friend gave an I-don't-know shrug of her shoulders.

"Let's go," Griff said, taking Hannah's hand. Laughing, ducking the shower of birdseed that rained down on them, they made their way to the waiting limo. Ensconced inside, they poked their heads out of the sun roof and waved as the car pulled out onto the street.

Jo and Elizabeth broke through the crowd and ran behind the car a few dozen feet, yelling something.

"What are they saying?" Griff asked.

Hannah smiled and waved harder. "Friends forever!" she yelled back. "Friends forever."

From her place on the sidewalk, Aunt Becky watched the car disappear around the corner, feeling like a cat who'd just lapped up spilt cream. "All in Your time, Lord," she said with a satisfied smile on her plump face. "All in Your time."

* * * * *

And now, turn the page for a sneak preview of
REASONABLE DOUBT,
the first book in
THE MAHONEY SISTERS
miniseries by Tracey Bateman,
part of Steeple Hill's exciting new line,
Love Inspired Suspense!

On sale in August 2005 from Steeple Hill Books.

Chapter One

Justin Kramer knew two things for certain.

One, he didn't murder his wife.

Two, the detectives weren't buying it.

The four-month-old memory of Amelia's body lying facedown on the blue living room carpet etched a horrifying image in his mind. An image Justin knew he wouldn't shake for the rest of his life—which, if the cops had their way, would be spent up the river, without possibility of parole.

The detectives stood over him like a couple of lions working together to bring down a zebra. Justin's glare swept them both. "What do you think my wife's killer is doing while you two are playing good cop/bad cop for the third time?"

Detective Raney slapped his hands flat on the table and rested his considerable weight on apelike arms. He leaned forward and stared Justin square in the eye.

Disgusted, Justin clamped his lips together and shifted backward. The guy's breath stank of cigarettes and coffee—one or the other was enough to gag a horse. Together they were nothing less than cruel and unusual punishment.

The detective pressed forward to close the distance caused by Justin's not-so-subtle retreat. "Just shut your smart mouth and answer the questions."

Without even trying to hide his amusement, Justin twisted his lips. "I can't shut my mouth and answer the questions at the same time." He knew he sounded like a delinquent punk, but he was getting pretty sick of being accused of murder when he'd done nothing worse than allow Amelia to run all over him for years.

Detective Appling clapped his partner on the shoulder, effectively getting him out of Justin's immediate air space.

Appling's face molded into an amiable expression—one carefully practiced and intended to instill confidence in the would-be criminal. "Come on, Justin. Don't you think it's time to tell the truth?"

The good-cop routine was getting old. Justin leveled his gaze at Appling. "Didn't you two switch roles? Seems like last time you hauled me in for questioning, you were the heavy."

Detective Appling's eyes glittered hard. His lips tensed and turned down at the corners. He perched on the edge of the table, no longer playing like a pal.

"Let's talk about where you were the night your wife was killed. Say...around eleven-thirty."

"He's told you where he was. Repeatedly." Bob Landau, a friend and the only attorney Justin knew, sat in a chair at the other end of the table, looking a lot more comfortable than he had any right to while Justin's freedom dangled from a worn-out thread.

Detective Raney sneered at Bob. He snagged a metal chair leg with his booted toes and pulled it out. With a grunt he plopped into the seat. "I'm tired of getting the same answer."

Too bad for him. Justin only had one answer to give—the truth. "For the third time, I was at the Victory Mission Men's Shelter. All night. I didn't leave until a little after six the next morning."

Raney jerked his head at Justin and picked up a manila file folder from the table. He waved it under Justin's nose like a filet mignon. "Know what I have here?"

"Not a clue. But I bet you're going to tell me."

In one fluid movement, the officer slapped the file open on the table with the flat of his hand, keeping the bottom of the page covered. "Signed testimony from two men who say you left during the night and came back later."

Triumph gleamed in the detective's eyes. Closing the file, he leaned back, lacing pudgy fingers over his ample gut.

Unwilling to give Raney the satisfaction of knowing how badly the news had rattled him, Justin forced himself to keep a bland expression. "You're bluffing."

The officer glared over the rim of an enormous coffee mug. He set the cup back down, gathered a long, slow breath and started again. "The cards are stacked against you, Kramer." He held up his thumb then one finger and another as he counted off the marks against Justin. "A murdered woman, no sign of forced entry and there are witnesses who demolish your alibi. And, I have to tell you, those separate bedrooms don't exactly speak of marital bliss."

Bob shifted forward. "Why don't you guys give him a break? You haven't even charged him with a crime."

"Yet."

Bob shot from his chair. "Do you realize that Mr. Kramer's cooperation is voluntary?"

"We hear you, Mr. Landau. But we have a good reason for questioning him about his so-called alibi. And like you said, he agreed to the questions, so he might as well answer the right ones, or there's really no point, is there?"

"Just watch how you phrase your sentences. I'd hate to slap you with a lawsuit." Bob grabbed his briefcase from the floor next to his vacated chair. "I think you've taken enough of Mr. Kramer's time today, so unless you plan to arrest him, we're going to walk out of here now."

The detectives exchanged looks that clearly revealed their reluctance to let him go. Justin's stomach churned.

A scowl twisted Detective Raney's fat face. "Get out of here," he snarled, his breath assaulting Justin's air space once more.

Justin balled his fists to keep his hands from trembling. "I'm free to go?"

"For now."

Deputy Keri Mahoney opened her mouth wide to take a bite of her on-the-go burger when her cell phone rang to the tune of "Deep in the Heart of Texas." She jumped, and ketchup escaped the bun, globbing onto her uniform before she could stop it. "Great." Why had she ever allowed Dad's Southern belle fiancée to program that stupid song into the phone? It nearly sent her through the roof every time it rang.

Negotiating the hamburger, to prevent another glob of ketchup from plopping onto her clothes, she tried to snatch her cell phone at the same time. Impossible. With a growl, she pulled into the nearest Wal-Mart store parking lot and located the phone.

"Yes?"

"Kere?"

Swiping at the ketchup stain on her tan slacks, Keri scowled.

"Who else?" she barked.

"Sheesh. Did you get up on the wrong side of the bed, or what?" Her sister Raven's voice only irritated her more, but she fought to keep her temper in check.

"What's up, Rave?"

"Are you sitting down?"

"Yeah, I'm in the Jeep."

"It's about Justin Kramer."

She stopped swiping and gave Raven her full attention. "What about him?"

"I think the KC police are getting close to an arrest."

Swallowing past the sudden thickness in her throat, Keri managed to croak, "How do you know?"

"Eugene. Who else?" Raven's contact at the Kansas City PD. A dispatcher with a crush on the annoyingly gorgeous TV reporter.

"Is it still off the record?"

"Yeah, for now. But he said Justin and his lawyer spent the better part of the afternoon in an interrogation room with the detectives working his wife's homicide."

"I just can't believe it," she breathed, almost to herself.

No longer in the mood for lunch, Keri wrapped her barely eaten sandwich and stuffed it back in the bag.

"I absolutely don't believe it," Raven said emphatically. "Justin Kramer is no killer."

"Not when he was fourteen, you mean." But considering her childhood friend never even bothered to come back to visit like he said he would before moving away, how could she really know if he was capable of murder at the ripe old age of twenty-nine?

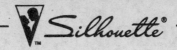

SILHOUETTE *Romance*

From first love to forever, these love stories
are fairy tale romances for today's woman.

Silhouette®
Desire

Modern, passionate reads that are powerful and provocative.

Silhouette®
SPECIAL EDITION™

Emotional, compelling stories that capture the intensity
of living, loving and creating a family in today's world.

Silhouette®
INTIMATE MOMENTS™

A roller-coaster read that delivers romantic thrills
in a world of suspense, adventure and more.

Love Inspired

THE PATH TO LOVE

BY

JANE MYERS PERRINE

Francie Calhoun found God when she was touched
by the words of "Amazing Grace." The former con
artist was determined to be wretched no longer.
But first, she had to convince her stiff-necked parole
officer—the very handsome Brandon Fairchild—
that her conversion was real…as real as her
growing feelings for him!

Don't miss THE PATH TO LOVE
On sale July 2005

Available at your favorite retail outlet.